THE MAN FROM MISERY

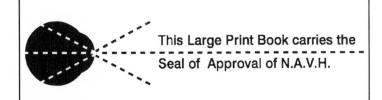
This Large Print Book carries the
Seal of Approval of N.A.V.H.

THE MAN FROM MISERY

DAVID C. NOONAN

THORNDIKE PRESS
A part of Gale, a Cengage Company

LIBRARY OF CONGRESS CIP DATA ON FILE.
CATALOGUING IN PUBLICATION FOR THIS BOOK
IS AVAILABLE FROM THE LIBRARY OF CONGRESS

ISBN-13: 978-1-4328-5191-0 (hardcover alk. paper)

Published in 2020 by arrangement with David C. Noonan

Printed in Mexico
Print Number: 01   Print Year: 2020

For all my "children"
John, Mark, Kristin, Cody, and Shane

Thanks to Sr. Paschala Noonan, Louisa Clerici, and Debbie Denney for sharing their love of writing with me, and special thanks to my editor, Gordon Aalborg.

"Who will rise up for me against the wicked? Who will stand by me against the evildoers?"

— Psalm 94:16

CHAPTER 1
DIXVILLE, TEXAS
SEPTEMBER 1870

The tall man in the brown slouch hat raced towards the Dixville Hotel as fast as his lean legs would allow, but it was too late. His first thought at the sound of the alarm had conjured up some sort of outlaw or Indian raid, so he'd paused long enough to grab his rifle. By the time he arrived at the town center, flames were shooting up the three-story wooden structure with unimpeded speed. Great billows of black smoke rose into the sky, blotting out the stars. Long ribbons of flame danced around the roof, shoving the heated air upwards, reddening the rim of the sky.

A bucket brigade threw pail after pail of water onto the inferno, but the intensifying broil kept pushing them farther back until they realized the futility of their efforts. Just as they dropped their buckets, a girl appeared on the third-floor balcony, screeching for help.

"Somebody do something!" a man yelled.

"We can't get near her," another man shouted back. "The flames are too hot."

Two women dropped to their knees and began to pray.

A long finger of fire caught the girl's dress. She smothered it with frantic slaps and continued to scream. The roar of the fire grew louder, and her voice became harder to hear.

"Jump!" people pleaded, but flames forced the girl away from the railing and back towards the doorway of her room. The crowd gasped when the tips of her long hair caught fire.

"For the love of God, somebody do something!" a man cried out.

The man in the slouch hat raised his rifle, aimed, fired. The shot pitched the girl backwards, and she disappeared into the smoke and flames. Moments later, the porch she'd been standing on trembled, twisted, and tumbled down on the two floors below in an avalanche of sparks and burning wood.

Speechless and glaring, the spectators turned to the man in the slouch hat. He returned their stares. A man emerged from the crowd, his tin star gleaming orange with reflected flame. He held out his hand for the rifle, and the man in the slouch hat

12

passed it to him.

"I'm sorry, Emmet," the sheriff said, "but you're going to have to come with me."

"I know," was his soft reply.

CHAPTER 2
DIABLO CANYON, TEXAS
SIX MONTHS LATER

"Faith, stay inside!"

The girl scrubbing dishes in the cabin's small kitchen rushed to the window. Never had she heard such barbed urgency in her father's voice, even after all the sermons she'd heard him preach. He stood outside a wooden shed in black hat, shirt, and pants, his hand cleaved against his spectacles to shield his eyes from the noontime sun, and watched four approaching horsemen. A dust devil swirled a dark shroud of grit around the riders.

"Destruction cometh as a whirlwind," she whispered to herself.

Her mother was hanging wash on a make-shift clothesline. She eyed the men and raced to her husband, leaving the white sheets snapping in the wind behind her. The foursome pulled up ten feet in front of her parents. The leader wore a bloodred sombrero encrusted with embroidered golden

14

circles. He tilted his hat back, revealing a sun-baked face pocked with black stubble, and deepset eyes, which glowed like coals. He had handsome features save for a brown, pea-sized wart nestled in the corner of his mouth.

Faith recognized him — a recent visitor to one of her father's revivals. The stranger had sat at the end of a bench under the ramada, staring at her with those same vexing eyes. He had never spoken a word to her or her parents — until now.

"Know why we're here, Preacher?" the stranger asked.

Two crows on a saltbush squawked. The wind chimes Faith had fashioned from a broken cowbell clanged on the porch. Her blonde hair was twisted into a long braid. She pulled it to the side and stroked it with quick, strong motions.

"Food?" her father asked.

The stranger laughed as he dismounted, shuffled over to her father, and squeezed his cheeks together with a hairy hand. "We're not here for food," he said. "We're here for your daughter."

"No!" The word burst from her mother's mouth like a gunshot, and she bolted for the cabin. But the stranger snatched her arm with his free hand and yanked her back.

15

"Don't hurt her," her mother begged.

The stranger glanced back at the riders, nodded towards the cabin. Faith shivered as a tall, lank man with a yellow sash around his waist slid off his horse and lurched towards the door. He flung it open and grabbed her with bony hands, his sour breath reeking of tobacco and whiskey. As he dragged her outside, she unleashed a shrill scream. "Poppa!"

"I beseech you, by everything that is holy," her father said. "Leave her alone. She's only sixteen."

With a powerful backhand, the stranger knocked her father to the ground. Her mother struggled to break free, but another blow sent her sprawling next to her husband. While her parents scrabbled on the ground, Faith shrieked and sobbed in spasms, her eyes two glassy streams.

"Shut her up," the stranger said. "I'll catch up with you."

The man with the yellow sash jammed his sweat-soaked bandana into Faith's mouth. Her breathing became fierce and frantic as she struggled for air. He hoisted her on to the back of his horse, and the group rode toward the foothills. Faith kept glancing back at her parents, straining to hear their words.

"Here's twenty pesos, Preacher," the stranger said, thrusting out the bills. "We're even."

"I don't want your money!" her father yelled, scratching at the air in front of him.

The stranger jammed the money into his pocket. "Well, there's always another choice," he said, removing the Peacemaker from its holster.

Faith's last image of her parents was of them kneeling, their hands raddled, their heads bowed. Now she was too far away to hear their words, but she could still hear their voices, distant but strangely rhythmic. She knew they were praying.

She looked at the stark beauty of the sun-seared landscape that had been her home for seven years, the steep rock cliffs that rose above the brown valley stippled with catclaw and greasewood. Two gunshots thundered through the canyon. Faith did not look back. Instead, trembling, she kept her eyes fixed on the horizon. For the first time in her life, as she sat on that black horse amid those menacing men, riding out under that vast sky, she knew she was utterly alone.

CHAPTER 3
DIXVILLE, TEXAS
FOUR DAYS LATER

Emmet T. Honeycut's gangly frame straddled a wooden chair as he listened to Wade Coleman across the table. A shaft of late morning sunlight slanted across the saloon floor. Emmet's leg cramped, and he needed to shift but didn't. Fidgeting, he believed, suggested desperation, and the last thing he wanted was for Wade to think he was desperate.

"I'm sorry, Emmet, I truly am, but business in the saloon is off, and we can't afford to keep you behind the bar any longer."

"If it's just a matter of me taking some time off until business . . ."

"No. It's over. This comes straight from Charley. He didn't have the guts to tell you. Made me do it."

"Level with me, Wade. I work here just three days a week. What's the real reason?"

"You know as well as I do."

"I'd like to hear it from your mouth."

18

Wade was stout as a horse and pushed himself back in the chair using the table for leverage. "You want me to spell it out for you? Business is off. Folks seem to prefer going to the Shady Lady these days — and you know why."

Emmet adjusted his body, and the cramp in his leg dissipated. "The trial ended a month ago, and I was found not guilty," he said in a low voice.

"Not guilty of murder. But you did shoot that little girl."

Emmet put his hands flat on the table and leaned forward. "Straight and true, Wade. I shot her straight and true. And if I found myself in the same situation tomorrow, I'd do exactly the same thing."

"You don't mean that."

"I almost always tell the truth."

Wade looked at the floorboards, shook his head. "I know you thought you were doing right, but a lot of folks around here think you were slapped out wrong."

Now it was Emmet's turn to lean back. "Since the trial, I've gradually lost every odd job I've had," he said. "And the verdict was in my favor. Shane Foster decided his fences didn't need no more mending. The Widow Riley said she found another fellow to take care of her chickens, and Stubby told me he found a cheaper source of fire-wood."

"I'm sure it was hard for them to tell you."

"Oh, folks have been polite enough when they tell me, but in truth they're digging me a hole I can't get out of. This saloon job is the last rope tying things together. You cut me loose, I got no other way to pay my debts here in Dixville."

"You should have thought of that before you pulled the trigger."

The comment sliced Emmet like a blade, but he didn't respond.

Wade slapped the table. "I'm sorry, that was uncalled for. I know living here hasn't been easy for you. Anyway, like I said, Charlie's mind is made up, and I was hand-picked to give you the regrettable news."

The sunshine pouring through the window warmed the inside air, intensifying the sour smell of beer, sweat, and sawdust. Emmet knew the smell well, and it had never bothered him, until now. A small wave of nausea pushed up, but he swallowed hard several times, and the feeling passed.

"What about another job where I ain't so visible," Emmet asked. "Washing dishes? Maybe working in the kitchen?"

Wade exhaled with such force that two cowboys sitting at a table in the back glanced over. "Charlie decided he doesn't want you anywhere in, around, or near the Dusty Rose, given what you did."

"What I did?" Emmet tensed and relaxed his right fist several times. "I put a girl who was about to burn to death out of her misery. She was headed for the same fiery end as the other victims in that hotel. I ended her suffering."

"That's your way of looking at it." Wade took out several dollar bills from his shirt pocket and pushed them across the table. "Here's last week's pay. All I can say is I wish you luck."

Emmet palmed the singles, untied his greasy apron, tossed it on the table. "You agree with what Charlie's doing?"

"Don't matter if I agree. It's business, Emmet. You got an albatross around your neck, and that ain't good for business. That's the nut of it."

"Well, thanks for the work while it lasted."

"You know, Emmet, some people believe when everything in a person's life is going wretchedly wrong all at once — love, family, work — it's because something new and exciting and transforming is trying to be born."

"I ain't one of those people, Wade." Emmet donned his brown slouch hat and pivoted towards the door.

"Wait," Wade called out. "One more thing. I almost forgot. Johnny Raincloud stopped by earlier. Says there's a telegram waiting for you at the station. Now, who'd be sending you a telegram?"

Emmet dropped his head a few inches and pondered the question. "I have absolutely no idea."

"Maybe it's good news," Wade suggested.

Emmet puffed out a small laugh of disgust. "How often does a telegram bring good news?" Then he pushed the batwing doors open and headed for the general store.

Three days of heavy rain had turned the main street into brown gravy. Emmet's boots, heavily caked with mud, squished as he crossed the street. He stomped them sideways against the wooden walkway outside the general store before he entered.

Cody Clarkson, the tall, thin proprietor, was sweeping the floor and looked up when he heard the tiny bell on the door ting. Rheumatism had rendered his body as stiff as a coat rack. He gave Emmet a quick nod and resumed sweeping. The general store was much darker than the saloon, having only two windows compared to the saloon's

22

six, but it smelled much better. The aromas of fresh coffee and tobacco mixed with those of spices and perfumed soaps. Emmet inhaled the scents as he studied the store. Two women examined bolts of calico and gingham on a large table. A young girl lingered in front of the hard candy display, her eyes sweeping over the multicolored sweets.

Emmet approached Cody. "A word?"

Cody stopped sweeping and leaned both arms on the broomstick. "What?"

"In private?"

Cody leaned the broom against a crate and motioned Emmet into a small side room. "I think I know what this is about," he said.

In a tone as businesslike as he could muster, Emmet said, "I just lost my job at the Dusty Rose, and I'm gonna need more time to pay off what I owe you."

The storeowner turned his head and scratched his ear. "How much time?"

"Not sure. I'm totally skint. The trial cost me all my savings. I've got no job right now, but you know I ain't afraid of hard work. I'll find something."

"Emmet, Emmet, Emmet . . ." Cody said, his voice trailing off. "What are we going to do? I've extended you as much credit as I can. Now that you're idle, it'll be quite some time before you can pay back what you owe."

"You know I'm good for it," Emmet said.

"No, I don't know you're good for it. Listen, I appreciate that you're a war veteran, and I appreciate the sacrifices you made for the southern cause. But I don't see any way you can pay me back."

Clarkson walked over to a small desk and stacked a couple of ledgers on top of each other, rubbed his eyes, turned around. "I'll make a deal. I'm willing to forgive all the money you owe me."

"That's quite an offer," Emmet said. "If?"

"You leave Dixville."

"And?"

"Never come back."

Emmet stroked two fingers over his moustache. "So all I have to do is turn tail and run?"

"That's not how I see it."

"And then you and Charlie and Wade and Smiggy and all the other fine citizens of Dixville can rest comfortable knowing you successfully ran me out of town."

"It's no good for you here."

"Yeah, folks are making me feel as welcome as a rattlesnake at a square dance."

Clarkson didn't laugh.

"Truth is, Cody, all I ever wanted was a place to settle down. I was just beginning to feel I had a home."

"Not here."

"So where should I go?"

"Some folks say you should go to the devil." The harshness of his own words seemed to surprise Clarkson, and he glanced down at his belt. Emmet walked over to the proprietor until they stood face to face, eyes inches apart.

"Well, I'd rather hear curses than be pitied, so I thank you for that. Now, where do *you* suggest I go?" Emmet's voice was not quite a whisper, not quite a hiss.

Clarkson gulped hard like he had swallowed a penny, shrugged his shoulders. "The world's a big place. You've got abilities as a long-range shooter. Might be time to think about getting back to it."

Emmet held his gaze a few seconds longer, then tapped the bottom of Clarkson's right arm. "I was hoping to shed that kind of life," he said, "but, to be honest, yours is the best offer I've had today, so let me think about it." Clarkson exhaled, relieved. Emmet left the side room, returned to the main store and stood next to the girl eyeing the sweets. He smiled at her, grabbed a handful of candy sticks from a large-mouthed jar, handed them to her. Then he plucked one out for himself.

"Put these on my tab," he yelled back to Clarkson.

The girl's mother rushed over and snatched the candy out of her hand. "We need to put these back, dear," she said.

"Aw, Momma, can't I have just one?" the girl pleaded.

"Okay," the mother said, "but I'll buy it for you."

Emmet stared at the woman and asked, "Do I know you?"

She wrapped her arm around her daughter and rubbed the girl's shoulder. "No, but I know you. Well, at least, I know who you are."

Emmet dropped his head, popped the stick in his mouth, sucked on it for a few seconds, removed it, and pointed the wet end at the door. "I've enjoyed talking with you too, ma'am, but right now you'll have to excuse me because I need to go fetch me a telegram."

What served as the telegraph office was just one long shelf along a wall of the stagecoach depot. Five people lounged in the waiting room. A well-dressed middle-aged couple sat on a bench with their teenage son. The woman held a closed, pink parasol in one hand, a red purse in the other. Across the room, Tug Roberts and Bobby Lee McIver sprawled across another bench. When Bobby Lee saw Emmet enter, he jumped up and strutted over.

"Well, if it isn't our famous citizen paying us a visit," McIver said.

"What are you boys doing here?" Emmet asked. "Somebody handing out free food?"

"We're waiting on a friend coming in on the next stage from Sweetwater. Damn, Honeycut, you look like the hindquarters of bad luck."

"I ain't here for your guff, Bobby Lee. I'm here for a telegram."

"So we've heard. You intending on going somewhere?"

"Would you like that?"

"Actually, Honeycut, I wouldn't. I'm hoping that you'll stick around a bit longer so you and me can settle some business."

"You and me got no business together."

"You shoot an innocent kid and give our town a bad name, you make it all our business," Bobby Lee said, throwing out his chest. "What do you say we step out in the street and take care of things?"

"That's not a question that needs an answer right now," Emmet said, and he walked over to Sam Toomey, who was perched on the edge of a chair beside the telegraph transcribing a message.

Sam, who'd been operating the telegraph office for the past three years, had a strong, square jaw and a thick shock of black hair. He dangled the telegram reception form out to Emmet without looking up.

Emmet unfolded the paper, read it: *Emmet. Meet me in Santa Sabino. Need help. Bring Betty. Ammo. Friends. Soapy on way. Big pay. Major K.* He studied the telegram for a few seconds to let the message soak in.

"Who's Major K?" Bobby Lee shouted from across the room so everybody could hear.

"Yeah, and what's Betty look like?" Tug chimed in. "We ain't seen you with a woman the whole time you've been in Dixville." He roared the throaty laugh of a heavy smoker.

"You boys best hobble your mouths and stop tormenting the air," Emmet said. Then he turned back to Sam, who was tapping out another message on the machine. Emmet pressed his hand down on Sam's hand and the telegraph so that the knob couldn't click.

"What are you doing?" Sam yelled. "You're ruining the message."

Emmet clenched his teeth and asked, "Do you usually share personal messages with anybody who happens to be around?" He pressed his hand down as hard as he could and then released it.

Sam rubbed the red circle the knob had impressed on his palm. "I work in a telegraph office," he said. "It's hard to keep a secret in this town."

Emmet shoved the telegram into his pocket and shrugged. "How do you think Tug over there's gonna react when I tell him you've been entertaining his wife? I hear that you're real fond of one of her desserts. Peach pie, ain't it?"

Sam's eyes went wide as poker chips, and his sore hand began to shake. "How do you know about that?"

"I work in a saloon — well, at least I used to — so I know you're exactly right. It's hard to keep a secret in this town."

"Please don't," Sam begged.

Emmet went over to the woman waiting for the stage and asked if he could borrow her parasol for a moment. When she obliged, he took it, flumped it open, closed it tight, and began twirling the curved handle around his right index finger as he walked over to Tug and Bobby Lee.

"Please don't," Sam yelled louder.

"Gentlemen, you've asked me a couple of good questions, even though it's none of your damned business," Emmet said, "but I'm gonna give you a couple of good answers anyway. First off, Major K is Major Arthur Kingston. The 'King' saved my life at Chickamauga — couple of minié balls struck my leg, put me back-flat, and a Yank's blade was perched at my throat when he appeared like an avenging angel and cut off that blue dog's head with his saber. So I truly owe him a debt I can't repay."

Emmet stopped twirling the parasol, gripped it with two hands, pretended it was a rifle. He swung his arms from right to left as he sighted lengthwise at an imaginary target on the far wall.

"Second, Betty is Big Betty — the name I gave my favorite long gun, a four-foot-long breech-loading Sharps. See, I was a marksman during the war. I can take down a man a thousand yards away. Imagine that? A thousand yards away." He feigned getting a shot off and recoiled his arms for effect.

"Third" — now Emmet was gripping the parasol like a club — "I'm pretty good up close, too, and I love the element of surprise, so don't ever taunt me again," and he swung it as hard as he could across Bobby Lee's skull, knocking him to the floor, senseless.

Tug made a move, but Emmet was quicker. He jammed the parasol in Tug's face, freezing him. With steady hands, Emmet pushed its metal tip into Tug's right nostril.

"If I had me a bayonet on the end of this bumbershoot," Emmet said, "I could pierce your skull and pin your brains against the back wall."

"Calm down, Honeycut," Tug whispered.

Emmet danced Tug backwards a couple of steps before withdrawing the tip from the man's nose.

"Fourth and final, instead of giving me a hard time, you should be taking Sam over yonder to task."

"Why?" Tug asked, wiping his nostrils with two curled fingers.

"Do you know where your wife was two Saturday nights ago? My guess is that she told you she was going to the church social. I bet she baked one of her famous peach pies to bring along."

"That's right," Tug said.

"The Widow Riley told me she loves peach pie and was looking forward to what your missus was bringing, except your wife left the social early and didn't leave the pie. Even more curious, somehow your wife and that pie ended up at Sam's house that Saturday night."

31

Tug grimaced, and his nose holes flared like a bull about to charge. "What are you saying?" he said with a snort.

"Ask Sam." Emmet took several steps backward, turned, and handed the parasol back to the woman with a "much obliged, ma'am," as Tug stormed across the room towards Sam.

"Is what he just told me true?" Tug screamed, jamming a finger in Sam's chest.

"I can explain," Sam said, his words coming out weak and wobbly.

Emmet left the telegraph office. Even outside, he could hear Tug shouting, and then came the muffled but unmistakable sound of furniture breaking apart. The waiting room door sprang open with such force that it sounded like a gunshot as the bottom rail slammed against the siding. Out staggered Bobby Lee, his body weaving side to side like a soused sailor.

"Honeycut, if you ever come back to Dixville," Bobby Lee screamed, "you'll find your cabin a pile of cinders and ash. You hear me?"

Emmet never looked back, never broke stride. He lifted his hand, flicked Bobby Lee a quick wave, and headed home to pack.

Emmet's cabin was a half mile outside Dixville. It was a humble two-room structure constructed with hand-hewn logs, the gaps stuffed with mud and moss chinking. The cabin had no foundation, no windows, and a hole in the roof for smoke to escape. Dozens of empty rusted cans that once contained beans, fruits, and vegetables littered the side yard, damning evidence that a bachelor lived on the premises.

Emmet entered the dark cabin and lit a kerosene lamp, which did little to cut the musty smell. The place had two rooms: a larger one that served as a kitchen and sitting area, and a small bedroom in the back. Furnishings were sparse: a wooden table with two chairs, a large pine chest that was nicked and weathered, and a wall of shelving. A stack of unwashed tin plates squatted in the sink.

He set the lamp down, knelt next to the chest, opened the lid. With both arms, he pulled out an oilskin blanket, unwrapped it, and let the long gun slip into his palms. *Hello, old girl,* he thought as he rested Big Betty on the table, *looks like our business ain't quite finished.* He reached into the chest again and removed four boxes of cartridges, taking time to shake each one, the bullets rattling like beans inside a maraca.

The fact that the King had reached out to

him after so many years pleased Emmet. He wished his eagerness to assist his former commander was based on loyalty, but, in truth, he knew it was all about the money. A significant payday would afford him a fresh start. He also knew the only reason the King wanted him was for his sharp-shooting, which struck Emmet as an honest enough swap.

He groped around the bottom of the chest until he found an old coffee can containing a few coins, some stray matches, and a photograph. He removed the photograph, which showed him standing behind a woman and a young girl, all three of them smartly dressed and smiling; Emmet in his black frock coat, the woman in a lilac silk dress, the girl in a fawn checked dress with a bustle pinafore. After straightening the dog-eared edge, he gently traced the outline of the woman's face with his thumb before slipping the picture into his shirt pocket.

He continued to pack, pulling a dozen cans of food off the shelf, jamming them into a gunnysack, setting it on the table. From the bedroom, he grabbed his bedroll and a change of clothes and tossed them on the floor. His eyes swept through the cabin one last time, and the sight saddened him. The soft sift of his years was slipping by with nothing to show but an old model Sharps, a few tin cans, and some loose change, his future long since emptied of natural promise. He scooped up the items on the table and floor, went outside, and stuffed them inside Ruby Red's saddlebags.

Returning to the cabin, he grabbed the lantern and hurled it into the far corner. The fire spread faster than he expected, forcing him outside. He cradled Big Betty and watched as the flickering tongues of flame licked along the chinking. The fire let out a small roar as the roof blazed up. Soon, the square brown cabin was a ball of orange flame.

You're too late, Bobby Lee, Emmet thought, as he watched the charred ribs of the roof collapse, pulling down two walls with it. A jack rafter and a ridgepole stuck out of the flames at odd angles, like the broken masts of a shipwreck. *I saved you the bother. Nothing left but a pile of cinders and ash, just like you said.*

A few hours of daylight remained, so Emmet checked the horse's girth, mounted up, and sprinted south with two clear-cut destinations: Sabo Canyon to recruit the Thompson twins, and then on to Santa Sabino to rendezvous with the King.

CHAPTER 4
THE HACIENDA

Faith rode in the middle of her captors staring straight ahead, afraid, and aching with sorrow. She had watched her mother, a nurse, deliver dozens of babies, and she had always marveled at how totally helpless infants were. She felt that way now, newly born into a world of evil and depravity, totally helpless.

The group rode for hours, stopping only to water the horses. Faith spoke Spanish and understood the crude comments and jokes the men were making at her expense but remained silent. Eventually they left the blazing hot flatlands and ascended the foothills, where tall white-pine trees provided welcome shade and relief. After an hour of upslope riding, the trail flattened out again.

"Almost there," the man in the yellow sash informed her.

In the distance she saw the roof of a large

house poking up from the tall adobe wall that surrounded it. The guard towers in the corners made the place look like a prison. Two vaqueros greeted the band of riders outside the giant archway to the hacienda.

"Welcome home, Yago," one said to the man in the red sombrero. "Open," yelled the other.

The large wooden gates swung in, and Faith saw the opulence of the estate. The main house was made of shimmering pink adobe with a white balustrade running across the top of the first floor. Birds splashed in a tall fountain in the front courtyard. In every corner and along every walkway, flowers spilled from pots and terra-cotta urns. In the distance, a bunkhouse and corral bustled with activity.

Faith noticed an older man sitting on the veranda of the main house. He looked to be in his sixties, the corners of his almond-shaped eyes puckered with sun wrinkles, his bushy mustache graying at the edges. As she rode closer to the veranda, a brindle-colored mastiff sitting next to the man began to growl.

"What did you bring us, Yago?" the older man asked.

Yago Garza removed his red sombrero, hung it on the horn of his saddle, and led

Faith's horse still closer. "See for yourself, Enrique."

"White skin. Yellow hair. Blue eyes," Enrique Salazar said. "Well done. Where did you find her?"

"Heard about a preacher living in Diablo Canyon who had a pretty daughter. I checked it out. Figured she'd make a nice addition to our family."

"Let her sit for a minute," Salazar said with a sweep of his hand.

Garza dismounted and directed Faith to get down. As she slid off the horse, Salazar extended an open palm in front of the seat next to him. She eased into the chair, welcoming the soft comfort compared to the hard saddle she'd been riding in.

'What's your name, señorita?" Salazar asked softly.

"Faith Wheeler." His welcoming manner made her even more fearful and uneasy.

Salazar angled his body in the chair and tilted his head back. "Armando, get Miss Wheeler a glass of lemonade."

The teenage attendant stationed next to the door disappeared inside the house.

Now, Faith studied the dog. Its head was massive, its eyes as black as olives, its body thick and sinewy. The sight of the dog's collar sickened her. She had seen a similar one

38

when she was a young girl in Tennessee, except it encircled the neck of an escaped slave boy who was being returned to a plantation. Her parents never owned slaves, and it had troubled her greatly to see a human being restrained that way: two strands of iron linked to a sleeve and secured by a locking pin. The name of the person who had previously worn the collar had been scratched off and replaced with "La Vibora." When she stared into the animal's eyes, its growl grew louder.

"Cálmese, Vibora," Salazar said as he petted the dog behind one of its cropped ears. The animal quieted but kept its eyes riveted on Faith. "This is Viper, *la Vibora.* He's a 'canary dog' — Spanish conquistadors brought them here from the Canary Islands. Great hunters."

Salazar scrunched down so he was at the dog's eye level and pointed to Faith. The canine approached her, sniffed her shoes. When the beast looked up, Faith noted how powerful its jaws were.

"These animals were bred to protect farms and cattle from wild dogs," Salazar said.

"I hate that animal," Garza said to Faith. "How about you?"

"You're the animal I hate," Faith said, and

then she slowly extended her trembling hand and patted the dog's back as if it were teeming with ticks. Its fur was thin, smooth.

Armando returned and passed her the lemonade. Her mouth was dry as dust, and her tongue felt like a hot stone. She accepted the glass and guzzled its contents.

"Vibora, ven," Salazar commanded. The dog spun around and returned to his side. "These dogs are strong, fierce, and loyal," he said. "What better traits could you ask for in a pet?"

"Or in a woman," Garza said with a smirk.

Salazar grinned and then let his eyes drift back to Faith. "You'll be staying with us for a while, señorita," he said.

Faith's body went rigid. "What are you going to do to me?"

"*To* you? Nothing," Salazar said. "*For* you? Everything. We're going to provide you a new life, a life of privilege and wealth."

"I loved the life I had."

"Really?" Salazar said. "You loved that hardscrabble life on that barren piece of rock, with nobody around for miles?"

A dark mix of revulsion and rage sprang up in her. She pointed a censuring finger at Garza. "He murdered my parents. Are you going to let him get away with that?"

"Yago is family," he said. "We're cousins.

What would you have me do?"

"He killed *my* family."

Garza spread his arms out, shrugged, and said, "I offered your parents money, but they refused."

"Blood money," she snapped. Anger began to overtake her fear. "You're murderers, kidnappers." She perched her body on the edge of the seat like a bird of prey, and then dove at Garza, swinging at him with flailing arms. The dog lunged at her, clamping its teeth on the hem of her yellow sun dress and whipping its neck back and forth until it tore off a piece of the garment, exposing part of her leg. When she felt the hot breath of the dog on her leg, Faith scampered backwards and flung herself into the chair before the enraged beast could break her skin with its teeth.

"Watch out, Enrique," Garza said. "This little mustang has spunk. She spat in my face earlier today."

"Spat in your face?" Salazar said, feigning shock. "Such bad manners from the daughter of a man of the cloth. Is that how she got the bruise and the swollen cheek?"

"She'll learn her manners," Garza said crossing his arms, "even if it has to be the hard way." He turned to Faith. "How do you like the dog now?"

Faith ignored him again, smoothed her damaged dress, rubbed her leg.

Salazar beckoned to the attendant. "Armando, bring Miss Wheeler to Juanita and get her settled. Miss Wheeler, I hope you adjust well to your new life here."

The attendant approached Faith and motioned her inside. She rose, glared first at Garza and then Salazar. "Murderers," she whispered, and then she turned and entered the darkness of the main house.

CHAPTER 5
MOONLIGHT ENCOUNTER

Emmet figured he had three more hours of riding before the moon rose out of the bluffs. This stretch of earth was known for hiding hostiles. Tonight's was a rustler's moon, full, with no clouds to cloak the light, and Emmet never traveled when a rustler's moon hung over dangerous terrain — too easy to become a target when all the landscape is backlit and still, and you're the only thing that's backlit and moving. He wanted no chance of getting bushwhacked by Comanches or desperados hiding in the bluffs. He estimated a daybreak start would put him in front of the headquarters of the Sabo Canyon Cattle Company by mid-morning.

Emmet mulled over the telegram. *Meet me in Santa Sabino. Need help. Bring Betty. Ammo. Friends. Soapy on way. Big pay. Major K.* He had brought Big Betty and the ammo, and if he successfully recruited the Thompson twins at Sabo Canyon, there'd be a couple more firebrands added to the shooting party.

Emmet was pleased that the King had reached out to Soapy Waters, who had also served in Major Kingston's regiment. Round-faced and ruddy, Soapy was burly as a bear, bald as a cannon ball, and friendly as hell, and he knew munitions better than any man alive. He could gab for hours about any aspect of military weapons: why the four-foot breech-loading Sharps was the choice of long-range marksman like Emmet, why the "Napoleon" was the cannon of choice in bad weather, or why canister shot was superior to grapeshot in *any* kind of weather.

The moon became a ghost riding the sky behind the mountains, and it climbed high enough into the stars to make further travel risky. Emmet spied a rocky outcrop with some scrub that provided enough cover to put down for the night. No fire — too risky. No clouds meant the desert cold would soon grab the night in its chilly fingers, so he wrapped a blanket around himself and broke out some hardtack for a late supper. After he ate, he leaned in against his saddle, pulled his blanket up, tipped his hat over his face, and nodded off.

Emmet slept a few hours before he was

jolted awake by the sound of wagon wheels flailing the ground and war whoops ringing the air. He rolled on his belly. In the moonlit landscape, he saw two men in a covered wagon trying to outrun an Indian attack party.

Of all the chicken-brained stunts, Emmet thought. When he counted five hostiles in pursuit, his instincts flared, and he reached for his long gun. Nestling his Sharps against a rock, he took a bead, pulled the trigger, and took down the closest Indian, who was at the back of the pack from his angle. He reloaded and fired again, making a second warrior pinwheel his arms before hitting the ground. As the wagon whizzed away from him, bouncing and bucking on uneven ground, he figured he had time for one more shot before they'd be out of range. He aimed, breathed in and out, and squeezed off another round, dispatching a third hostile to hell.

Now they were too far away, but Emmet wasn't finished. He knew he could ride as well as any man on horseback and shoot almost as straight from an attacking gallop. He saddled Ruby Red, unsheathed his repeater, and lit out towards the wagon.

He passed the body of the first downed Indian and recognized the markings as

Comanche. They were able riders, and Emmet realized it would be hard to gain enough ground to have decent shots at the remaining two. As he raced towards the wagon, he heard a crack and watched another Indian go earthbound. Emmet figured the man sitting shotgun had finally gotten around to doing his job. When the last Comanche realized his medicine had gone bad, he pulled off to the east and rode back towards the bluffs, disappearing into the scrub wood and shadows.

The wagon slowed, and then creaked to a stop, just as Emmet caught up to it. Two Mexican men sat up front. "Señor," the driver said, "my brother and I say *muchas gracias.* We are grateful that you shoot so well."

The driver was filthy and grizzled with animated eyes. His brother was just as ragged, with jagged teeth sticking out of black-licorice gums. The horses' panting eased, and Emmet heard muffled sobbing coming from inside the wagon.

"Who's back there?" he asked.

The shotgun man smiled, and his gold-capped tooth flashed in the moonlight. He pushed the canvas flap back with the barrel of his carbine. Two teenage girls were huddled together, whimpering like frightened animals. Emmet could tell from their ragged clothing they were the children of peasants, likely poor and uneducated.

"You girls okay?" Emmet asked. Neither answered, and they hugged each other more tightly.

"They don't speak English," the driver said. "They don't understand you."

"Who are they, and where are you taking them?"

Emmet noticed the driver's brother had swiveled the Springfield around and was lap-leaning it so that the business end was now pointing at him. No time for discussion. In one motion Emmet snatched the barrel with his left hand and pushed it down while jamming his repeater against the man's throat with his right.

"You saw what I did from a distance," Emmet said. "You better watch how you hold that gun, or you'll see how much damage I can do up close."

"Easy, amigo," the driver said. "We're running from trouble, not looking for it." He turned to his brother and said: "Do what he says, Paco. This man won't hurt us."

Paco cradled the weapon in his arms, pointing the muzzle towards the sky.

"My name is Diego," the driver said. "We're bringing these girls to Sierra Cabrera. It's a tiny village just south of Santa Sabino. Father Ramirez, our priest, has a school for orphaned children up there. We're bringing these girls to him."

"You took one hell of a chance hauling innocents over unsafe ground like this during the night," Emmet told him. "In fact, it was flat-out reckless."

Diego nodded. "We thought we could make good time by switching off drivers during the night and be up in Sierra Cabrera by mid-morning. We never planned on those Indians, though." He grinned. "You gave these señoritas and my brother and me *a nuevo dia* . . . a new day."

At this point, Emmet's mind bustled with thoughts as to what was going on. Diego told his story with a good dose of conviction, and Emmet didn't detect any signs that he was flim-flamming, but it did strike him odd that there weren't any trunks inside the wagon, almost as if the only items these girls had in this life were the clothes on their backs. As Emmet chewed on the situation, the driver asked where he was headed.

"That's not a question that needs an answer right now," Emmet replied.

"If you ever get up to Sierra Cabrera, you should make it a point to come to see the school," Diego said. "Father is a most gracious man, and I'm sure he would like to thank you in person for saving his precious cargo from these savages." As he spoke, he swept his hand behind him in the general direction of the four downed warriors.

Emmet perceived Diego to be a slick talker, his manner a curious mix of grease and grace. He would have loved to chaperone the two brothers back to the orphanage and confirm what they were telling him. But Major Kingston's plight remained paramount, and that meant picking up the twins in Sabo Canyon and hightailing it to Santa Sabino.

"I'll try to get up to that school some day," Emmet answered.

"What's your name, so I can tell Father when I see him?"

"My name is nobody's bother," Emmet said. "You can tell him what I look like. Even better, you can tell him what my long range looks like." He pulled Big Betty out of her sling and held her up. Her long metal barrel glinted in the moon glow.

The brothers looked at each other before turning back to Emmet.

"As you wish, señor. Let us say once more, *muchas gracias.*" Diego flipped the reins, and the wagon wheeled south toward the foothills.

49

The night's events left Emmet too riled to sleep, so he decided to move out. The odds of a second war party lurking in the same area were slim. He was further encouraged by the fact that dawn was due in an hour's time, given the morning star's hover on the eastern horizon. He pointed Ruby Red towards Sabo Canyon and eased her on. But as he glanced back one last time, the wagon now just a brown shadow blurring into the brightening landscape, he wondered whether he would ever meet up with those ragged men or those frightened girls again.

CHAPTER 6
SANTA SABINO

It hadn't taken long for Emmet to convince the Thompson twins to join him. Times were hard, and the craving for a dollar cuts deep and makes people more willing to take big risks, especially for big rewards.

Emmet first met the twins when he hired them into his buffalo-hunting outfit. Their father abandoned them at an early age, and their mother raised them by herself. She was a churchgoer and gave her red-headed sons good Bible names: Absalom and Zachariah. But everybody called them Abe and Zack, which, to Emmet's mind, scumbled the Good-Book gloss off her intent.

Life on the prairie had made them able killers — perfect, Emmet figured, for this mission. Red hair is a prize in any Indian's scalp belt, so the twins learned as many tricks as possible to prevent their hair from parting company with their skulls. Abe was a wizard with a blade. He could whirl Arkansas toothpicks and Bowie knives with equal flash and flair. Nobody could gut a buffalo, or skin the hide, quicker and cleaner. Zack handled a Sharps rifle well and improved under Emmet's tutoring, learning how to work the arc of the earth into his aim.

Emmet knew giving the twins the opportunity to make some good money using those skills would be an easy sell. They took leave of the Sabo Canyon Cattle Company that morning and had made good time in the saddle. They were now on the main road into Santa Sabino from the north, which required crossing the Santa Sabino bridge, a large wooden span that arched the San Rafael River.

Emmet saw the bridge in the distance. "Almost there, boys," he said.

"I can't believe I'm riding with you again, Mr. Honeycut," Zack said. "Just like old times."

Emmet smiled. Abe grunted.

The trio reached the bridge in the early afternoon, crossed, and trotted uphill along the main road into town. Franciscan friars founded Santa Sabino after Spanish soldiers gave up looking for gold and went home. San Lazaro, the original adobe church, remained the centerpiece of the main square. The San Rafael River was good sized — fifty feet across at its widest, five feet down at its deepest — and offered numerous watering points for large cattle herds. And even though the town was a quarter the size of Juarez, its main street was an explosion of bustle, dust, and dung.

"Boys, welcome to Santa Sabino," Emmet said.

They sat their horses and soaked up the view. Open-air vendors jammed both sides of the main road yammering and haggling — and pushing their wares. Wicker baskets stuffed with chickens sat next to vegetables splayed out in rows on the ground. Carts churned up rust-colored dirt, and smoke from cook fires drifted in gray clouds from whitewashed adobe buildings. The smell of roasting meat scented the air. Colorful flowers burst from pots perched on sills and railings. Donkeys with panniers strained against their loads. Drunks curled up in alleyways, while children squealed and laughed and chased animals through tiny yards. Three scruffy waifs ran up begging for money, so Abe shucked them a few coins.

Emmet liked what he saw and felt. Santa Sabino was centuries old with a rich history, unlike Dixville, which sprang up from nothing ten years ago and was still trying to find its identity, or to create one in the middle of the mesquite and sagebrush. Santa Sabino's buildings were solid, established, well-constructed, not thrown together like most of the wooden structures and canvas tents in Dixville. Most important, nobody here knew who he was, so he could ride along the streets without affront or insult.

"Mr. Honeycut, your friend is somewhere in this beehive," Zack said. "How we gonna find him?"

"My guess is that he'll find us."

A wagon went by, its wheels grinding and screeching. Once it passed, Emmet could hear a guitar being strummed from inside a cantina to his right. A small slate sign with *Carmen's* painted on it hung from a large nail. He decided it was as good a place as any to throw down, so they dismounted, tied up, and walked towards the music.

The inside of the cantina was dark, and it took a few moments for Emmet's eyes to adjust. An old man with a trim salt and pepper moustache was playing the guitar against the back wall, the creases in his forehead as thin and distinct as the strings he was plucking. A dozen men and women clustered around small wooden tables, and a half-dozen more leaned on a long pine plank that served as a bar. Strings of red chili peppers hung from the ceiling, and baskets of fresh bread were lined up on a small table next to the kitchen. The inviting smells of beans and onions frying on a stove set Emmet's mouth to watering. He and the twins commandeered the last empty table, and an animated young woman hurried over as soon as they sat down.

"What can I get you?" she asked, widening her eyes.

"What exactly are you offering?" Zack asked with a wink.

Emmet shook his head, chuckled, and said, "I'm sorry, ma'am, but Zack here has always loved a pretty ankle, and everything else that comes attached to it. Pay him no mind. We'll have a bottle of pulque and three glasses, and as many tacos and enchiladas as you can muster to fill three hungry men."

As the woman disappeared into the kitchen, Emmet turned to Zack. "You'll always be part hound dog, won't you?"

Zack spanked his knee. "Come on, Mr. Honeycut. Tell me she ain't as pretty as a painted wagon."

Abe leaned in. "Forget that. What can you tell us about this Major Kingston? What does he look like?"

"He's a couple of inches shorter than me, but wider. Black hair. Strong jaw. He's got the eyes of a hawk and the memory of an elephant. He's confident, but he ain't arrogant. He's quiet, but he ain't soft."

"How did he make all his money?" Abe asked.

"Family business. Dry goods — wholesale, then retail. The Kingstons were one of the few Tennessee families that the war didn't bankrupt. The King told me his daddy started salting wagon loads of money away six months before Fort Sumter."

"So Major Kingston's a businessman," Abe said.

"Don't mistake yourself. Just because he knows commerce don't mean he ain't got plenty of sand in his craw. He's the best darned soldier I ever seen. He wields a saber easier than most men do a soupspoon. I rode with him in the war, although it'd be more exact to say I rode behind him."

"Sounds like you have a lot of respect for him," Zack said.

"Yep. He'd work out all the details of our battle plans and leave nothing to chance. We soldiers grasped what we was supposed to do, and when, and where. You boys can rest easy knowing that whatever's going on up here, the King's nailed down every last detail to win whatever battle we're gonna be fighting."

"I wonder how much money we're going to get paid," Zack said, rubbing his hands together.

"Depends on how much fighting we have to do," Emmet advised him.

To Emmet, the twins were two needles off the same cactus, impossible to tell apart save for a couple of scars that were hidden, by clothing in Zack's case, or hair, in Abe's. The big difference was in their personalities. Zack was the talker. He could spin a good yarn around the campfire and hold his own with the rowdiest cowboy storytellers. Some of his best stories were about how folks would mistake him for his brother, or the other way around, and how that would lead to a whole lot of misunderstanding and mayhem. One of his skills was honey-talking young ladies into haystacks for some necking. Abe's was a different tale: he kept to himself and always seemed to be spoiling for a fight.

The woman brought the bottle and glasses over. After he poured three shots, Emmet raised his glass: "To our dead rebel brothers." He threw back the pulque in one burst and gave a loud hoot. The snake water burned and made him clench his teeth like he had a horse's bit in his mouth.

"That is some awful gullet-wash," he said, screwing up his face.

Zack stood and said, "I'll be right back. I'm out of tobacco. You boys need anything from next door?"

"The señorita will be here with the food any time now," Emmet said. "You don't want to miss her, do you?"

"I'll want to smoke after we eat. I'll just be gone a couple of minutes. Tell her to keep it hot for me," he said, bugging out his eyes and licking his lips.

Emmet poured another shot for Abe and himself, but this time he sipped it, twisting the glass back and forth in his hand. As he examined its murky color, two white men rose from a corner table, their meals finished. The larger one wore a denim jacket with a bright red patch on the elbow. The shorter one had long, blond hair that spilled out from beneath his straw hat. They passed Emmet's table just as the server dropped off the food.

"Thanks, Carmen," the man in denim said to her, glancing at Emmet and Abe as he spoke.

She responded with another enthusiastic smile.

The man took two more steps towards the door, stopped short, then turned around.

"Wait a minute," he said pointing at Abe. "I know you."

Abe pulled his head up from his food, studied the man's face, bit into a taco, and said, "Never saw you before in my life."

"No, boy. I know you. Your name's Zack Thompson."

"Believe me, sir, we've never met."

Emmet knew that Abe was anything but a genteel man, and calling anyone "sir" was completely out of character for him. He realized what Abe was doing and, more importantly, where the conversation was headed.

"You're a liar!" the large man bellowed.

The guitarist stopped playing, stood up, and scampered into the kitchen, holding the guitar against his body to protect it. Several couples opted not to finish their meals, eased away from their tables, slinked towards the door, and rushed outside. Five men at two other tables sat and watched, expectant.

Emmet held his hand out a few inches from the large man's stomach. "Easy, friend. There ain't no cause for that kind of talk."

"No cause?" the man said, his voice swollen with rage. "No cause? This reckless good-for-nothing gets my daughter pregnant and then hightails it out of town, leaving me and her mother to manage the mess, and you say there's no cause?"

"I never touched your daughter, sir," Abe said, still chewing.

Emmet noticed the blond man in the straw hat positioning himself behind Abe's chair, his hands resting on his guns, ready to pull.

"I think we got a case of mistaken identity, here," Emmet said. "This boy's name is Abe."

"You're a liar, too."

Emmet stood and squinted into his accuser's eyes. "Folks that know me will tell you I almost always tell the truth."

The man in denim would not back down. "His name is Zack," he said. "I never forget a face, especially an ugly, freckled one."

"An ugly, freckled one?" another voice boomed.

The large man spun towards the door to see Zack walk in.

"An ugly, freckled one?" Zack repeated. "Let me just say two things. First, Mr. Danny Brown, I think you got the wrong pig by the tail."

Brown's eyes flipped back and forth between Abe and Zack.

"Second, that doesn't say much about

your daughter's taste in men, does it? Rita Ann is her name, isn't it? Or is it Rita Marie? Something like that."

"How dare you mock her," Brown said.

"No, I'm serious," Zack said. "I don't quite remember her name."

"Her name was Rita Ann, you worthless scum." His voice was low but oozing with venom.

"Does it matter?" Zack said, and when he smiled, the moment turned.

In the time it takes to wink, Zack and Danny Brown drew iron, but Zack was quicker and sparked the pistol out of Brown's hand. The bullet had no sooner ricocheted off the gun and embedded itself into the wall than Abe's knife was out of his sleeve and jammed into the blond man's thigh, causing him to crumple to the floor, howling. The table overturned, and food flew and plates shattered as Abe heaved himself on top of the blond man, one hand a flailing fist, the other reaching for his boot knife, which he snatched and pressed against the man's throat.

"Easy, Goldilocks," Abe whispered. "Easy."

Zack stared at Danny Brown. "Next bullet's going to be through your brisket."

As he arched his hands over his head,

Brown glared back and said, "My girl drowned herself over you. Killed the unborn baby inside her. The grief split her mother and me up. I just wanted you to know that."

Zack blanched, swallowed, gave no reply. Emmet heard the uncomfortable silence growing louder, so he moved towards the door and said, "One thing I know, Mr. Brown, is that since you caused this mess, you can pay for our meal. Let's go, Abe."

"One second," Abe said, and then, with a short grunt, he plucked the knife out of the blond man's thigh, who let out a piercing scream, followed by a spray of cuss words. Abe gazed down and smiled. "Just needed my knife back." He turned to Emmet. "Now we can go."

Emmet yelled over to Carmen, who was cowering in the kitchen. "Thanks for the food, darling. You can expect a nice tip from our table." Emmet glanced back at Danny Brown. "Can't she?"

Brown didn't answer, so Zack cocked his pistol and said, "Didn't hear you."

"Yes," Danny Brown answered, his eyes bulging with hate.

Emmet tipped his hat and walked out the door and into the street with the twins behind. "Let's get the hell away from here," he said as they mounted up.

"Boot knives sure come in handy," Abe said as he slipped the weapon back into its fold.

In a sour voice, Zack said, "Knives are good for cutting things. Guns are good for killing things. A man with a knife going up against a man with a gun will lose every time."

"Not every time," Abe said. "Sometimes if the man with a knife is quick enough, it can end in a tie, or better — a knife never jams."

Seconds later, Emmet noticed a man rushing at them from the opposite side of the street.

"Wait!" the man shouted. "Please wait."

The trio turned towards a short Mexican in a striped cotton shirt and brown pants, about fifty years old. He had a prominent jaw and a bit more flab on his bones than his height needed.

"Tarnation, Zack, how many women have you been with?" Emmet asked.

"I swear I've never been to Santa Sabino before," Zack said as the stranger caught up to them.

"Excuse me, señor. Are you Emmet Honeycut?"

Emmet glanced at both sides of the street to see if the man had brought friends.

"Who's asking?"

"I'm Reno Alvarez, a friend of Major Kingston's. I've been waiting several days for you to show up. Please come with me — and quickly."

Reno led them around a corner off the main street, down an alley, and out of sight of *Carmen*'s cantina. He peered up at the men on horseback and said, "Major Kingston told me to watch for a tall, lean man coming in from the north with a few other strangers. I heard the gunshot and wondered if you had something to do with it."

Zack glanced over at Emmet. "Could be a trap."

Emmet nodded. "Alvarez, assure me and the boys that you're on the square."

"Major Kingston understood that you'd want a sign. He told me to tell you the password the both of you used on the night patrol just before the Battle of Chickenmonga."

"Chickamauga," Emmet corrected him, smiling. "Leave it to the King to think of everything. Tell me the password."

Reno straightened up, beamed, and said, "Camelot."

Emmet slapped his knee and hooted, because Reno said it just like the major, with an overstated English accent.

"Do you know where the word comes

from, Alvarez?"

"I don't, Mr. Honeycut. And, please, call me Reno."

"Call me Emmet. This here's Zack and Abe. Camelot was where King Arthur and the knights of the Round Table held court. There were a lot of stories about how those chivalrous fellers saved fair maidens and fought off evildoers. Major Kingston committed the stories to memory and would recite them around the campfires at night for us soldiers. It boosted morale. We used that password a lot."

"Have you saved young women and battled bad men?" Reno asked.

"I've tried."

Reno nodded. "How appropriate, given the situation here."

Emmet cocked a quizzical eyebrow. "Got something to tell us?"

"Not here."

"Where's Major Kingston?" Zack asked.

This time it was Alvarez who looked around. "He's away on business but will return tonight. He instructed me to bring you and your men to my home, where he'll join us. Please come with me."

"Wait a minute," Zack protested. "I never got my lunch, and my belly's growling like a ticked-off tiger. I say we find another cantina."

"Señor, the less the three of you are seen on the streets of Santa Sabino, the safer it will be for all of us," Reno said. "You've already brought unwanted attention to yourselves with the gunfight. The commotion that brought me running could have brought others. You best stay out of sight. Please, come with me, meet my daughter, Mariana, and enjoy our humble hospitality."

Emmet noticed a tall, thin man observing them from fifty yards ahead who hadn't been there a minute ago. The bright yellow sash cinched around his waist flapped in the light breeze.

"Let's go, boys." Emmet said. "Reno knows what's going on up here, and it's time we got the full picture."

Reno climbed atop a tan bay he had tied up in the alley, and the four departed Santa Sabino on the same road they came in.

CHAPTER 7
RENO'S BUNGALOW

A few miles outside town, the group switched off the main road and onto a small trail that angled east. Reno led the way, Zack followed, then Abe, with Emmet bringing up the rear. They passed under numerous groves of piñyon pine, and Emmet relished the comfortable cool of the shade after riding in the hard sun. The woods were quiet except for the distant peal of the angelus bells at San Lazaro. Nobody was talking, so Emmet grabbed the opportunity to ask Reno how he met Major Kingston.

"My daughter spotted a stranger in town who was inquiring about a man with a red sombrero," Reno said. "He didn't appear to be a gunfighter. I approached him by the livery and warned him that it wasn't safe to be asking questions like the ones he was asking. I told him the man in the red sombrero was named Garza. When I asked why he was searching for Garza, Major Kingston said 'unfinished business.' I told him I knew Garza and couldn't wait for the day when somebody would come along and crush him. When the major realized he had a partner, he told me why he came to Santa Sabino."

"What's the unfinished business?" Emmet asked.

"Garza abducted his niece. The two of us have been plotting how to rescue her. I'll tell you more when we reach my home."

Thirty minutes later, they approached another fork. The main trail kept ascending to the east, but they veered to the north toward a steep slope leading down. Up ahead lay a tangle of deadfall, and the trail seemed to disappear. Reno pushed his bay forward, and the animal dropped down the slope, scattering stones and sand and snapping brush as it went. The drop in elevation was more than two hundred feet.

Once over the rise, they heard the soothing sound of water rushing over rock. The air filled with mist, and the scent of pine intensified. They followed Reno down the defile. At the bottom, the trail widened as it snaked along the stream. Through the trees Emmet saw a one-story bungalow nestled in a stand of old cottonwoods. An enormous vegetable garden stretched between the house and the stream.

As they emerged from a small glade, Reno yelled, "Mariana, more guests have arrived, and they are thirsty, hungry, and tired."

They dismounted, and Reno escorted Emmet and the twins to a small porch in the front and pointed out where to sit. Emmet's sore backside welcomed the relief of the soft pillows on wicker chairs. Minutes later, a woman came out balancing huge plates of food on her left arm and toting a straw-covered wine bottle in her right. She wore a white cotton blouse and black skirt, both embroidered around the edges with beads formed into the shapes of flowers.

"This is my daughter," Reno said.

Emmet and the twins doffed their hats. Mariana was about thirty years old, slight of stature, and desperately beautiful. She had raven hair, warm, brown eyes, and a welcoming smile. Emmet stood like a stone statue, smitten.

"My friends, eat, drink, rest," Reno said, as he took the bottle from her and splashed wine into the glasses.

Zack kicked off his boots and propped back in his chair. "I'm so hungry I could eat a saddle blanket. Now this is more like it, ain't it, Abe?"

Abe lifted his head from the plate of red beans, rice, and pork he was plowing through and nodded it was so.

Emmet couldn't help noticing the generous portion of pork on each plate — he suspected meat was a luxury for such simple people. "Thanks for staking us to a feed," he said, and then he took a huge swallow from the glass. "What can you tell us, Reno?"

"Enrique Salazar and Yago Garza abducted Major Kingston's niece, Faith, and are holding her at their estate south of here. Salazar and Garza are cousins who run this town. They're powerful men. Salazar is the brains, Garza, the strong arm."

Emmet set the glass down and picked up his plate. "How did they get control?"

"Border-jumping Indians and *bandoleros* tormented the people of Santa Sabino for years until the cousins assembled a gang of gunmen and finally put an end to the raids. At first, the villagers enjoyed the peace, but the cousins seized control of the town, bit by bit, shop by shop. They take a cut from just about every business as tribute money."

Emmet forked some rice and beans into his mouth. "They control everything?"

"Just about. Saloons, hotels, brothels. There are many uncooperative business owners buried in these hills. Even Father Ramirez has to pay — the cousins get a cut from his weekly collection plate."

"What do they want with Faith? Ransom?"

Reno ran his fingers through his hair, leaned forward. "Greed drove them into new ventures. About three years ago, the cousins began selling girls as sex slaves. Once a year, they sweep the territory for young women — typically unmarried girls living with their parents. If they find one in a village, they pay off her parents for a pittance. In remote places, they simply murder them."

"Faith's parents?" Emmet asked.

"Murdered."

"I get the picture."

"After they've rounded up a dozen or so girls, they hold an auction at their estate and sell them off as if they were swine. The bidders are wealthy landowners who travel great distances to buy these untouched women. Major Kingston is hoping the cousins will let him ransom his niece. More wine?"

"No, thanks." Emmet wiped his mouth with a small scrap of cloth that served as a napkin. "Why doesn't the law get involved?"

"Salazar and Garza *are* the law."

"What happens to the girls before the bidders arrive?"

"These rich men will pay great sums for a young virgin, so the cousins make sure the girls remain intact before the bidders arrive. Anybody stupid enough to get frisky with the females gets a bullet in the head for his trouble."

Emmet noticed Reno's eyes were haunted with fatigue that hinted at a life of hard but honest work. "So the women ain't harmed?"

"Just the opposite. Salazar wants them looking their best, and that includes providing them good food, a safe house, and even going so far as to curl their hair and put them in fancy dresses. Two wagons of girls arrived this week. The landowners are expected to arrive in four days. Perfect timing."

Emmet shook his head. "How do you know all this?"

Reno thumbed towards the village. "Pedro, the baker, and Pepe, the tailor. Salazar told Pedro to start making basketfuls of tortillas a week ago. He'll work his ovens day and night until the bidders and soldiers arrive. He's summoned Pepe to the hacienda to measure the girls for new dresses later today."

"Two wagons of girls came in this week?"
"Yes."

Emmet's gut turned queasy, and he set his glass down. "There's something eating at me, Reno, and I got to ask you about it. You mentioned a Father Ramirez. Does he run an orphanage?"

"Orphanage? No. What gave you that idea?"

Emmet related his moonlight meeting with the two brothers in the wagon. Then he clenched his fist and said, "I could've saved those girls." He slammed his fist on the table, knocking the glass on its side. Mariana rushed over to mop the spill, the wine turning her sop cloth red. He apologized to her and took several calming breaths.

Reno said, "Don't blame yourself. You didn't know who the girls were, or what was happening to them."

"Is the major alone? Has he recruited anyone else?"

"Several men from town have been giving Major Kingston information and helping him move around the perimeter of the estate. But they're peasants, simple men like me, not gunfighters. I'm grateful that you three have come to help. Major Kingston is expecting Soapy Waters and possibly others to join him."

"And if I know Soapy," Emmet said, "he'll

be showing up with a wagon load of fire and brimstone."

"How many men?" Reno asked.

"Your guess is as good as mine," Emmet said.

Reno persisted. "Well, are we talking a half a dozen, a dozen, more?"

"I told you I don't know," Emmet said. "Why are you so interested in the exact number?"

Reno backed off. "So I can make sure I have enough food for them, that's all." His tone carried a thin bitterness.

"We could know as early as tomorrow," Emmet assured him.

"I've posted a friend on Chimney Rock," Reno said, "which offers an open view of the valley. He'll spot any wagons an hour before they get to the base of the overlook, ride down to meet your friends, and direct them here."

"Soapy was right there alongside me the night before Chickamauga," Emmet said, "so I expect Major Kingston told you to give him the same password."

"Camelot," Reno replied with a smile.

"Sure enough," Emmet said, "Soapy will give you the same knowing hoot that I did when he hears it."

"Major Kingston will return tonight,"

Reno said, "and provide more details on what's happened — and what's going to happen. For now, I ask you to excuse me. I must see to business, including making preparations for Señor Soapy and the others. Please continue to relax. You might want to sleep before you meet with Major Kingston. My house is small, but you're welcome to sleep in it."

"Thanks, Reno, but me and the boys will put down under the trees. I ain't quite ready to settle in yet. In the meantime, would it be okay if I chat with Miss Mariana for a spell?" Emmet said it loud enough for her to hear.

"Of course," Reno said, a twinkle in his eye.

"Let me clear the table," Mariana said. She stacked the plates, collected the forks, and went inside the house.

"Abe, Zack," Emmet said, "now that you finished your meals, it might be a good time to start breaking down your gear."

"Right now?" Abe whined.

"Maybe *I'd* like to spend some time with Mariana," Zack whispered.

"Looking to put another notch on your pistol, are you?" Emmet said. "She's too old for you."

"She's too young for you."

"Time will tell, son," Emmet said. "Time will tell." He jerked his thumb twice towards the cottonwoods. "Go stow your gear."

"Let's go, Abe," Zack said, "I know when we ain't wanted."

The twins stepped off the porch and ambled towards the horses. When Mariana returned, Emmet poured her a glass of wine. She smiled, hung a damp cloth over the railing to dry, and took a seat across from him.

When she was bustling about the bungalow or tending to her guests, Mariana seemed as comfortable as a house cat on a rainy afternoon. But all that comfort disappeared as soon as she sat down. She stared at her lap and fingered the embroidery on her skirt. Emmet suspected she enjoyed working behind the scenes and didn't welcome any attention on herself, pretty as she was, so he tried to put her at ease.

"You've been so gracious to me and the boys, I just wanted to take a minute to thank you."

He gestured with his hand to have some wine. The sip she took barely wet her lips.

"How do you know Major Kingston?" she asked.

"I fought under him during the war."

"You were a soldier."

"Yep."

"Were you a hero, Mr. Honeycut?"

"Call me Emmet. The real heroes were my brothers who died during battle."

"I'm sure you're glad it's over."

"Yep."

"Are you able to put it out of your mind?"

"Actually, Miss Mariana, I've seen all the horrors of war, and I do my best to try to remember, especially my brothers who didn't make it home. Watch this."

He lifted his glass and told her to do the same. "To my dead rebel brothers," he said, and then he tossed the rest of the wine down and gave a loud hoot.

His yawp startled her, but then she relaxed and took a bigger sip.

"It's good that you remember them," she said. "It's good to think of those who are no longer here." Her voice trailed off, and her eyes drifted to the horizon.

Emmet noticed a tiny cross around her neck. "Are you a churchgoer?"

Her eyes crisped back into focus. "Yes. Father Ramirez is a wonderful priest. I've known him all my life. He baptized me. He hears my confessions and gives me Communion. He was the priest who married me."

Those last two words wedged themselves

inside Emmet's ears like half-eaten corn-cobs. He scanned her fingers and didn't see a ring or any skin discoloration from where one used to be.

"Where's your husband?"

"Dead."

"I'm sorry to hear that, Miss Mariana. What was his name?"

"Miguel."

"What happened?"

She twizzled the cross around her finger. "He drowned."

Emmet jammed his tongue against the roof of his mouth and let her go on.

She let the cross drop. "I moved back in with my parents after he died. My mother got sick and died a few months after that. It was hard to lose my husband and my mother so closely together. I've taken care of my father ever since."

Some of the brightness had left her face. Emmet regretted kindling the conversation and intended to chase her sadness away, but she changed the subject before he could.

"Are you a religious man, Emmet?"

"No ma'am, I ain't a churchgoer, but I got a grip on what's right and what's wrong."

"You have an easy way about you," she said. "You let people talk, and your ears really listen."

Emmet chuckled at that one. "Not everybody thinks my way is that easy, or that I listen as good as I should. Plus some folks say there's no better way to conceal yourself than to sit back and listen to everybody else talk. Maybe that's my way of remaining mysterious."

She nestled back in her chair, and her shoulders slackened. She rubbed her hands together and then reached for her glass. "Are you a mystery man?"

"I got nothing to hide, Miss Mariana."

She brushed some crumbs off the table. "Where's your home?"

"I have a cabin outside Dixville." In his mind, Emmet saw the charred remains of the structure, the acrid smell rising from the smoldering timbers. "I ain't particularly happy there, and I'll be looking for a new place to settle down once our business in Santa Sabino is done. I'd like to make some changes in my life."

"What kind of changes?"

"For starters, staying in one place for a long spell. All my life, I've moved from place to place and slept wherever I had to — cabins, bunkhouses, hotels, barns, tents, under the stars. I guess I was meant to be a rover, at least when I wore a younger man's chaps. But I'm on the dusky side of forty now and aching to settle down in one location. I'd like to develop a sense of place."

He set his napkin on the table. "Excuse me for asking, Miss Mariana, but have you ever thought of remarrying? I mean, you're still young and beautiful. If Soapy were here, he'd call you flat-out handsome."

Her skin was brown, but Emmet saw her blush.

"No," she whispered, "I don't think so."

"Well, it's one thing to think it, and another to feel it. Thinking in the head and feeling in the heart are two different animals, and a lot of times they can get to clawing at each other. It's best to keep an open mind about matters of the heart."

"Sounds like maybe you've been married?"

"No. Never married. Engaged once."

Now it was Emmet's eyes that turned glossy and distant. He began to reach for the photograph in his shirt pocket, decided against it. Several moments passed in silence.

"I'm sorry it didn't work out," she said.

Emmet snapped back to attention. "I'm keeping an open mind. Soapy's been married twenty years, and he kids me about it: 'Why bother getting married at your age,

Emmet?' And I tell him: 'Soapy, if I get the right one, she'll be worth the wait, and if I don't, I won't have so long to live with her.' "

Mariana uncorked a hearty laugh that warmed Emmet's innards. He continued to savor her beauty and the flash of her smile.

"Miss Mariana, I was never exposed to a lot of kindness in my travels, and I know my lines of work had a lot to do with that. It's pleasing to be in your sweet company if only for a short spell."

"I've enjoyed talking with you, too," she said, "but I must get back to work."

The wine and food had made Emmet drowsy. He yawned, thanked her for her hospitality, and excused himself. She went back to the kitchen while he slipped off under the trees, figuring some shut-eye would sharpen him up for his meeting with the major in a few hours, and since he hadn't seen the King in six years, he wanted to be razor sharp when he did.

CHAPTER 8
THE TAILOR

A well-dressed woman in her fifties stood in the doorway of Salazar's office and announced, "The tailor's here. Shall I bring him up?"

Salazar hunched over his desk for a few seconds longer. Bookcases lined the walls, and piles of papers covered his desk. The room smelled of leather, pipe smoke, and pencil shavings.

"Thank you, Juanita. I'll come down."

He left the den, turned the corner, and descended the steps to where the tailor was waiting on the first floor. The tailor was a slight man with a thin mustache that angled out from beneath his nostrils in two small triangles. He doffed a small bowler and said, "Good morning, señor. Lovely day, isn't it?"

Salazar brushed past him and said, "Let's go."

The two strode down several long hallways, past the great room, the dining room, and several guest quarters, their footfalls clacking on the large tiles and echoing off the high ceilings. They stopped in front of a large wooden door guarded by a man with bandoleers crossing his chest.

"The tailor's here to measure the girls," Salazar said.

The door groaned as it swung into an enormous storage room that had been emptied and transformed into sleeping quarters. Girls in white smocks sat on cots and chairs that lined the walls. One window with bars across it divided the back wall.

"How many girls?" the tailor asked.

"There's nine here now with a tenth on the way," Salazar answered. "You know what to do. Give each girl a different look. Use different colors and styles. Juanita will see to their hair and jewelry, and work with you on the final display. I want my girls to sparkle."

Salazar reached in his pocket and removed a piece of paper containing the girls' names. "Valencia," he bellowed, and a black-haired girl came running over. She was on the chubby side of sixteen, her body no longer that of a child. She stared at the floor. Salazar put his forefinger under her chin and edged her head up, tilted it to the left, to the right. He felt her body trembling beneath his fingers. "Say *ah,*" he ordered.

The girl opened her mouth, and he peered inside, his head moving back and forth for a better view. He pulled his hand back and let her chin drop. Then he placed both of his hands on her breasts from outside her smock. She flinched at his touch but remained silent. Salazar fondled her for a few more seconds and then leaned in until his lips touched her ear. "Very nice," he whispered. "Very beautiful."

He turned to the tailor. "Give Valencia a lower neckline to showcase her bosom."

The tailor sparked to work, unfurling his tape measure and opening his worn notebook. He vaulted back and forth between measuring her bust, waist, the width of her hips — and jotting down numbers. He worked with great efficiency, his index finger beneath the tape measure, his thumb on top.

"I've got what I need from this one, señor," he said.

Salazar told Valencia to sit down, and then yelled, "Faith."

Faith marched over to him.

"So, how is our wild mustang today?" he asked. "Have you shed some of your sassiness?"

Faith thrust out her chin and said, "You'll be punished for what you've done."

84

"Really?" Salazar laughed. "By who?"

"The wrath of God will avenge my parents," she answered with words crusted with contempt, "unless my uncle gets to you first."

"Your uncle?"

"He was an officer during the war, and he knows how to fight. He'll come for me. And you'll be sorry."

"Little mustang, I would welcome an opportunity to meet your uncle — unless my men get to *him* first."

"The Lord says 'I will punish you according to the fruits of your doings.' "

"And what fruits are those?" he asked.

She had bathed that morning, and the fragrant scent of bluebonnets filled his nostrils. He sunk his hands into her soft hips and tried to lift her up, so he could gaze into her eyes, but she slapped him across the face. He staggered back, raised his hand to hit her, but stopped. Instead, he rubbed his reddened cheek and said, "Such spirit. I just may outbid the others so I can have you all to myself. Measure her, Pepe, and put her in your fanciest gown. She might fetch a greater price than all the others combined."

Faith stared at the wall, blank-faced, as the tailor snapped off her dimensions.

After the tailor finished, Salazar said, "Stay well, señorita. You and I just might be spending a lot of time together." He scanned the list and yelled "Toya."

A small, wiry girl slinked over to him as Faith returned to her cot.

Before he began his examination, Salazar glanced over at the guard and winked. "I *do* enjoy looking over the beautiful flowers in my garden."

The guard smirked and held out his hand in a gesture that said "be my guest."

CHAPTER 9
THE REUNION

Emmet woke from a cleansing sleep refreshed and alert. The sun was just easing down behind the trees, so he reasoned he'd been out for at least five hours. Mariana was making a batch of corn tortillas in the kitchen and yelled to him from the window that Major Kingston had arrived and was waiting down by the stream.

Emmet's blood surged when he saw Lamrye tied up with the rest of the horses, confirming that he was going to make eye contact with his former commander for the first time in six years. Emmet thought Lamrye was a ridiculous name for a warhorse when he first heard it, until the King told him that it was the name King Arthur gave his mare.

Emmet studied the animal. She was old but still a magnificent beast. She didn't smell like the typical barn-kept horse. Her scent was a sweet mix of earth, sweat, and wild honey. The Friesian was dark as pitch and strong in stature, and Emmet would have recognized her anywhere. In battle, Emmet remembered the horse and the King moving as one — a striking whirlwind of fire and fury.

He patted Lam-rye on the withers and sauntered toward the stream. In the fading light, he saw the shadow of Kingston lounging in a chair, puffing on a pipe, and watching the dying sun-fire kindle a rosy glow between the hills. Kingston turned when he heard Emmet's foot crack a twig.

"Major, I know I ain't the quietest redskin in the forest when it comes to sneaking up on people."

"Emmet Honeycut, you tall bundle of rags."

They clamped their left hands on each other's shoulder and shook hands with their right, squeezing and pumping several times before letting go.

"Major, it's been a long time. Sorry our reunion is under such sad circumstances."

"It's bittersweet to be sure," Kingston said. "Sit, please."

He pointed to a second chair. A jug of whiskey and two glasses waited for them on a small table. Emmet glanced at the setup and said, "Looks like you were expecting company."

"I was."

Kingston poured three fingers worth in each glass and said, "I knew you'd come, Emmet."

"Reno told me about your niece, and your sister and her husband. I'm sorry for your loss."

Recognizing the grimness of the situation, Emmet foreswore his usual toast and hoot and sipped from the glass. He knew the King was not a man to fribble, so he got down to business.

"How did you find out about your sister, Major?"

Kingston took a small sip from the glass and a huge puff off the pipe.

"Telegram. When I got the terrible news, I immediately left for Texas. It took me an extra day to find their small cabin because it was in such a remote canyon. Chubby McDaniels, a neighbor, met me and told me what he knew. He'd been riding up the main road to my sister's for a drop-by when he spied a group of men headed in the direction of Santa Sabino with Faith in the middle of them. The leader wore a red sombrero."

"That would be Garza," Emmet said.

Kingston nodded. "McDaniels found Bart

and Celie outside the shed. Emmet, you and I have seen a lot of killing, but it was war, not murder. He said Bart and Celie died quickly, shot close up, black muzzle burns on their foreheads. He gave my sister and her husband a proper Christian burial and then telegrammed me. I've been in Santa Sabino ever since, trying to figure out the best way to rescue Faith."

"Major, you know that I'm in this with you to the end."

"Emmet, you're a true Lancelot."

"Thank you, your grace," Emmet joked, "but that ain't the nickname most folks call me these days. Anyway, it looks like we're gonna be rescuing us a damsel."

They both laughed and eased back into their chairs. Kingston recounted his years since the war, which he had devoted to running the family business. Emmet noted the major was wearing his gold West Point graduation ring with the eagle on it on his right hand, but his wedding ring was missing from the left.

Kingston followed Emmet's eyes and smiled. "Yes, Elsie's gone. We wrangled a lot over the years but managed to keep patching things up, until we both grew too tired to bother any more. She got her share of what she was after, then re-married and settled in Vicksburg. How about you, Emmet? You got a woman. Did you ever marry?"

"Nope. Came close once. Things didn't work out the way I'd planned." Emmet cleared his throat. "Major, if I didn't have buzzard luck, I'd have no luck a-tall. But I got no bitterness inside me. I'm pretty sure of it. And you never know. Beauty could be right next door in places you'd least expect to find it."

"I take it you've met Mariana," Kingston said.

"I reckon I have."

Kingston sipped his whiskey as Emmet told him about his years after the war: how long-range shooting became his means to earning a living; how the railroads hired him to provide buffalo meat for the work crews in the ragtowns, and hides at two and a half dollars a piece for rich easterners riding the rails; how he grew weary of the vagabond life and abandoned it in the hope of settling down.

Emmet paused and gazed at the stream. The moon was spinning silver curls on top of the gurgling black water.

"You and me ain't seen each other in years, Major. How'd you know enough to send the telegram to Dixville?"

Kingston sighed, looked Emmet in the eyes. "I read the newspapers."

"Well, don't believe all the hot ink you read."

"I read you were found not guilty."

"Not guilty of murder, but I did shoot that little girl. I'll always be guilty of that."

Kingston slumped in his chair, looked down at his boots. "I can't imagine what that must have been like for you."

Emmet drained the glass. Kingston poured him another measure and waited.

"An outside alarm bell woke me from a deep sleep," Emmet said. "My first thought was that it might be an Indian raid, so I grabbed my gun. As soon as I stepped outside, though, I saw the light from the fire clear across town. It was night, but the whole sky was lit up red as a sunset. By the time I reached the hotel, flames had pretty much swallowed up the building. The eye-balling crowd backed up every few minutes as the heat grew worse.

"Somebody screamed when a girl appeared on the third-floor porch. People shouted at her to jump, but the poor thing was in shock. Never matter. The heat was hotter than the furies of hell, and the flames below her were every bit as big as those above, so nobody could get near enough to catch her. Through breaks in the smoke, I saw her silhouette cowering in the doorway. Her long hair was blowing in the heat swirls. She screeched for someone to help her. It was awful."

Kingston tapped the pipe stem against his teeth. "I read there were five victims in all."

"Turns out her momma and uncle and two other guests were already dead, and the girl was about to join them. Nothing could be done. So people stood there helpless as lame beggars and waited for her to burn. Some folks blocked their eyes. Some prayed. Some covered their ears. When I seen her hair catch fire, I couldn't watch no more, so I picked up my rifle and done what I done."

Kingston shifted in his chair, drew hard on the pipe several times. "You know there's a lot of people who still think what you did was wrong."

Emmet steeled himself when he heard the change in Kingston's tone. "I ended that innocent's torment as quick as that bullet could fly," he said in a fevered voice, "and I don't care what you or anybody else thinks."

"Can killing a child ever be right?"

"No living creature should have to endure that kind of suffering," Emmet said. "No living creature. Her name was Amy Baxter. She was twelve years old."

Kingston hoisted both hands in front of him, palms up: "Well, the jury agreed with you."

"Major, sooner or later, we'll all have to sit down with a plateful of consequences. I know most people in town didn't cotton to what I did, and some folks were aiming to make me a guest of the state because they claimed that somebody was fetching a ladder to save the girl, and if I had only waited, she'd be alive, but it was a lie. Once the newspapers learned I was born in Mount Misery, Tennessee, they had themselves a feast and gave me a new nickname."

"The Man from Misery," Kingston said in a voice as heavy as stone.

"Leave it to the newspapers to get only half my birthplace right," Emmet said with a shrug and a cropped laugh.

"Catchy names sell more newspapers."

"I suppose. Anyway, I was living in a cabin just outside of town when your telegram reached me. Your timing couldn't have been better. Let me be honest, Major. I can sure use the money you're offering."

"I sent for you because I may need your sharpshooter's eye," Kingston said, "and I'm willing to pay well for it. Pay very well."

"I've always been good at killing," Emmet said. He lowered the glass into his lap.

Kingston sucked several quick puffs on the pipe before he set it down and said, "Don't cumber me with your self pity. Let *me* be honest. A bullet in the head seems to be your solution to a lot of problems. That wasn't the first time you mercy-killed somebody."

Emmet's body went stiff as oak. He glared at the King and said, "Perryville?"

"Yes," Kingston said with a quick nod. "Micah True."

Emmet leaned over and jabbed his finger into Kingston's chest. "I never agreed with General Bragg's decision to leave nine hundred wounded men behind while we withdrew to Harrodsburg."

"And I never agreed with you killing that soldier. Dominican sisters from a nearby convent were already tending the wounded."

"How could two dozen women take care of nine hundred men? Micah True was a boyhood friend. You saw how that cannon shot sliced him open. He was gut-holed and dying the most painful death there is, and he knew it, too."

"Emmet, you heard me ask Doc Clayton for opium to ease Micah's pain, but he said no. Drug supplies were low and had to be rationed among those with a chance of living."

"So where'd that leave us? Huh? The doc also said Micah had maybe another hour of agony left before he died. My friend's fists were stuffed with dirt and leaves from where he'd scratched up the ground in his torment. I heard the moans coming out of his mouth with every breath, and if I tried touching him, he'd scream."

Kingston turned his head towards the river.

"Micah was one of my best shooters, Major. He begged me to help him die easy. 'Please don't let the pigs eat me,' he said. He knew once we retreated, the farmers would let the hogs loose to root through the dead and the wounded. He was afraid the animals were coming for him, and he'd still be alive when they did. You knew that, didn't you?"

Kingston turned and looked at Emmet. "I knew, but I still couldn't bring myself to kill him."

"Not everybody has the stomach for it. That's what separates you and me. That's why I suggested you check back in with the big brass while I took care of business. You knew I meant to give him the simple gift of a quick death."

"That doesn't mean you were right."

"I got no regrets, Major. I'd do it for a

dumb animal. Seemed cruel to withhold it from one of our own. How many of our men do you think were killed by friendly fire during the course of the war?"

"I have no idea. I hate to think about it."

"Well, consider it this way. Micah True was just one more Johnny Reb killed by friendly fire."

Kingston took a moment to glance up at the sky then looked back at Emmet. "Maybe if I had stopped you at Perryville, you'd have thought twice about shooting Amy Baxter. Do you regret killing her?"

Once again, Emmet drained the remainder of his whiskey in one gulp but this time slammed the glass on the table. "No."

"An honest answer," Kingston said as he gently set his glass down.

"Well, you know me. I almost always tell the truth."

"Here again, I can't say I agree with you, but I'm not going to judge you either."

"Judge me, Major, or judge me not. I don't care. Just as long as you pay me for services rendered."

Kingston jumped to his feet. "Well, that's probably enough reminiscing for one night."

"You didn't finish your whiskey."

"I've had enough," Kingston said in a waspish tone. "Tomorrow, I'm going to show you and the twins Salazar's compound. I'm meeting with Salazar the day after tomorrow at his hacienda. That's the business I was on today. I hope to pay a ransom for Faith and leave here without bloodshed. If I succeed, I'll give you and the others a handsome reward for showing up. But if I fail, then we'll take her by force. I've brought enough money to either ransom her or pay you and the others. Good night, Emmet."

"Good night, Major." He watched Kingston tramp towards the house with heavy steps, the gait of a war-weary soldier. Emmet wasn't ready to turn in, so he repaired to the porch and rolled a smoke. As he puffed in the shadowed quiet, his cheeks flushed, his mind awhirl from the liquor, his thoughts turned darksome as he brooded on his past: the war, the hotel fire, the trial, and the woman he never got to marry.

CHAPTER 10
THE DINING ROOM

Faith and Valencia huddled on their cots at the far end of the storage room while the other girls conversed in hushed voices.

"I wonder why they're letting us eat in the main dining room tonight?" Valencia asked.

"Don't know," Faith said. "Don't care."

Valencia brushed several strands of jet-black hair out of her face and said, "I hope the food will be good."

"How can you even think about food?" Faith asked.

Valencia blushed, bit her lip. "There's nothing we can do, so we should do what they say."

"Maybe for now," Faith said, "but there's always something we can do. I just need to think of what it is."

"How old are you, Faith?"

"Sixteen."

"Same as me," Valencia said, a pulse of energy lifting her voice. "My father was working in the Dolores silver mine when Garza and his men came. They paid my mother twenty pesos for me."

"She didn't put up a fight?" Faith asked, the black memory of her own abduction seared into her consciousness.

"What could she do? I have five younger brothers and sisters. She had to worry about them, too. I think they would have killed her if she didn't accept the money. Twenty pesos was better than nothing."

"Twenty pesos? That buys five chickens," Faith said. "Is that all you're worth to your family?"

Valencia dropped her head, and tears rolled down her cheeks.

"I'm sorry," Faith said. "That was unkind. I know you had no control over what happened." Faith kneaded Valencia's shoulder with her right hand.

The dark-haired girl sniffled, wiped her eyes, and offered a faint smile. "Do you have brothers and sisters?"

"I'm an only child. My parents served the South during the war and tended the wounded. My father helped with the soldiers' prayers. My mother was a nurse."

"Do you remember the war?"

"I was too young. When the war ended, we moved to Texas so my parents could continue helping other people. That decision caused a lot of problems with my grandfather. He was rich, and he resented my mother walking away from her inheritance."

"Why did she do it?"

"She was more interested in healing. I learned a lot about nursing from her. She delivered babies, stitched wounds, made medicines. Folks would come from far away to see her and listen to my father. He preached to them that God loves us all."

"Do you think God loves Garza?"

A chill shot up Faith's spine, and she gritted her teeth. "I don't know," she said, choking on the words. Just the sound of the killer's name stirred the bile in her stomach.

"Did your parents take the money?"

Faith's temples started to ache. Warring thoughts and emotions jostled inside her brain, some of them unholy, contemptible. She opened her mouth, but no words came out. She glanced at the ceiling, trying not to think about the horror she had experienced, but she couldn't put it out of her mind. She shuddered and fought back sobs.

Now Valencia's comforting hand rubbed Faith's shoulder. Faith opened her mouth again, and, this time, words came out. "They refused to take the blood money, and

Garza killed them. Your mother was right to take it. At least she's still alive."

"So you're an orphan now," Valencia said, still massaging her shoulder.

Once again, Faith was unable to speak. She nodded as tears dripped off her cheeks.

A heavy rap on the door startled the girls. From the other side, a voice yelled, "Dinner." The door swung open. A guard entered and pointed the girls towards the hallway.

Faith dried her eyes with the backs of her hands and followed the eight other girls into a large dining room. She marveled at the extravagance. A marble fireplace dominated one wall of the room. On the opposite wall, a ten-foot-wide hutch carved from Mexican pine displayed multiple place settings, pitchers, serving dishes, and glasses. Two wrought iron chandeliers hung from the ceiling, each with six red pillar candles. Three lit candelabras on the table accentuated the yellow tablecloth. Salazar and Garza occupied chairs at either end of the table. The girls took their seats in the hand-carved chairs, and two older women served them steaming bowls of soup.

"Juanita will be observing your table manners," Salazar said, "and teaching you proper etiquette as you eat. Your new homes will be quite grand compared to what you're used to, and you don't want to embarrass yourselves. We had you skip lunch today so you'd be extra hungry for this *comida.* Now, ladies, you may begin."

"Shouldn't we say grace?" Faith asked.

"No," Salazar snapped, tapping his chest and then pointing to Garza. "*We* are the creators of *this* feast."

The girls picked up spoons and attacked their bowls. Faith savored the blend of chicken broth, onions, garlic, and celery. She saw one of the girls pick up the bowl with both hands and slurp its contents. At once, Salazar cued Juanita, who approached the girl and lowered her arms with one hand and passed her the spoon with the other. As the girl glanced at the smirking faces around the table, Juanita said, "It's okay, dear, you're here to learn."

Garza reached over and picked up a guitar resting against the wall. He smiled and said, "Let me play something to enhance your meal," and then he filled the room with the sweet notes of a romantic song.

As Garza played, Salazar said, "Ladies, if you cooperate, you'll live fine lives indeed. Soon, you'll be wearing beautiful dresses and expensive jewelry and living like queens."

After the girls finished the first course, Salazar rang a small bell, and Armando entered through the right door to collect the bowls. Faith recognized him as the boy who had brought her the welcome glass of lemonade when she first arrived. The two women reappeared at the left door with skillets of food. A third woman entered, opened the hutch, and removed a stack of plates. The girls received heaping portions of beef, beans, tortillas, and salsa, and they shared pitchers of juice squeezed from bananas and mangoes.

"These will be exciting days for you," Garza said as he plucked at the strings. "New romance is always exciting."

Faith sneered at him. Garza finished the song and transitioned to a slower ballad. His fingers rolled up and down the instrument as he hummed in a relaxed tone. Faith could tell that several girls were enchanted by the music but noticed Marisol peering down at her plate and stifling a sob.

"Yago, perhaps something more upbeat, yes?" Salazar said as he pumped his head twice at the doleful girl.

Garza nodded and truncated the song with a flourish of strums before launching into a more spirited tune. In perfect tempo, he moved down and across the strings with his index finger, and then slapped the upper bout of the guitar. The effect enlivened the notes and, at the same time, showcased his musical prowess.

Showoff, Faith thought.

Juanita circled the table, offering assistance and pointing out mistakes. "Head up, Jacinda," she said to one girl whose face hung inches from her plate. "Chew with your mouth closed," she told another as she squeezed her own lips together with her thumb and forefinger. "Here's the proper way to cut meat with a knife," she said to a third and demonstrated with the girl's utensils.

Juanita lifted a tiny wooden cross hanging from Toya's neck with one finger and asked, "Señor Salazar?"

Salazar nodded. "I must have missed that when I was with the tailor."

Juanita removed the cross from the girl's neck.

"But my parents gave it to me," Toya protested.

"We'll replace that with a much more expensive necklace, señorita," Salazar assured her. "Soon you'll be wearing gold instead of wood. Right now, we're going to take a short rest before we enjoy dessert. Juanita, while we digest our food, tell us what you've learned from your talks with our new guests."

Juanita removed a folded piece of paper from her apron pocket and recited each girl's abilities. Six cooked. Six sewed. Three were literate. Valencia could bend her fingers back until they touched the top of her hand. Belinda knew how to juggle. Faith spoke English and Spanish and also had excellent nursing skills. None of the nine girls admitted to ever having sex.

"Miss Wheeler," Salazar said. Faith turned to him and noticed his eyes strolling up and down her. "You put these girls to shame, my little mustang. You speak two languages. You read. You cook. You sew. You know how to take care of sick people. You are truly remarkable. Now if we can just drive that Bible babble out of you."

Garza chuckled. "Watch out, Enrique. Bible thumpers have queer religious notions, and they rarely smile."

Faith wasn't listening. Her mind was set on filching the steak knife on her plate.

Garza leaned the guitar against the wall. Faith watched his eyes float from girl to girl before they settled on Belinda. He clapped his hands together and said, "So you know how to juggle." He walked over to a straw basket in a corner of the room, pulled out three balls of colored yarn, and tossed them to the girl. "Please, show us."

"I need to be standing," Belinda said with a pained look.

"Of course," Garza said. He extended his palm and invited her to rise by wiggling his fingers.

Faith saw her chance. When she believed all eyes were on Belinda, she snatched the knife and slipped it under her napkin. With two fingers she hiked the hem of her smock up several inches, leaned forward to slide her chair closer to the table, and tucked the knife beneath her garment. She glanced up at Garza who, like Salazar, was watching Belinda.

She started to exhale a sigh of relief but stopped abruptly — Armando was in the doorway, staring at her. Pangs of panic wracked her, and she went numb as he walked around the table towards her. He leaned in on her right side and asked, "May I take your dish, señorita?" He winked at her so only she could see. Her numbness disappeared, and a warm feeling of calm descended on her when she realized he wasn't going to expose her.

"Thank you," she whispered. "That would be fine."

Belinda juggled for several minutes and

ended with some fancy flourishes without dropping a ball. When she stopped, the group clapped at her dexterity. She bowed at the applause, looked at the floor, and said that her brother had taught her.

"Can you juggle four balls?" Garza asked, as he pointed to the basket of yarn.

"Not yet, but my brother says he's going to teach . . ." She stopped speaking, her small smile disappeared, and she sat down.

Armando removed the remaining dishes and silverware just as the older women brought in dessert — *sopapilla,* two layers of fried dough with honey drizzled between them. Faith heard several girls gasp with delight at seeing the pastries.

"Wait until everyone is served," Juanita advised, anticipating their eagerness. They began eating as soon as the last dessert plate touched the table. "Like ladies," Juanita reminded them. "Like ladies."

Salazar jammed his thumbs in his belt and poured his voice around the table. "After you finish your desserts, Juanita will discuss with you what to expect in the bedroom. Ask Juanita as many questions as you'd like." Salazar yanked his thumbs out and stood. "I'm done here. Yago, are you coming?"

Garza leaned back in his chair and

grinned. "No, I think I'll stay. I'm curious as to what kind of questions these girls might have. And who knows? Maybe I can help answer them and put their minds at ease. They might benefit from hearing a man's point of view on what is expected."

"As you wish," Salazar said. "Enjoy your chat." He turned on his heel and left the room.

Garza placed three water glasses before him, dipped his index fingers in the water, and moved them around the rims of the glasses until the vessels began to sing in high-pitched harmony. All of the girls purred their amazement that water glasses could sing — all except Faith.

"You think you make beautiful music," she said.

Garza ignored her and played for a minute more before withdrawing his hands and wiping them on his pants.

"Yes, I think I do," he said. Then he picked up a carafe of wine, filled his goblet, looked around the table, and said, "Ladies, it's time to talk about doing the Aztec nug-a-nug."

CHAPTER 11
RECONNAISSANCE

"Breakfast," Reno yelled from the porch. Emmet and the twins roused themselves from the ground and stowed their bedding. It was a beautiful morning, but Emmet knew another hard sun would make it a scorcher by midday. The three drifted down to the stream, splashed their faces with cold wake-up water, and headed for the welcoming aroma of griddlecakes and fried sausages floating out the kitchen window.

Kingston was already at the table. After the twins and Emmet sat down, Reno asked Mariana to serve. She hefted a big frying pan, taking time to smile at each guest before piling up his plate.

Emmet ignored Kingston on purpose and looked at Mariana. "It seems like all you've done since we got here is feed us," he said.

"I'm the type of person who likes to cook," Mariana said. "Really likes it."

"Gentlemen," Kingston said, "today you'll

get to see the hacienda. It took me a long time to find the vantage point we're going to. It's a tricky route but worth the effort."

Emmet attacked his breakfast. "What about Soapy and the others?" he asked between mouthfuls.

"I'll take them there if time allows. At least this way, you and the twins get to see the place."

The men quickly downed their meals, thanked Mariana and Reno again for their hospitality, and went outside to gather their gear. Emmet watched Kingston stuff a brass spyglass and several rolled-up maps into his saddlebag before mounting up.

The four wended east off the main trails for several hours. They had ventured far out into the backcountry when Kingston ducked up a side trail that wasn't visible from the road.

"Major, it's plain as a pack saddle that you know the terrain," Emmet said as he spurred Ruby Red upward.

Kingston guided them along a series of narrow trails and switchbacks for another hour until they reached a small glade, where they picketed the horses and footed it the rest of the way up.

After a twenty-minute climb, they came to a small clearing with an outcrop of rimrock on the lip of a deep ravine. The ledge could only accommodate two people at a time, so Kingston and Emmet went first, and the twins laid back. Emmet scrambled on his belly to keep hidden. He scrunched behind the rock and then eased his head up to get his first glimpse of Salazar's hacienda.

It was staggeringly beautiful. The main house was a sprawling, two-story building of pink adobe with several open patios shaded by Mexican plum and redbud trees. A half-dozen chimneys poked out at different points in the clay-tiled roof. A large cobbled courtyard shimmered in front, and a tall fountain bubbled water over two sculpted basins. A second smaller courtyard on the east side faced them.

"Well, ain't this a little hunk of heaven," Emmet whispered.

"And a well guarded one at that," Kingston replied.

Both men took turns peering through the spyglass. A seven-foot-high wall surrounded the hacienda. Emmet could see the sentries shifting in the shade in the two watchtowers that loomed over the front gate. A large arch framed the entrance, and beneath it hung a wooden door as thick as a drawbridge.

"There's two more guards patrolling the inside yard that we can't see from here,"

Kingston said, "and at least another half a dozen inside the hacienda. If I can't ransom Faith tomorrow and we're forced to fight, then the key will be to isolate the bunkhouse from the hacienda and keep those vaqueros at bay. Check out the bunkhouse."

In the back, a hundred yards outside the wall, was a long log cabin with a porch in front, and stables and a corral to the side. Emmet saw a row of outhouses lining the edge of the woods. A narrow road snaked off to the west towards a small humpback bridge crossing the river.

"That cabin can bunk a lot of men," Kingston said. "I've counted up to twenty horses in the corral. This compound has only two ways in or out, which simplifies matters: the main gate in front, and the wooden bridge to the rear."

"Where are the girls?" Emmet asked.

"In a large storage room on the far corner of the house on the first floor. The room opens on a long hallway that connects to the great room. There's always one guard outside the door."

"How do you know the inside so well?"

"A little bird told me," Kingston said, and then he smiled. "A little bird that carries a sewing needle and a tape measure. Salazar lives on the second floor on the side closest to us. Garza lives on the far side. Now look at the back room on the second story. That's Salazar's den. That's where he works. The den overlooks the smaller courtyard. He's an early riser, and he spends a lot of time in there. I'll say this about him, he works hard at being a bad person. Do you think you can make a head shot on Salazar if we're forced to go that route?"

"It's a cherry, Major," Emmet assured him.

At that moment the female captives appeared in the yard, rubbing their eyes to adjust to the bright sunlight.

"Daily exercise," Kingston said.

The girls looped around the inside perimeter of the wall, stretching their arms and legs as they went. A guard in the yard watched them, and two more vaqueros sauntered over to a nearby hitching post to watch the procession. One was gnawing on a chicken wing, the other smoking a cigarette.

"I count nine girls," Emmet said, "and I'll bet a dollar to a doorknob I know which one is Faith."

"That's two more girls than I saw last time," Kingston said. "I want to avoid a fight. Salazar has to be willing to negotiate tomorrow. If it's money that he wants, it's money I'll give him. If we have to attack, who knows what will happen to Faith or any of those girls."

Through the spyglass, Emmet saw the vaqueros joking and backslapping each other every time the girls passed in front of them. *Laugh now, you lizards,* Emmet thought.

They eyed the terrain for ten more minutes before crabbing sideways to the waiting twins. Emmet dusted himself off with his hat while Kingston explained to the brothers what to look for. After the boys finished their look-about, the four retraced their steps to the horses and descended the foothills.

As they were about to rejoin the main road, loud hoofbeats came hammering down the trail. Kingston held his hand up. "Keep hidden," he whispered. Minutes later, Emmet recognized the men racing past as Danny Brown and his blond companion. He looked at the twins, and the three of them hooked eyes.

Kingston noticed the eye contact. "Know them?" he asked.

Emmet spoke up. "Yeah, we got into a tight crease with them at a cantina our first day in Santa Sabino."

"About what, Emmet?" Kingston asked.

"Who was gonna pay for lunch."

Kingston looked back at the twins. "Are they after you?"

"Might be," Zack said with a smile.

"It ain't funny," Emmet snapped. "I know you two relish the confusion you cause, but somebody could've gotten killed back in that cantina for no good reason. Plus, Zack, I don't see no humor in what happened to that man's daughter and her unborn baby."

Zack's smirk wilted, and his face darkened.

Kingston shook his head. "We'd best stay on the back trails. The safe bet is to lay low at Reno's and wait for Soapy and the others to show up. On the way back, you three are going to tell me exactly what happened in that cantina."

The foursome crossed the main road to a different side trail, accepting that the longer route would keep them in the saddle for an extra hour.

CHAPTER 12
VIPER

Faith and Valencia paired up while they exercised. As they walked around the inside wall of the estate behind the other girls, Faith studied the yard, searching for a way out. The wall was too high to scale, but she noticed several wooden water barrels beneath a ramada. As she circled the yard, she noted the guards in the front towers had a blind spot — the right back corner of the big house near the water pump.

"Hey, blondie," the vaquero with the chicken bone yelled. "Where did you come from?"

Faith ignored him, kept walking.

"Something that beautiful must have dropped from heaven," his companion said.

The first vaquero tossed the bone on the ground and licked his greasy fingers. "She may be from heaven, but she's landed in hell."

"Better not let Señor Salazar hear you talk

that way," the guard warned.

The words had no sooner left the man's mouth than Salazar and Juanita exited the big house from the side courtyard with the mastiff hulking behind them.

"Moco. Chimo," Salazar shouted. "Back to work." The men made no reply and returned to the bunkhouse through the rear gate.

"Ladies, exercise is over," Juanita said. "Time to wash up."

The group followed her to the west side of the yard where she pointed to the water pump that was surrounded by several basins and a stack of washcloths. Sweat coated Faith's upper lip, and the mix of dust and perspiration formed a film over her skin. She was eager to rinse off, but the station could only accommodate three girls at a time. She backed off to let the other girls go and ducked under the ramada to get out of the direct sun.

"Viper," Salazar shouted.

Faith spun around to see the dog staggering across the yard as if it were drunk. She found the sight comical at first, until the mastiff stopped cold and pushed its head towards the ground trying to retch.

"Something's wrong," Salazar said in a panicked voice.

The dog stood motionless for several minutes and then jerked its head in a frantic spasm. Saliva oozed from its mouth in thick drops. Salazar approached the animal with an outstretched hand to comfort it. He knelt next to the distressed dog, the knees of his brown canvas pants now coated with dust.

"Something's wrong," he repeated. The animal remained rigid, afraid to move its head, teeth clenched, slobber dripping from its maw in long, syrupy strands.

Faith sprinted from the shadow of the ramada and stopped behind Salazar. "The dog's choking to death," she informed him. Her tone was flat, unemotional.

The unexpected proximity of Faith's voice startled Salazar. Juanita's voice pierced the air. "Get back here now." The guard raced over, grabbed Faith by the arm, and pushed her back towards the other girls.

"Wait," Salazar said. "Miss Wheeler, can you help him?"

Faith didn't answer. She turned and squatted next to the dog, set her quivering hands on its muscular shoulders. The dog pulled back its lips to show the yellowed tips of its fangs and growled, but Faith did not take her hands away.

She spoke reassuring words to the dog, looked into its eyes, tried to ignore the powerful jut of its jaw just inches from her face, jaws that could mutilate her in seconds. The girl's gentle strokes silenced the growling. The animal blinked its black eyes, sidled closer to her.

She slid the pin out and unlocked the slave collar. The iron links made a chinking sound when they hit the ground. "Smell that?" Faith asked. A strong foul odor hung around the beast like a cloud. "He's scared. Dogs leak when they're frightened. It's the stink of fear."

"Save him," Salazar said.

Faith placed her hands on the dog's ears, stroked them backwards, kept speaking in a soothing voice. The animal began to shake, its head now drooping at a lower angle.

She set one hand on the back of the dog's head, the other on its massive chest, distributing the energy in her hands across the dog's body.

Now she placed both hands on the dog's neck and, with stronger pressure and greater deliberation, worked them up towards its muzzle. Her hands were halfway up the dog's throat when she heard a loud crack. The dog swallowed hard, and whatever was lodged in its throat was gone. The animal's behavior changed in a flash. Its long tail lashed the air, and the dog washed Faith's face with whiskered licks.

"You saved him!" Salazar shouted. He pivoted towards the guard. "She saved him." Turning back to Faith, he said, "You're a healer. You have gifts."

He offered his hand to Faith to help her up, but she refused it.

The snub angered Salazar, and his tone turned. "I intend to find out what he was choking on," he muttered, "and punish the person responsible."

"The dog is okay," Faith offered. "There's no need to punish anybody."

"I pride myself on taking great care of this animal. Something almost killed him, and I'm going to get to the bottom of it, if I have to claw through his shit for the next week to find out what it was."

"You must have a lot of time on your hands," Faith said and smiled to herself. "But my guess is that a man like you will have someone else do the clawing for you." Faith waited for his reaction.

Salazar did a double take, and his eyes brightened. "You're different from the rest," he said. "You're making me rethink what to do with you. Thank you for saving my dog."

Faith ignored his words of gratitude and walked back to the other girls with a flush of satisfaction.

"Don't ever try a stunt like that again," Juanita warned her. "Never approach Señor Salazar unless told to."

Faith ignored Juanita, too, and picked up a basin, pumping water into it. Then she plunged her hands into the cold liquid and splashed it over her face. The feeling was one of sublime refreshment. It dispersed the hotness and grime, just like a thunderstorm cleanses the air after a sweltering heat wave.

CHAPTER 13
THE SHOOTING CONTEST

As Kingston, Emmet, and the twins neared the steep trail down to Reno's bungalow, they heard gut-busting laughter booming through the trees.

Kingston glanced at Emmet. "Sounds like Soapy has arrived."

At the bottom of the defile, the four riders noticed a limber hitched to six horses in the yard, and another hitched to six mules. A smooth-bore cannon gleamed behind the horses, and a Gatling gun behind the mules. A third wagon covered with canvas brought up the rear. The newcomers were sprawled out in tree shade, and they swiveled their heads when Kingston sauntered over.

"Well, I'll be a giddy goat," Soapy yelled. He hopped up and hustled over to Kingston. "Major, it's been a long time."

"Soapy, you old scalawag," Kingston said.

Emmet saw Soapy's eyes key on him next. "Emmet, you rebel devil," he said. "It's been years." They thumped each other's backs like long lost brothers.

Soapy continued the introductions. "Boys, this is Frank Mackenzie. He's big enough to hunt bears with a switch. This here's Emmet Honeycut."

Frank Mackenzie was about thirty years old, and, after he stood, Emmet realized he was without exception the heftiest human being he'd ever come across. His legs were solid as road markers, and his hands were like two ham hocks hanging by his sides. He was wide as a wagon, and his enormous bulk seemed bolted to his bones. He was stuffed into gray pants and a black shirt. A hawk feather stuck out of his hatband. Emmet ranged a few inches over six feet, but Frank was another head above him.

"You're a big one, Frank," Emmet said. "I'm glad you're on our side."

Frank said nothing, staring at Emmet with cold, unsparing eyes.

"Something wrong?" Emmet asked.

"You tell me," he said, his voice as prickly as a cactus.

Soapy sensed the chill and moved the how-do-you-dos along. "This here's Chiquito," he said. "He's a fierce warrior."

An Apache with two long, black braids, dressed in a red shirt and black cotton pants, walked over to Emmet. He was rawboned, with a pointy face ending at a chin that looked sharp enough to split wood. His handshake was strong, the skin on his hands as scaly as a lizard's.

"Chiquito," Emmet said.

The Indian nodded. Emmet got the immediate sense that none of these men were big talkers, which was fine by him.

As Chiquito went over to greet Kingston, Zack leaned into Emmet. "You never said there'd be red niggers."

"Mind your manners, boy," Soapy piped in. "He's with us, not against us."

Chiquito had apparently heard what Zack said and stepped toward him. He pointed to Zack's head. "Red hair," he said and then pointed to his own waist. "Would look good on my belt."

Zack glowered at the Apache.

"Aw, he's just joshing you, son," Soapy said with a dismissive wave.

Now Abe pushed in. "Apache, huh? You're a long way from home, ain't you?"

Chiquito studied Abe's face. "You know your geography," he said. "What else do you know?"

"I know Zack hates Apaches, and because I'm his brother, I probably do, too."

Soapy sped the final introduction along.

"Last but not least, we got Billy. He's a top rail muleskinner."

Now Emmet gave a disapproving glare. "Not him," he said, shaking his head.

"The man I hoped to get couldn't come on such short notice," Soapy said. "Billy's the best I could do."

Billy Bigby was tall and skinny, his Stetson too big for his head. Emmet had met Billy several years before at one of Soapy's gun shows and considered him harmless. But worse, Billy was slow, which Emmet recognized as a liability going against men like Garza and Salazar. He decided nothing could be done about it now.

"I guess we have to dance with who we brung," he said under his breath.

Now it was Kingston's turn to speak. "Please, all of you, sit. I want to thank you for traveling here on such short notice and with so little information. Soapy and Emmet, you did a fine job assembling this bunch. Reno explained why I needed you here. Salazar and Garza abducted my niece. Their plan is to auction her off. Our time is short. An army unit escorting the bidders will arrive in three days."

"Army?" Billy yelped. "Are we planning on fighting an army?"

"I hope not to," Kingston replied. "I'm

meeting with Salazar tomorrow. I intend to pay a ransom for my niece and then depart Santa Sabino long before the army gets here, but not before I pay each of you five hundred dollars for showing up."

The men smiled and nodded, pleased at such generous compensation for merely taking a few days' ride into the hills. Emmet, in particular, found the offer compelling. Money is power in the pocket, and that was enough to pay off all his debts and then some — and zero risk of ending up with holes in his body that weren't natural.

"What about the other girls?" Zack asked.

"I'm here for Faith. If I can free her, my job here is done."

"So the rest of the girls are on their own?" Emmet said. He realized his tone might have come across as judgmental, but he didn't care.

"I have only so much money," Kingston replied. "I had no idea of the size of Salazar's operation and how many girls were involved until I arrived."

"What happens if Salazar won't deal?" Soapy asked.

"Then we'll storm the compound. I'm prepared to pay each of you two thousand dollars to help me take her by force."

Kingston took a moment to let the men

consider his offer. Billy piped a loud whistle, and the others looked at each other with bulging eyes and laughs of approval.

"Make no mistake," Kingston continued. "We're greatly outnumbered even without the army's arrival. Salazar and Garza have at least two dozen gunslingers and ex-soldiers guarding the estate. But we've got the bulge on them because of the element of surprise and, from what I see behind those wagons" — Kingston flashed a huge grin — "superior firepower."

"I hope we'll only have to fight this battle once to win it," Soapy said.

"I do, too," Kingston replied. "For now, I commend you to Reno, our gracious host. Is there anything you'd like to say to our guests, Reno?"

"Yes, Major Kingston. Gentlemen, I have three simple words for you: Eat, drink, rest." Reno stretched his arms out in a warm gesture of welcome.

"Soapy," Emmet said, "how about showing us the Christmas presents you got hidden under them tarps."

Soapy's face brightened. "Emmet, get ready to rub your flabbergasted eyes till you see spots."

"My munitions business is booming," Soapy

said as he undid the slipknots on the last wagon. "I can't keep up with the demand. I got me one customer — a Mexican army captain garrisoned at Colonia Nueva — who'll buy just about anything I can get my hands on."

While Kingston examined the Gatling gun, Emmet ran his hand along the smooth metal neck of the cannon muzzle.

"That captain is especially crazy about big guns like these," Soapy said, "and he can break your ears once he starts talking about them." He untied the last knot and flipped back the tarp, revealing a wagon crammed with crates of guns, cartons of ammunition, and boxes of dynamite.

Kingston's mouth fell open. "Damnation," he said.

"Soapy, you done good," Emmet said. "You left the major one word short of speechless."

"Look at these," Soapy said, lunging into the wagon. He snapped a wooden slat off one of the crates, reached in, and handed each man a Spencer repeating carbine. "I got two crates full."

Emmet held the weapon as if it were an expensive vase, admiring its red-walnut stock and compact, twenty-inch barrel. He had mixed feelings about the guns. The

129

Yanks favored Spencers because they were magazine-fed. Many of the soldiers Emmet fought beside toted muskets and powder, which were no match against repeating action weapons like these, and the casualty lists proved it. He aimed it and marveled at its balance, liking how the gun felt snug against his body.

Soapy made a circuit around the wagons pointing out the shot, dynamite, fuses, canisters, shells, powder, and, most impressive, the belts for the Gatling gun. "That gun will spit out four hundred rounds a minute," he said. "I brought enough cartridges to take down an army."

"I hope it doesn't come to that," Kingston joked.

The wagon contained army-issued tents, medical supplies, and rations, mostly hard tack and jerky. Soapy even thought to bring a small box of shaving mirrors for long-range signaling.

Kingston walked over to Soapy and put his right arm around him. "You're amazing, Mister Waters. I think you've got us all feeling quite inspired right now."

"One more thing, Major." Soapy broke free of Kingston's arm, reached into the wagon just behind the jockey box, and pulled out a brass bugle strung on a blue rope.

"Remember this?" He put the bugle to his lips and played the rebel "Charge" call. The noise made Reno laugh, but it chilled Emmet. Hearing that sound after so many years triggered images of hundreds of Confederate soldiers falling to the ground like dead leaves, and it weighed on his heart.

"Stop that racket," Frank yelled, "and put that damned thing down."

Soapy lowered the horn. "Sorry about that, Frank. I forgot you fought for the North."

"What?" Emmet sputtered. "You're a Yank?"

"The war's over, Honeycut," Frank said with a snarl. "Get over it. Or maybe you still wish you were living in the land of cotton?"

The tips of Emmet's ears started to burn. Reno tried to calm the situation by pointing to a large cask. "What's in there?"

"Brandy," Soapy told him, eager once again to move the conversation along. "When this thing's over, this here brandy is going to flow like buttermilk. We're going to paint our tonsils until we're whittled white, and that keg is dry."

"I don't drink with Yanks," Emmet said

and spat on the ground.

Kingston stepped over, set his hand on Emmet's shoulder, and whispered in his ear, "I know how far your hatred goes. I know the world will always be colored gray and blue for you; I understand that. But we need all the help we can get."

Emmet decided to let things float and turned away.

"Billy, picket the mules and horses by the creek," Kingston ordered.

"Wait," Zack called out. "Can I try out one of them Spencers?"

Soapy handed him a rifle but held on to the box of cartridges. Zack whirled around, aiming the shining new weapon at imaginary targets. Emmet knew he had trained him well when he heard Zack remark to himself "nice balance."

"Give me some ammo, Soapy," Zack said, holding out his hand.

"Reno, is it okay to shoot on the premises?" Soapy asked.

"Not here. The shots would echo right up this canyon. Go a quarter mile down the road past that curve where there are plenty of open fields, the view opens up, and the sound of the shots won't carry."

Soapy tossed Zack the box. "Have at it, son."

"Mr. Honeycut, are you up to a challenge?" Zack asked.

"What you got in mind?"

"Strike the match."

Emmet would be the first to admit that sharpshooters love to compete against each other. During the war, he had heard about the Berdan Sharpshooters of the North. Just to get into that group meant being able to fire ten rounds into a circle ten inches wide at a distance of two hundred yards. Emmet fought with Maney's Brigade. They preferred a game of "Drive the Nail," which required hitting a fat-head nail stuck in a tree from a hundred yards, with the intent of repeatedly hitting the nail until it was flush with the bark.

But the contest Emmet loved the most was "Strike the Match," where the shooter tries to hit the head off three matchsticks stuck in a post a hundred yards away. Extra money is usually wagered on the third match, daring the shooter to actually light it instead of knocking the head off.

"You're on, Zack," Emmet said. "Two dollars for hits on the sticks and ten for a fire-strike on the third. Ten practice shots apiece. Anybody else want in?"

"I got the moxie," Frank said, grabbing a rifle and a box of bullets.

"Careful, Frank," Soapy warned. "Emmet here was a sharpshooter during the war. He never misses. He can toss an apple in the air and shoot out all the seeds before it hits the ground. God gave him the gift of an uncommon eye."

"I know he's a sharpshooter," Frank said with a curled lip. "Let's see what you got, Honeycut."

Emmet, Zack, Billy, and Frank walked down the road until the trees gave way to an open meadow filled with the pungent smell of newly cut hay. Soapy lagged behind a few yards, whistling "Buffalo Gal" and strolling like he was on his way to his favorite fishing hole. A low fence made of posts and wire cut across the field. Soapy directed Billy to run out and set up the targets and, most important, keep his head down afterwards.

While Billy ran into the field with a box of wooden matches, the men each fired ten practice shots into the bole of a huge oak to get comfortable with the Spencers. Emmet found the barrel shorter than what he was used to, but it didn't take long for him to get the knack.

What he loved about these weapons was that they could be fitted with a Stabler cutoff, a gadget that blocked the magazine. If careful, aimed fire was needed — like they were doing now — the magazine could be blocked and single cartridges fed into the breech, one at a time. That way, the shooter can keep the magazine full until rapid fire was needed. For rapid fire, the shooter slid the cut-off aside and fired at will.

They flipped coins to determine the shooting order. Frank lost and went first. The rifle was a toy in his hands. He assumed his firing stance and spent a long minute lining up his shot. He squeezed the trigger, and the gun recoiled. Billy popped his head up and said, "Miss." Emmet heard Frank mutter something under his breath before taking aim on his second shot. When that turned out to be a miss as well, Emmet could hear the big man's cussing loud and clear.

"This is hard," he growled before taking aim a third time. He fired again. Three was Frank's lucky number, because Billy yelled "Hit." Frank gave a huge sigh of relief. "At least I'm in the running for some of the money," he said.

"You keep believing that, Frank," Soapy said.

Zack went second. As he aimed at the target, Billy popped his head up right in

Zack's line of fire and shouted, "Who's shooting next?"

"Keep your head down, you damned fool," Soapy yelled.

Zack stared at Soapy in disbelief. "Is he a dingus? I almost blew him to hell on a shutter."

"God forgive me for saying this, because he's my sister's kid. Billy's great with the mules, but he's a couple of biscuits short of a picnic, if you know what I mean. I'm awful sorry, Zack."

"Stay down," Zack hollered at Billy. He aimed and fired. "Miss," Billy yelled as the shot chipped the wood in the post. Emmet figured Zack might have been a bit rattled given he had almost separated Billy's head from his body a minute earlier.

Zack aimed his second shot, but this time he bided his time, patient as an undertaker until the shot felt right, and then fired. "Hit," Billy said. A big smile stretched across Zack's face. Decision time had now arrived: it's safer to go for the direct hit on the match head on the third try. Trying to light it almost always ends in a miss.

Emmet knew that Zack would play it safe. "I'll throw in an extra twenty dollars if you light the match," he said, hoping Zack would bite.

"Not this time, Mr. Honeycut. I'm still a bit awkward with the Spencer. I'm going for the easier shot."

He squinted, aimed, and fired. "Hit," Billy confirmed. The men clapped and slapped Zack on the back. "The pressure's on, Mr. Honeycut," he said.

Emmet took up his position. "Gentlemen, I'm gonna let you in on a little secret about sharpshooting," he said. "It's all about breathing right. I sight and then breathe out normally, making sure not to take up any tension in my arms. Once I lock on my target, I breathe deep in and out. I track how the rifle moves slightly in the up and down direction. On the breath out, I'll have five to ten seconds before the breathing reflex triggers the need for more air. During that brief calm, I know that any up and down wobble will be small. I wait for the calm, and then I squeeze the trigger."

He aimed, breathed in, out, waited for the calm, and fired.

"Hit," Billy yelled.

Emmet repeated his routine.

"Hit," Billy yelled.

"Now, stop right there," Zack said. "I'll throw in an extra twenty dollars if *you* light the match."

Emmet had already made up his mind to

137

go for the strike. "You're on," he told him. As Zack reached into his wallet, removed some paper bills, and tossed them on a log, Emmet asked, "Anybody else want in?"

"Wait a minute," Frank said, puzzled. "You intend to light the match and just not hit the head off? That's damn near impossible. I'm in for twenty dollars." He jammed his fist into his pocket, plucked out some cash, and pitched it on the pile. "Twenty dollars is nothing compared to the money the major promised us."

Emmet settled in, letting all the tension seep out of his arms and hands. Even with all the men's eyes focused on him, he felt poised, loose. He locked on, breathed in, waited for the calming moment, then squeezed off. The crack of the shot echoed across the field.

Billy jumped up and shouted, "Jerusalem's crickets, he lit the match, Uncle Soapy. He lit the damned match."

Frank raced out to the fence post and scowled when he saw the flame burning its way down the matchstick. The rest of the men congratulated Emmet.

"You still got the goods, Mr. Honeycut," Zack said.

Emmet scooped up his winnings, slapped him on the back, and said, "So do you."

"Double or nothing?" Zack asked.

"I'm gonna let that little display stand for now. You boys keep at it. And let me know if anybody lights a match. I'll give twenty dollars to any man who does."

Soapy and Zack were chattering away about "the shot," but Frank was silent as the Sphinx, so Emmet decided to needle him.

"Better luck next time," he called over.

Frank's face went dark as a winter night. He glared at Emmet and said, "So you were a sniper during the war, huh?"

"I prefer the word sharpshooter."

"I bet you do. Which did you do to the Baxter girl — snipe her or sharpshoot her?"

Soapy and Zack went quiet.

"You got something you want to say?" Emmet asked.

"I got a question for you. Is it harder to shoot a Union soldier from a distance, or a child? I mean, if you're far enough away, I'd expect there'd be no difference, because you can't see their faces."

Soapy moved in between them. "Hey now, Frank, that wasn't called for."

"I ended her pain," Emmet said in a clipped tone.

"Is that what you do?" Frank scoffed. "Put people out of their misery?"

"You weren't there."

Frank pointed at Emmet. "Who made you God?"

"I wasn't playing God. But I got eyes to see and ears to hear, and I see and hear a lot of needless suffering in this world."

"Well, I got eyes and ears, too, but I don't go around killing kids," he answered back.

"You'd best let things sit," Emmet warned.

"Or what? What you going to do? You're good with a gun, sitting up in a tree, or sneaking around in the shadows. Let me see what you can do with your fists, man to man."

"I ain't gonna fight you, Frank."

"What's the matter? Guts turning to fiddle strings?"

"You got my bristles up, but I ain't mad enough to be stupid. You're bigger and stronger than me. You'd clean my plow. I know my limits."

"You're damn right I'd clean your plow."

"Plus, if you give me a whupping, you'd have to spend the rest of your time here watching your back. Nobody here knows you that good, or cares a rap about you, but I got some personal loyalties working in my favor. You saw what Zack can do with a gun. You should see what Abe can do in the dead of night with a knife and some proper motivation."

"Enough threats," Soapy said. "This is utter nonsense. Let's go back to the house."

Soapy grabbed Emmet's arm and spun him back towards the bungalow. Frank mumbled something neither one could hear. Emmet ignored it, because he saw Reno running down the road towards them.

"Emmet, the major and I need to talk to you right away," Reno said.

Emmet could tell from Reno's fevered words and chalk-white face that there was a problem. "Something wrong?"

"Very wrong," Reno said.

The trio hustled up the road to the bungalow.

CHAPTER 14
MOCO AND CHIMO

Salazar and Garza lolled in the shade of the side courtyard. A small breeze kicked up and wafted a fine mist off the bubbling fountain. Garza enjoyed the thin veil of vapor against his leathery face.

"We have a visitor coming tomorrow morning," Salazar said.

Garza dug his thumb into an orange and began peeling it, the scent of citrus sweetening the air.

"Who?"

"Arthur Kingston."

"What's he want?"

"To buy my little mustang, Yago."

Garza smiled. "You mean *our* little mustang. The girl is a gold mine — the real simon-pure. Tell him to wait until Captain Ortega gets here with our other guests."

"This one is different. Claims he's family. My guess is that he's the uncle Faith mentioned to me, so this would be more like a ransom."

Garza tossed a piece of rind on the ground. "Faith, huh? So now we're on a first name basis? Since when did you and her get so chummy?"

Salazar ignored the comment. "The meeting is mid-morning."

"How much is he willing to pay?" Garza asked. He popped an orange slice into his mouth and chewed.

"It doesn't matter. I'm not selling."

Garza stopped in mid-chew. The tips of his ears started to tingle. "What do you mean? To him? Or to anybody?"

"To anybody. That girl is special."

Garza swallowed, wiped the juice on his hands onto his pants, and pointed his finger. "Listen to me. I told you that girl is a gold mine. I was the one who found her. I was the one who took her. I sure as hell intend to get my cut. If you want her so badly, outbid everybody else and then give me my share."

"Easy, Yago. I haven't decided what I'm going to do yet. But don't worry; you'll get your cut. Haven't I always done right by you?"

"So far. But don't ever let that change."

Salazar squinted his eyes. "Is that a threat?

I'm still the one calling the shots. Remember that."

Garza resented his cousin's hard tone and decided to push back. "You wear your power like a robe, Enrique, but you're losing your edge. Your hands are turning as soft as a woman's. You rely on me to do the dirty work. You remember *that.*"

Salazar glared. "I'm not losing my edge."

"At least hear Kingston's offer. Otherwise, why bother meeting with him?"

Salazar rubbed his forehead. "I'll listen to what he has to say, but I also want to find out what else he's up to. Tito spotted him in town a week ago. He'll be joining us tomorrow morning before the meeting to tell us anything new he's learned about Kingston."

"You think there's more to him than meets the eye?"

"Just a suspicion. In the meantime, look at this." He handed Garza a sheet of paper. "We have several new guests this year. We need to make them feel welcome so they'll come back. More bidders, more money."

Garza spent several minutes silently studying the paper. "The men are coming from farther and farther away," he noted.

"Our fame spreads," Salazar said, throwing out his chest.

"Our success might make Captain Ortega greedier," Garza suggested.

"You mean his political aspirations? If he wants more money, we'll give it to him. All politicians are as crooked as a dog's hind leg, and Ortega is no exception. We could use a friend in the governor's mansion."

Juanita emerged from the side yard with Viper stumping beside her. "We're back," she said. The dog lowered its bulk down to the tiled floor next to Salazar's left boot.

"How was your walk?" he asked.

"Informative."

"What did you learn?"

"It was a chicken bone the dog was choking on. I saw the evidence. I assumed I didn't have to bring it back to show you."

"A chicken bone?" Salazar's eyes went dark as dolmens. "Was it Moco or Chimo who was eating the chicken bone in the yard while the girls were exercising?"

"I don't remember," Juanita replied.

"Have Armando tell both of them to come here."

Juanita went inside, and, a minute later, Armando came out and sprinted for the bunkhouse.

"So you think I've lost my edge, Yago?" Salazar asked.

"Enrique, it seems these days you focus

on paper more than anything."

"We run a good business, and we've done well, no? And we did it ourselves, the hard way. We risked everything because we wouldn't settle for the ordinary. Others talked. We acted."

"We've prospered like princes," Garza said.

"Since we've taken control, this valley is thriving. No more Indian raids. No more *pistolero* attacks. Santa Sabino lives in peace."

"Santa Sabino lives in fear," Garza said, his voice calm, confident.

"That too, cousin. And I thank you for being the forceful hand that makes the villagers tremble."

"Ours is a two-handed operation, Enrique. You extend your palm for money, and I extend my fist if people refuse to contribute. All I'm saying is, in the future, you could do more to help me obtain the women, especially if you intend to keep some of the fruits of my labor for yourself."

"I'll think about it."

Minutes later, Moco and Chimo strode into the courtyard and stood between the cousins and the fountain.

"Which one of you dropped a chicken bone in the main yard?" Salazar asked. His voice was playful.

The vaqueros glanced at each other. Neither responded.

Salazar reached into his hip pocket, slid out a Remington Over-Under derringer, and cocked the trigger. "Once more, which of you dropped a chicken bone in the yard?" He widened his grin.

Chimo pointed at Moco with both hands. Moco threw his arms in the air and, with a puzzled look, asked, "What's this all about?"

"You tried to kill my dog."

"No, I didn't," Moco protested. "We were just having some fun with the girls. I never touched your dog." He pressed his hands together.

"He almost died choking on the chicken bone you tossed." The playfulness in Salazar's voice was gone, and the smile had drained from his face. His eyes darkened, and he glared at Moco.

"I'm sorry I dropped it on the ground, Señor Salazar. I wasn't thinking. Plus, the dog is fine. I saw it running around here earlier," Moco said, running his sentences together.

"Vibora," Salazar shouted. The dog sparked to attention.

"Listo."

The animal issued a low growl, bared its

fangs, and crouched several inches closer to the patio floor. Chimo quick-footed several feet backwards.

"Ataque!"

The mastiff raced towards Moco and lunged. The vaquero thrust his arm up to protect his face, and the dog clamped its jaws on his forearm. Moco flipped the dog loose, but the animal dug its back paws into the grout between the tiles for traction and lurched again. This time the dog's clutch was tighter, and it hung off his arm in mid-air, trying to drag him to the ground. The weight of the animal buckled Moco to one knee. Viper lashed its head right and left, trying to rip the arm from the vaquero's body.

Moco punched the dog's nose, and it disengaged, only to regain its balance and attack again. It leaped, and its momentum shoved the vaquero onto his back. Moco screamed and thrashed, trying to keep the dog's teeth from his throat. Only after the vaquero's arm had been bitten into a pulpy mess did Salazar finally yell *"basta."* At once, the dog released its grip and returned to Salazar's side panting, its mouth slick and red.

"Get up," Salazar ordered.

Moco wobbled as he rose, holding his

mangled arm up with his other hand.

"Before I turn you into a memory," Salazar said, "do you have any last words?"

"Last words?"

"Oh, Moco," Salazar said. "Not very memorable." He raised the derringer and fired point blank into the vaquero's chest, dropping him backwards into the fountain. Moco writhed and splashed for several seconds, his blood tinting the water pink, and then he went still as stone.

Salazar slid the gun back into his pocket and glanced at Garza. "Losing my edge?" he asked. He turned back to Chimo. "Take him away."

Garza could see Chimo's hands trembling as he grabbed the body under the arms. He dragged Moco from the patio and then across the main yard, the dead man's heels carving two thin furrows in the sand behind him.

"You do love that damn dog, Enrique," Garza said.

"I love him to death," Salazar answered. "Unfortunately, today it had to be Moco's."

They latched eyes for a second, and then their liquid laughter flooded the courtyard.

CHAPTER 15
RAGO

Reno, Soapy, and Emmet rushed into the bungalow and found Kingston sitting at a kitchen table cluttered with maps and drawings.

"Reno says we got trouble. What's wrong?" Emmet asked.

Kingston spoke without looking up. "It seems we have a mystery guest. There's a bounty on Chiquito's head."

"What?" Emmet asked. "Are you sure?"

"There's a Wanted poster of him nailed outside the Ox-Cart Saloon," Reno said. "I thought I recognized him when he showed up here. I went back to the saloon to double-check. It's him, all right."

"What'd he do?" Emmet asked.

"Deserted the army and murdered somebody," Kingston said. "His real name is Rago."

Emmet chewed his lip. "This ain't good."

"A wanted man can draw lightning,"

Kingston said. "The last thing we need here is a bunch of blue coats or a posse itching to lynch a redskin. I've got to believe that you didn't know anything about this, Soapy."

"Major, I swear on a ton of Bibles."

"This Indian could be a Jonah," Emmet offered, "so maybe it's best to let that bad luck ride away. Otherwise, pray he's good at covering his tracks, or else saving Faith could get a lot more complicated."

"The fact that there's a reward means the army has probably given up hunting for him," Soapy said. "It also means bounty hunters could've already tracked him here and are watching us right now."

"I guess we should have expected at least one bad hat in the bunch," Kingston said. "Have a seat. I'll go get our Indian friend. It's time we had a chat." A few minutes later, Chiquito pushed through the doorway.

Kingston wasted no time. "Is Chiquito your real name?"

The Apache gave him a wary once-over. "Yes."

Kingston cleared his throat and peered into Chiquito's eyes. "Look. This is serious. Are you Rago?"

The Apache sighed and dropped his head. Kingston tapped the top of a ladder-back chair twice with the palm of his hand, signaling him to sit.

"Now that you know who I am," Chiquito said, "my guess is that you also know there's a bounty on my head. But before you do anything, Major Kingston, you need to understand what happened."

"It doesn't matter."

"It matters to me."

Kingston gave a dull nod, scratched another chair across the floor, and set it next to the table. "Go ahead."

"It's a long story."

"Shorten it," Kingston said.

Chiquito pointed at Emmet. "Do you have tobacco?"

Emmet reached into his pants pocket, yanked out a pouch and a leaf from his book, and slid them across the table. "Any other last wishes?" he asked.

Chiquito didn't react. He rolled a smoke and pushed the pouch back to Emmet. He sparked a wooden match with his thumbnail, lit the cigarette, took a long poke, and puffed out a small, blue cloud that hung shiftless in the air. The smell made Emmet crave a cigarette, but he decided to let the Apache smoke alone.

"Enough!'" Kingston shouted. "Talk."

"I'd signed on for a six-month enlistment

as a tracker," Chiquito said, "under Lieutenant Charles Winthrop at Fort Currier. One day, my cousin Red Deer rode in and told me my father had been killed by a tribesman named Pojo. My father and Pojo were drinking and arguing. Their voices turned to shouts, the shouts turned to threats, and the threats turned to gunshots."

Chiquito straightened in the chair, stiffening his backbone against the wooden slats. "Revenge is a sacred duty to an Apache. As my father's only surviving son, that responsibility fell to me. I left the fort and tracked down Pojo."

"And my guess," Kingston said, "is that you didn't let anybody at the fort know where you were."

"No, I didn't," the Apache said in a deflated voice. He flicked ashes into an empty cup. "I had seven days left in my enlistment. My time was almost up. But I wasn't thinking of that. I was only thinking of my duty to my family."

"Did you find Pojo?" Emmet asked.

Chiquito leaned toward Emmet and grinned. "Of course I found Pojo. He was easy to track. I simply followed the trail of whiskey bottles. Even though he had a two-day head start, I caught up to him in three days. To prove his killing was no accident, I shot him twice, just like he did to my father."

"Interesting," Emmet said. "I'll have to remember that next time I want to make the same point."

"What happened when you returned to the fort?" Kingston asked.

Chiquito pulled a piece of tobacco off his lip. "Lieutenant Winthrop charged me with leaving my post without authorization, dereliction of duty, and . . . desertion."

"That'll get you posing in front of a firing squad," Soapy said.

"That was Winthrop's intent," Chiquito said. "I offered to extend my enlistment for the number of days I was gone, but he wouldn't consider it."

"That explains the desertion," Kingston said. "What about the murder?"

Chiquito took two quick puffs. "Thompson tried to take me by force. Red Deer and I drew our weapons and took off for the gate. Winthrop shot Red Deer, and I put three bullets in Winthrop's chest. Once I was outside the fort, I zigzagged my horse to avoid the gunfire from the towers. When I reached the tree line, I knew they'd never find me. I figured the army would pursue me south and west, so I came east."

"I met up with Chiquito in Sweetwater,"

Soapy said, "but I never knew anything about this."

Chiquito took one last drag off the cigarette before crushing it inside the cup. "Major Kingston, who told you I'm a wanted man?"

Before Kingston could answer, Reno jumped in. "I saw your face on a Wanted poster."

"How much is the reward?" Emmet asked.

"One hundred and fifty dollars," Chiquito said.

"Actually, now you're worth two hundred dollars according to the poster I saw," Reno said.

"Dead or alive?" Emmet asked.

Reno looked down at the floor. "Yes."

"What are you planning to do with me, Major?" Chiquito asked.

"If you've played us false, Rago, there's any number of men here who'll kill you on the spot."

"I do not speak in two directions. And please, continue to call me Chiquito. You understand — for safety reasons, and to avoid confusing the others."

"Okay," Kingston said. "If we have to fight, we'll need every man we can get, so even though you're a man on the dodge, you're still in. Stay out of sight. No need for you to show your face anywhere in town. There's nothing we can do if bounty hunters have already trailed you here. You best be watching your back."

"I always do," Chiquito said.

"And you're right; we'll keep this our little secret. No point in whipping the others up right now. You can go."

The Indian rose and left the room. A slow burn had been building inside Emmet. When Chiquito was out of earshot, he launched into Soapy. "What the hell did you bring us? A buffle-brained boy, an ornery Yank, and a wanted redskin?"

"Now you just hold on there, Emmet," Soapy snapped back. "Major Kingston asked me to find him some able men. He never said they had to have pedigrees, otherwise this place would be emptier than a church."

"Soapy's right, Emmet," Kingston said. "He did his best on short order."

"Remember what these men bring to the party," Soapy said in a voice that was still on the peck. "Billy is a top-rail muleskinner — just what we need. Frank knows how to fire a Gatler better than anyone — just what we need. And Chiquito is one fierce fighter — just what we need. So don't try busting me because they ain't exactly what you wanted. I brought you what you needed."

Emmet sat in thought for a few moments and realized his second-guessing Soapy was out of line, that he had done the best he could. "I appreciate your efforts," he said. "We'll try to make this work."

Soapy's shoulders eased down several inches. "Apology accepted," he said. "Now, I think we're all a bit cranky because we're hungry. Out in those wagons are the fixings for my TNT stew, and I aim to whip up a batch for tonight's supper."

Emmet's stomach growled at the thought of Soapy's specialty dish — sweetbreads and choice pieces of calf simmering in a thick brown gravy with beans and peppers. Just the smell of it cooking could drive cowboys crazy. He clapped Soapy on the back as they walked outside.

"Now where'd you happen to get fresh meat for that stew?" Emmet asked.

"I grabbed a steer down by the San Rafael River. Unfortunately, I think it was standing on Salazar's graze at the time."

"Ain't that stealing?" Emmet asked, smothering a laugh.

"I didn't steal it — just took borrow of it. He'll get it all back tomorrow in one form or another," Soapy said in a voice as serious as a senator. And then the two of them broke up laughing.

Mariana was kneeling in the garden, and the men's noise attracted her attention. She popped her head up and wagged a minatory finger at them, as if they were misbehaving schoolboys.

"Actually, Soapy, do you need anything else for that stew?" Emmet asked. "Some other fresh vegetables might sweeten the pot, no?" He was smiling at Mariana as he spoke.

Soapy noticed where Emmet's eyes were fixed, smirked, and said, "Tossing some fresh vegetables into the mix is just what the recipe calls for. Emmet, she is one flat-out handsome woman."

Emmet winked at him and said, "I thought you might think that." Then he headed towards the garden.

"Can I help with the picking?"

Mariana glanced up from where she was kneeling and offered Emmet a smile as warm as a sun-dried towel. "Of course," she said.

"You missed some fancy shooting today," he told her.

"Emmet, maybe you could pull up some carrots while I pick the beans." She handed him a brown basket. "Yes, I hear you're an amazing shooter."

Emmet gazed at row after row of carrots, their green leafy crowns sticking out of the rich black earth, filling the air with the fresh smell of springtime growth. He squatted and started yanking the vegetables out of the ground.

"My Pa learned me to shoot long before the war ever started," he said.

"Have you killed a lot of men?" She had lowered her voice when she posed the question, almost as if she didn't want anybody to hear.

"I've killed my share but never bothered to count. I figure when I meet my Maker I'll just issue one big apology for the lot of them, in case any of them deaths was undeserved. But I'll tell you this: I never killed nobody who wasn't trying to kill me first."

Emmet knew this was a lie, but he wanted to get closer to Mariana, not drive her away.

"Me and Big Betty have logged lots of time together," he said.

"Big Betty?"

"My favorite rifle. She was good to me all during the war and the years after. Big Betty's put food on my table and silver in my pocket on account of the buffalo."

"I've never seen a real buffalo."

Emmet brushed the dirt off the end of a carrot and took a bite. "They're big hairy beasts. To my mind, they're better animals than steers," he said between crunches. "They taste as good and don't need a lot of pampering like cows. They can go a long time without water; they can handle the toughest winters, and — believe what I'm telling you — they're the best darn swimmers. They can cross a river a half-mile wide without so much as sneezing.

"I prefer cows," she said.

"Cows are stupid beasts that need a lot of water. Plus they wither up in the cold. Downright fragile critters, to my mind, compared to the bison."

"You know a lot about buffaloes," Mariana said. "Are they dangerous?"

Emmet swallowed the last bite. "Buffaloes are unpredictable animals. One moment, they're peaceable enough and give you a look as bored as a kid at a Sunday sermon. Next thing, you know, for no apparent reason they'll attack you hard."

"Ever been attacked?"

"Lots of times. They are frightening beasts when they want to be and ain't a-feared of any other living thing walking the earth. Well, except for a man toting a gun."

"How many buffalo have you killed?"

160

Mariana shook her basket to settle the contents and make room for more.

"Hundreds. Back in the old days, these animals was so dumb of us that we could take them down one by one without any of them so much as turning a beard in our direction. But as the herds thinned, I swear they recognized the danger we posed, and they would turn tail and scatter at the first crack of gunfire."

Emmet needed to stand up because his leg had gone numb but didn't. He shifted and waited until the tingling passed and then switched to a new row.

"Miss Mariana, I've spent most of my life killing, and I'm sick of it. I'm hoping to change, maybe start growing something, raising something, like you do with this here vegetable patch. It takes time to grow things. It takes no time to kill."

"Do you know anything about farming?"

"Enough to know I'd like to learn more."

"It's hard work. Our plots are small, yet my father and I still work from dawn to dusk to make things grow."

"I think I got the gizzard for it. I've got two strong arms and a will that won't quit."

"Perhaps you'll be lucky enough to fulfill your destiny." Emmet sensed a change in her tone. It was flat, resigned. It almost seemed like she was losing interest in what he was trying to tell her.

"It ain't a matter of luck," he said. "It's a matter of choice. I just need to set my mind to things."

Emmet's instincts were right — she wasn't listening. She examined the beans in the basket for a few seconds. Her face darkened, and her tone turned touchy. "Well, don't plan on settling around here as long as Salazar and Garza control things. Don't plan on living a normal life. Don't make any plans for the future." She dropped the basket, cupped her face in her hands, and sobbed.

"What's wrong?" Emmet asked. He set his basket down and draped an arm around her heaving shoulders. A breeze brushed her hair against his hand, and the strands felt as soft as spider silk.

"You asked me if I would ever remarry, and I told you no," she said. "The reason is that I can't, because of Garza."

"Garza?" Emmet scratched his head. "Chew it finer, if you would, Miss Mariana."

"I didn't tell you the whole story. When I was younger, Garza fell in love with me. I never wanted his affections. Never encouraged them. Never returned them. But that didn't stop him from coming after me."

"So you and Garza go way back," Emmet said. "What did you do?"

"I told him to leave me alone, that I wanted nothing to do with him, ever. He said if he couldn't have me, nobody could. I fooled him though, or at least I thought I had. I met a wonderful boy — Miguel — who was kind, gentle, a hard worker. We fell in love, and Father Ramirez married us on a beautiful summer day."

Emmet tried to imagine how stunning she must have appeared clutching a bouquet of colorful flowers, her wedding dress billowing about her, her black hair in blissful contrast to the white veil.

"When Garza found out, he was furious," Mariana said. "Two weeks after our wedding, Miguel visited his mother and never came back. Two women doing their wash by the river saw him floating by. To this day, people believe that his drowning was an accident."

"You don't think so?"

"I know that Garza and Tito killed him. They kidnapped my husband, staked him in an arroyo, and waited for rainwater to flood the canyon and drown him."

"How do you know that?"

"Garza told me," she said, her voice cracking.

"I'm so sorry, Miss Mariana," was all Emmet could muster. Inside though, what he wanted most in the world was to have Garza's head in the middle of Big Betty's sights.

Mariana aproned away her tears. "He told me he would kill any man who approached me, and that if I told anybody that he drowned Miguel, my father would be the next man to be found floating in the river. That was my punishment. A life sentence born out of spite."

"I'm so sorry," Emmet repeated.

"He didn't want me after he learned I had married, but he wouldn't let anybody else have me either. Not long after, my mother got sick and died, and my father was lost without her, so I decided to make him my first duty. Over the years, I've never had another man because no man in Santa Sabino would dare come near me."

"So you and your pappy have your own reasons for seeing Garza dead," Emmet said. "Did Miguel know about Garza's threats?"

"Yes."

"He wasn't afraid?"

"No."

"Sounds to me like your husband was willing to die for love."

She flashed a weak smile. "That's a kind thing to say."

"Does Major Kingston know?"

"He's the only one, besides my father. And now you."

"Thanks for telling me," Emmet said with a nod.

"Now you know that I've lived most of my life in fear and shame."

"That's nonsense. I don't blame you and your pappy for not taking on Garza yourselves."

Emmet's words did not have their intended effect. Mariana grabbed her basket and stooped to pick more beans. "It doesn't matter. Nobody will take on Garza. All Major Kingston wants is to save his niece. Once he ransoms her, he'll pay you for showing up, and then you'll all go home. *Nothing* here will change."

"We all hope things will go well tomorrow, but there ain't no guarantees. Personally, I think Major Kingston's a fool to go in there alone, because the cousins don't play square. And just so you know, I have no home no more, so I may have to stick around here for a spell."

Emmet hoped for a warm reaction at the mention of staying on. She dismissed his suggestion with a faint frown and a quick wave. "Do what you want. It doesn't matter."

"It will matter if Salazar won't come to terms. Let's not get ahead of ourselves. Let's see what happens tomorrow. We just may need to unleash the firepower sitting in front of your father's house."

She remained silent, snapping off the beans in quick, brusque strokes.

Emmet realized words were no longer of use, that he might as well reason with the rain. "Hand me your basket, and I'll fetch them over to Soapy," he said with a sigh.

She passed her basket and thanked him without looking up.

Emmet walked over to Soapy, who was leaning over the cookpot. The smell of the stew diverted Emmet's thoughts and reminded him how hungry he was. He closed his eyes, inhaled, and savored the delicious aroma. When he re-opened them, he noticed Abe off to the side, squatting on his haunches and snickering at a fly on the ground. The fly's wings were missing on one side, causing it to flap and flit in a jagged circle.

"Did you pull the wings off that bug, boy?" Emmet asked.

"Yeah," Abe said with a quick laugh. "Look at it dance." He poked at the insect with his finger.

Emmet tilted the toe of his armadillo-skin boot over the fly and then pushed down hard on it like he was crushing out a lit smoke. Abe didn't draw his finger back in time, and Emmet caught the tip of it.

"Ow! What are you doing, Mr. Honeycut? That hurt."

Emmet's eyes fixed on Abe. "Never laugh at suffering, boy. Especially if it's suffering you helped make."

Abe sucked on his finger and then shook it in the air. "It was only a stupid fly. I was just having some fun."

"Find it some other way."

Soapy snatched the baskets of vegetables from Emmet and took each vegetable out, cleaned it by wiping it on his pants, and set it on a large cutting board he'd placed on a stump. After he diced the pickings into thumb-sized pieces, he slid them into the pot with the flat side of the knife.

"Trouble with Abe?" he asked.

"I worry about that boy. Might be a bad seed like his daddy."

"What do you mean?"

"I mean plant a tater, get a tater. His daddy got his neck lengthened for robbing a stage."

Soapy stirred the stew with a large wooden

spoon. "Zack isn't so bad," he said.

"I like Zack. Never cottoned to Abe though. Something in his eyes betrays the kind of man he is."

"What kind of man is that?"

"Merciless," Emmet said with conviction. "Abe prefers stabbing a man to shooting him. He likes to do his killing up close."

"I best be staying on his good side then."

"Probably a good idea."

Kingston appeared on the porch and asked if supper was ready.

"Good timing, Major," Soapy said. "M'lords and m'ladies," he called out as he bowed and made a fancy flourish with his hand, "your banquet awaits. Time to tuck on in."

The men jumped up, holding their plates in front of them like dowsing sticks and clustered around the kettle. Emmet waited his turn, plated up, propped his back against a tree, and slid down the trunk until he was sitting. Just as he was about to plunge his spoon into the stew, Kingston walked over and sat beside him.

"Salazar said to come alone, Emmet, but I'd feel better knowing you're up at that lookout tomorrow, watching what happens."

"I'll be there, Major."

"You know, in case something goes wrong."

Emmet looked up at the sky and shook his head. "Not that I could do anything about it if it did, but what could possibly go wrong? You always think of everything."

"I might not come back," Kingston said.

Emmet gave no reply. He looked down and lowered his spoon into the bowl of stew.

CHAPTER 16
CAPTAIN ORTEGA

Captain Javier Ortega led the column of carriages and soldiers towards Rio Rojano, the last village of any size before reaching Santa Sabino from the west. Even after the long journey, his blue tunic and white pants maintained their crisp, laundered look. Gold epaulettes, chunky as shaving brushes, perched atop his shoulders and gleamed like canaries in the late afternoon sun. The caravan included two dozen cavalrymen, half of them lancers, filing on either side of five town carriages and two fancy buckboards.

Inside the vehicles, well-dressed men with well-trimmed beards and ivory-topped canes lolled on thick, red cushions and peered out at the hills. As the column lumbered across a wooden bridge, the steady rhythm of rolling wheels and heavy hooves rumbled along the planks, and the deck beams groaned and heaved under the weight of the wagons and horses.

The parade proceeded up the main road and into the center of town. Ortega's detachment had departed from the garrison at Colonia Nueva with singular purpose: to escort the landowners to the Salazar estate so they could conduct their business and return them without incident.

The townsfolk stared as the group passed. People on the street edged backwards to make room for the cavalcade. Ortega stared ahead with resolve, as if gazing on the locals would somehow damage his eyes. The peasants didn't know the strangers under escort but could guess from the ornate carvings and brass fittings on the outside of the carriages that they were men of wealth and power.

A boy on horseback wearing a white *guayabera* and black pants approached the column from the rear and made his way to the front, shouting, "A message for Captain Ortega."

Ortega held his hand up, and the caravan rumbled to a stop. Lieutenant Torres intercepted the boy before he reached Ortega, took the letter, and passed it to the captain, who ripped open the envelope and read:

Dear Captain Ortega:

I have changed my mind and am not going to Santa Sabino. I have decided I want nothing to do with Enrique Salazar or Yago Garza. This will save you time because you don't have to come get me. I've only recently learned that a granddaughter of one of my long-term laborers was included in the last auction. Salazar's is a dirty business, Javier, and I don't want to be part of it anymore — and neither should you. I know you harbor political ambitions, and, when you are ready, I am ready to offer you financial backing to help you get elected. In the meantime, I urge you to end your association with the cousins. Nothing good can come of it. Consider your long-term future.

With respect,
Luis Muñoz

Ortega shoved the letter back into the envelope and said, "Lieutenant Torres, it seems Señor Munoz has other plans and will not be making the trip with us. Send a man ahead to Salazar to tell him we'll be arriving a day earlier, but with one less bidder. We don't want to surprise our host, eh? The sooner we get there and transact our business, the sooner we depart."

Torres saluted and turned his horse back to the line of soldiers. "Romero," he hollered. A soldier atop a black and white Appaloosa disengaged from the formation. Torres gave him the order, and Romero took off at full-pelt towards Santa Sabino.

Ortega watched the horse and soldier disappear over a crest in the road. He turned and eyed the line of fancy carriages trailing him. Personally, he found the auction a foul business, but these men were rich and powerful. He catered to them for his own selfish ends — financial support if he decided to run for governor of the territory. Escorting the gentry to Salazar's auctions for three years had ingratiated him, not to mention enriched him far beyond his meager military pay. Muñoz was the first person to distance himself from the unsavory enterprise. Ortega wondered if others would follow.

The captain motioned the caravan forward and continued to mull over the contents of the letter. He knew Muñoz was right. If exposed, his seeming complicity in the abductions could destroy any chance for elected office. He spent the next three hours fretting over his situation, stopping only when the group reached the outskirts of Rio Rojano.

Ortega turned back to Lieutenant Torres. "We'll be staying here tonight," he said. "Have the men pitch their tents around the plaza. Find rooms for our guests. We'll leave at daybreak."

The lieutenant snapped off another salute, spun around, and yelled orders to the men. Ortega dismounted. His back and neck were stiff from the long ride. He twisted his body to one side, then the other, swiveled his head back and forth, squatted up and down. Although he never participated in the auctions, he was always interested in seeing the girls. The more appealing they were, the more money they would bring in. His take was a direct percentage, so if this was going to be his last auction, he hoped all the girls were beautiful, or at least shapely. He doffed his shako, wiped the ring of sweat from his forehead with a handkerchief, and sat down in the shade of an enormous elm. A soldier hurried over with a gourd filled with cold well water. Ortega took a long drink and wiped his mouth with his hand. Tonight he anticipated a good meal and a bottle of fine local wine, knowing Salazar's hospitality tomorrow would be even better.

Chapter 17
Breakfast

Faith remained in the large room that served as a dormitory while the rest of the girls breakfasted. She had fashioned a long pocket on the inside of her smock using strips of a facecloth stitched together with a needle the tailor accidentally dropped on the floor. Now she hunched over, stitching the pocket into one of the inside seams of her smock. The door opened, and the girls poured in just as Faith flipped her smock over and flattened it out.

"Why you didn't eat with us?" Valencia asked.

"I got told I have to eat with Salazar this morning."

"Just you and him?" Toya asked with a wary look.

"I don't know what he has planned," Faith said, and then she noticed Calida in the corner, stooped over, clutching her stomach. "Are you okay?"

"Terrible cramping," Calida said with a gasp. She was a slight girl with sparkling green eyes and wiry hair. Faith yanked a cot over for Calida to sit. The ailing girl said, "I'm going to be sick."

Faith grabbed a chamber pot and slid it in front of the girl just before she threw up. As Faith stroked Calida's back, the outside guard stormed in.

"Not again," he bellowed. "You were sick yesterday, too."

"We've been eating a lot of rich food," Faith explained. "Her stomach's having a tough time adjusting."

"Give me that bucket," the guard said. "It stinks in here."

After the guard left, Faith helped the girl lie back on the cot and then placed her hands on either side of Calida's face. Faith leaned in so none of the other girls could hear and smelled the sour odor of the girl's bile. "Are you pregnant?" she asked.

Calida blinked back tears and nodded.

"Who is the father?"

"A boy in my village."

"Why did you say you were a virgin?"

"I was scared. I didn't know what to say. What will they do to me when they find out?"

Faith knew what they would do: kill her

and the baby inside her, but she couldn't tell the frightened girl the truth. "They won't find out," she said. "We'll do everything we can to make sure they don't find out."

The guard opened the door again and pointed at Faith. "Señor Salazar is ready for you." Just as he turned his back to leave, Faith reached under the sheet of her cot, snatched the steak knife she had stolen, and dropped it into the secret pocket.

Valencia observed her concealing the blade and called out, "Be careful."

Faith nodded, patted the pocket, and glided out the door.

Faith sat across from Salazar at the small table in the side courtyard, her spine as stiff as a cactus. Juanita set a plate of eggs and bacon before each of them. Salazar was smartly dressed in a forest green frock coat with pewter buttons and high black trousers. A scarf of green checkerpane hung from his neck.

He scooped up some eggs with his fork and swallowed them. Picking up a rasher of bacon, he nibbled it to a nub, which he then fed to Viper. The dog licked his fingers with its huge black tongue and then sat rigid as a statue, waiting for more.

Salazar pointed at Faith's plate with his fork. "Eat, Miss Wheeler. Mrs. Medina has made the bacon extra crispy."

Faith stared down at her plate. She had a stabbing hunger, and the aroma of the bacon was enticing, but she chose not to eat right then. Instead she asked, "What did you do to the man who dropped the chicken bone?"

Salazar sipped some coffee and set the small cup down. "How did you know it was a chicken bone?"

"I saw one of the cowboys eating. He dropped it on the ground just before you came outside."

"Why didn't you tell me?"

"Because I didn't want you to hurt him."

Salazar dipped his head in a gesture of understanding. "I sent him away."

"You lie," she said pointing to the pink tinge of the fountain water. "You killed him or you had him killed. I asked you not to harm him. I saved your dog, but you wouldn't spare him."

"I was upset," Salazar said. "I apologize." He re-focused on his breakfast. Then: "Tell me, Miss Wheeler, what would you like to do with your life?"

Faith realized he was changing the subject, so she decided to eat. She carved up both eggs with the edge of her fork and scooped up a mouthful. "I want to be a nurse, like my mother," she said.

Salazar's eyes brightened, half moons of brown skin sagging beneath them. "My grandmother was a healer, all five feet one inch of her," he said. "She also believed in God, like you, no?"

Faith reached for a glass of water that had two lemon wedges bobbing on top. "I believe in God," she said, "and the damnation of the wicked." She took two loud gulps.

"Such harsh words," Salazar said with a quizzical look. "Isn't forgiveness part of your religion?"

"For those who ask for forgiveness."

Salazar dabbed his lips with the linen napkin, gently set it down, and creased it with the side of his hand. "How would you like to take on a greater role at the hacienda?" he asked.

"What kind of role?"

"You're a healer, which is a tremendous gift. You could help tend sick animals, sick people even. You could assume the role your mother had, except you could do it here, in great comfort, in great luxury. Every morning could start this way for you."

The voice of her dead father resounded in

her ears: *A flattering mouth worketh ruin, Faith. Remember: the devil is a flatterer.*

She leaned forward and said, "You killed my mother and father."

Salazar held one hand up. "Garza killed them."

"He works for you."

"I'm sorry about your parents."

"You speak of them as if I'd lost a pet, instead of the people who brought me into this world."

Juanita returned to the patio to clear the plates and freshen the water glasses. She waited while Viper licked Salazar's plate clean before removing it. "More coffee?" she asked.

"No," Salazar replied. "Please bring the dog inside."

Juanita nodded, brought the plates into the house, and then returned for the animal, leaving Salazar and Faith alone. After several silent moments, Salazar rose and sauntered towards her side of the table. Cat-like, she tightened her leg muscles, ready to move in any direction.

"I'm sorry Garza killed them. All I'm asking is that you give *me* a chance," Salazar said. "Wouldn't you like to live here?"

"No," Faith said. She reached under her smock and fingered the handle of the knife.

When he stepped closer, she could smell bay rum on his skin. "I would like to be your benefactor," he said. "In fact, I'd like to be more than a benefactor."

With a trembling hand, Faith eased the knife from the hidden pocket. "What do you want?" she asked.

"You know I would never harm you," he said in a soothing voice, "or let anyone else harm you." He slid his hand along the table as he inched closer. "You and I could be friends. Perhaps, more than friends."

"Never."

"I hope to make you mine one day."

Faith jumped from the chair, brandishing the knife. He back-stepped when he saw the blade. "Oh, my little mustang, what do you intend to do with that?"

"Come closer and I'll kill you," she said, jabbing the air.

He shook his head, laughing. "No, you won't. You don't have it in you."

He tried to move closer, but she kept her distance by circling the table, knife extended.

He squinted, smiled, and extended his palm. "Give me the knife."

"You smirk because you know I won't kill you, but I can hurt you — by hurting myself." She pressed the knife against her own cheek. "I can fix it so I'm worth a lot less to the men that are coming."

Salazar froze, his smile melted, and the color leached from his face. "Don't do anything foolish," he said, wiggling his hands in front of him. "I think God would consider it a sin for you to harm yourself, don't you? He was the one that blessed you with that beauty."

"No man will pay for a whore with a hideous scar across her face."

"You're not a whore."

"Not yet."

They had danced a three-quarters turn around the table, so that Faith's back was to the house. She hovered with the knife in her right hand, tense, poised to cut. They stood motionless for several seconds. The only sound was the fountain swashing in the background.

From the corner of her eye the girl saw movement as Juanita burst from the shadows. With two quick thrusts, Faith sliced two deep gashes in her left cheek in the shape of a cross before Juanita toppled her to the floor, the knife clattering across the tiles out of Faith's reach. Viper charged out of the house and gnashed at Juanita's hand, its bark fanged and feral, its eyes yellow and frantic.

"Basta," Salazar screamed at the dog, and the animal backed off.

Juanita jumped up, cradling her chewed hand, and yelled, "That monster bit me."

Salazar rushed to Faith with a handkerchief. "What have you done? Why, Faith? Why?"

When he tried to dab at her face, she pushed his hand away. She raised herself on one elbow, her eyes glassy and distant, the shoulder of her smock spattered with blood, her cheek stinging with fire.

Vexed, Salazar rested a hand against his forehead, before motioning to Juanita. "Help me get her inside," he said.

They lifted Faith from the floor. Her head spun, and her legs wobbled. "My uncle will come for me," she mumbled, and then she staggered into the house, pressing her hands against her bloody cheek.

CHAPTER 18
RIDING TO THE MEETING

Emmet and Kingston had five more miles to travel before the road forked and they parted company. In the distance, a layer of clouds wreathed the hills. Patches of blue sky poked through the gray where the sun had burned off the morning mist.

"Thanks again for coming," Kingston said.

"You know my feelings about this," Emmet said. "You're going in there with blind hope. You might come out a sheared sheep."

"I'd rather put myself in danger instead of Faith. A bad peace is better than a good war. If they agree to ransom, there'll be no need to fight."

"Not unless we want to free the other girls," Emmet said.

"We can make that decision after Faith is safe."

"Too bad the other females don't have rich uncles," Emmet said. He reached for his canteen, popped the cap, and took a swig.

"What are you saying? That I'm heartless because I don't help all the girls?"

Emmet sleeved his mouth. "I know that you'd tear the world apart for your family's sake. But Faith ain't my kin, so it's hard for me to isolate her plight from the rest of the girls."

"What do you suggest?"

"Those girls are all in the same wagon that's about to roll off the same cliff. Each of us is guilty of the good we don't do, Major. To my mind, we're obliged to help them all."

"If I had enough money, I'd ransom them all; you know that, Emmet. But that won't stop Salazar and Garza from abducting more girls after we've gone."

"That's my point," Emmet said. "You could ransom Faith and call it a day, or we could rescue those girls and run for the hills. Or we could take the cousins on and wipe them out. We could end Salazar's reign of terror. We have the men, the weapons, *and* the element of surprise."

"Rescuing those girls is a tricky business, Emmet, let alone with bullets and cannonballs flying through the air. What if something went wrong? Would you want the blood of an innocent child on your hands?" Kingston caught himself. "I'm sorry. That's not what I meant."

Emmet spat on the ground. "I know what you meant."

Neither man spoke for several minutes, listening instead to the soft squeak of saddle leather and the hollow clop of hooves on hardpan. Emmet caught the sweet scent of purple wisteria and took a deep breath just as a cottontail raced across the trail.

Kingston broke the silence. "Every man has a madness of his own. Reno told me that for Salazar, it's money."

"Reno told you that, huh? And what if he's wrong. What if Salazar is about power or lust or something else?"

"I need to try and ransom Faith. It's the safest way to free her."

"You're going in with no weapon. That's suicide."

"Listen, Emmet. I have to make this deal. Once I get Faith out of harm's way, we'll attack Salazar and rescue the rest of the girls. Let me share with you my battle plan for doing just that."

For the next twenty minutes, Emmet listened as Kingston described his strategy to attack the estate and free the girls. He marveled at the King's attention to detail, and his sense of timing and positioning. When he finished, Kingston asked, "Got it?"

The idea of attacking the estate quickened Emmet's pulse. He harbored a burning ache to go to battle, free all the girls, crush the cousins' operation, kill Garza, and, to top it, avenge Mariana. "Got it," he replied.

The men reached the fork. Kingston's southern trail continued forward to Salazar's hacienda; Emmet's western trail veered to the right. Kingston slid his spyglass out of a saddlebag, handed it to Emmet, and said, "I'll meet you back at Reno's after Salazar and I conclude our business — with or without Faith. As my dear departed sister would say, hope for a miracle." Kingston doffed his black Stetson as he rode away.

"I'll hope for a miracle," Emmet yelled back, "but I ain't gonna rely on one." He stuffed the spyglass into his saddlebag, reined Ruby Red onto the high trail, and began his climb into the hills.

CHAPTER 19
AT FAITH'S BEDSIDE

Salazar stood outside the guest bedroom and rapped the door twice with his knuckle.

"Come in."

He eased the door open and saw Faith sleeping, with Juanita perched beside the bed in an elbowed armchair. Sunlight flooded the room, and a vase of fresh roses occupied the windowsill. Salazar winced when he saw the strips of fresh gauze across the girl's cheek. He noticed her bloody smock had been replaced.

"How is she?" he asked, as he closed the door and stood next to Juanita.

"The bleeding's stopped, but the cuts are deep. She will always have a nasty scar."

Salazar detected the acrid smell of carbolic acid in the air before he noticed the bottle of crystals on the bed stand. "Did you also put *aloe vera* on the bandages?"

Juanita nodded.

"Is there anything else we can do?"

"The wounds will take time to heal. Once the scabs form, I'll treat them with mimosa extract. It's supposed to promote healthy scar tissue."

"How is your arm?"

The chair creaked when Juanita slid back in it. "That vicious animal took a bite out of me," she said without looking up.

"I'm sorry. You saw the girl save the dog when he was choking. I think Viper was only trying to protect her."

"I'll be all right," Juanita said, but Salazar still detected irritation in her voice. He moved to the foot of the bed.

"The girl will be all right, too," Juanita said. "She'll heal. She's strong. The difficult part will be looking at her face."

He closed his eyes, tilted his head back, sighed. "Why did she do it?"

"To hurt you."

"But I would never harm her."

"She doesn't know that. Her parents are dead because of . . ."

"Garza." Salazar interjected the word before Juanita could finish the sentence. He twisted his body to look at the older woman. "Do you think I'd ever harm her?"

Juanita rubbed her hands across her apron and lifted her tired eyes. "You'd never harm her. In fact, I believe you care for her."

Salazar turned back to the sleeping girl. "I do," he said. "I have big plans for her. I believe she has a gift for healing."

"I'm not sure she wants to be part of your plans."

Salazar glared at Juanita but then softened his look. "My grandmother was a *curandero,*" he said. "She knew much about natural medicine, although she'd be treating those cuts with spider webs instead of *aloe vera.*"

"Medicine has changed since your grandmother's time."

"And this girl knows a lot about the modern ways, and it's not just what her mother taught her. She has a sympathy that I marvel at. It's like she understands pain — physical and mental — and how to relieve it."

"Yet she disfigures herself," Juanita said sweeping her right hand over the girl.

"The bandages don't bother me," Salazar said, "and neither will the scar. Different kinds of power exist in the world: physical strength, wealth, knowledge. But it's the power inside her I desire the most. It's the power my grandmother had — a type of fearlessness."

Juanita stroked the girl's hair. "I met your grandmother once," she said. "My mother brought me to her when I was a child."

"What was wrong with you?"

"Fever. I remember entering her house. It was dark and cluttered and smelled of orange blossoms and rosemary sprigs. She gave me something to drink. I fell asleep, and when I woke, the fever was gone."

"I remember her gnarled hands," Salazar said. "She never let the rheumatism get the best of her. Her fingers may have been curled and knobbed, but they gave off warmth, and I could feel the healing begin as soon as she touched me. Other people said the same thing."

"She was good to everybody, Señor, just like you."

Salazar smiled at the compliment.

"I'll always be grateful to you," Juanita continued, "for taking me in when I lost my family."

"I had money and was able to help you," Salazar answered, "although you may disagree with how I make my money."

"It's none of my business how you make your money."

"You've always been a good servant, Juanita. You tend this place with great care."

"I had once hoped to be more than just a good servant to you."

He shook his head. "I never thought of

you that way."

Her face went dark. She bowed her head, and her shoulders sagged. Salazar knew his words hurt her and decided to shift the subject.

"Any advice on how I can win Miss Wheeler over?"

Juanita's face went darker still. "Release the rest of the girls," she said in a cold, snow-crusted voice.

Salazar shook his head. "Impossible. Too much money at stake."

"Must you make money that way?"

Her comment triggered Salazar's temper. He leaned into the woman and said, "You were right the first time. It's none of your business how I make my money."

Juanita clasped her hands and looked away. "Then treat her kindly," she whispered. "Her family is dead, and she's all alone."

Salazar straightened and looked down at the older woman, her eyes now brimming with tears, her skin paper thin, her hair pulled tight against her skull. He let her squirm under his gaze for several more moments. The quiet broke when the girl began to stir.

"I'm going now," he said. "I'm sure Miss

Wheeler doesn't want to wake up to a crowd."

Salazar maneuvered around Juanita without touching her. He opened the door but swiveled his head back. "She's not completely alone, you know. She has an uncle, and, as it turns out, I'm going to meet with him right now." He shut the door behind him with a soft click.

CHAPTER 20
THE RANSOM MEETING

Kingston entered Salazar's estate escorted by two guards, who motioned him with their gun muzzles towards the big house. The hacienda looked even grander than it had from the lookout. Kingston could see the fine details of the woodwork and the designs etched into the fountain. As the guards frisked him, he observed Garza and Salazar slouched in wicker chairs on the veranda sipping from coffee mugs and smoking long-nines. A third man hung back in the shadows leaning against a wall, chewing on a matchstick. Kingston strolled through the front yard until he reached the bottom step of the veranda.

"Good morning, Mr. Kingston," Salazar said.

"Morning," Kingston replied. "Thanks for meeting with me." He noticed there were no extra chairs. "May I sit, or do you prefer I stand?"

"I don't think this will take long," Salazar said, "so there's no point in you getting too comfortable."

"I've come to ransom my niece."

"You mean Faith?" Garza said, and then he smirked at Salazar.

"Yes," Kingston said.

Salazar studied the glowing end of his cigar. "She's not for sale."

"What do you mean? You're planning to sell her to one of your bidders. All I'm asking is to give me first consideration, and I'll pay you a premium."

"How do you know about the bidders?" Salazar asked. "Who have you been talking to?"

"The people of Santa Sabino know what you're up to. And so do I."

"And even with that knowledge, you still have the courage to approach me?"

"I don't approach you with courage — but with money." Kingston angled his boot against the edge of the starter step. "Isn't that what this is all about?"

Salazar took a huge puff from the cigar and blew out a thick, silvery cloud. "Maybe. Maybe not. Since you know so much about our business, tell me how much you would be willing to pay."

"Whatever you think she'll bring at your

auction . . . plus two thousand dollars."

"What these men will be willing to pay is anybody's guess. One of them could take an incredible shine to her and drive the price up."

"This isn't the first girl you've sold. You know what she's worth."

Salazar pointed at Kingston with his index and middle fingers, the cigar wedged between them. "I don't like your tone."

Kingston regretted his words at once and backed off, because they weren't helping his cause. "Look, you and I are businessmen," he said. "Let's do some business. I'll give you four thousand dollars."

Salazar turned to Garza, "Seems low, no?"

"Six thousand dollars," Kingston said before Garza could answer.

Garza pressed his left boot against the flute of one of the carved columns and tipped his chair back a few inches. "You say she's different from the others, Enrique."

"Eight thousand," Kingston said.

Salazar shifted in the chair and stroked his beard with his free hand. "That's quite a sum. I don't see you holding any sacks of money, though. Or maybe you're thinking of paying us with Confederate shinplasters?"

"The money is nearby. You'll have it later today."

Salazar snorted.

"You scoff," Kingston said, "but I'd be a fool to come here with the money. What's to prevent you from stealing it and killing me?"

"There's that tone again, Enrique," Garza said. His long-nine was out, so he lit a match against his boot and fired up the smoke, taking time to make sure it was glowing red hot.

Kingston swallowed hard, shifted his weight from one foot to the other, and tried again. "Faith is the only family I have left. I've made you an incredible offer. May I see her?"

Salazar held the cigar to his lips for several seconds, puffing as he mulled over the offer and request, then shook his head. "No, she's not for sale; not to you, not to the bidders, not to any man. She's special, and I'm crafting my own plans for her. And, no, you may not see her. Anything else?"

"Ten thousand dollars."

"No," Salazar said.

Kingston felt the situation slipping through his fingers like sand. "I'm begging you to make this deal."

The man leaning against the post finally

emerged from the shadows and spoke. "Or what?"

"This is Tito," Salazar said. "He helps us watch over Santa Sabino. He brought me all kinds of information this morning, about you and your friends."

Tito was a tall, spare man with scowling eyes and a bright-yellow sash tied around his waist. He stepped towards Kingston and said, "Or what? You'll sic your gang on us?"

"What gang?"

Salazar grinned and said, "I don't know, maybe a gang that includes a man named Emmet Honeycut. That's his name, isn't it Tito?"

Tito nodded.

"He's . . . we fought in the war together," Kingston said.

Salazar glanced at Garza. "And he just happens to be in Santa Sabino the same time as you?" he said, faking amazement.

"How about Abe and Zack Thompson?" Tito said.

Kingston felt blood draining from his face and sweat creasing his brow; he sensed a black net being drawn around him.

Tito twirled the matchstick in his mouth and said, "Did you really think a tall stranger and a pair of red-headed bookends wouldn't be noticed in Santa Sabino, especially after they shot up a cantina?"

Kingston shook his head. "I don't know about that. I wasn't there."

Salazar's nostrils flared. "When is Soapy Waters arriving? And how many men is he bringing?"

Kingston's stomach soured, and his legs jellied, because at that instant, he realized he had a traitor in his ranks.

Tito rose, stepped off the porch, and drew his Colt Dragoon as he swaggered over to Kingston. "He asked you a question," he said, and then he brought the side of the revolver crashing down on the major's skull. The blow shot a bolt of lightning through Kingston's head, dropping him to the ground.

Salazar leaned forward in his chair. "Know what I think? I think you're planning some surprises for us, Mr. Kingston. I think you're here for more than your niece. I think you're here to take all our girls."

Kingston felt blood, warm and sticky, dripping down his forehead. His head wavered side to side as he tried to lift it up. "Trust me. Make this deal, and I'll head back to Texas tonight."

"I don't believe you," Salazar said. "When are the other men due?"

At this point, Kingston realized it was best

to stay silent. He eased his head back on the ground and stared up at the bright blue sky.

Tito stared down at Kingston. "When do they arrive?" he said with a withering snarl.

The next flash of pain Kingston felt came from a powerful kick in the ribs, which made him roll on his side. He moaned as fire flooded his abdomen.

Tito squatted on his heels. "How many more, and when are they coming?"

Kingston curled up like a pill bug. He had failed, and that knowledge was more hurtful than Tito's body blows. All the successful business strategies and war campaigns of his life mattered little now. He had failed Faith, his family, his army buddies. Salazar and Garza would keep him alive only until they found out what they wanted. He knew that. He also knew that Emmet was watching from up in the hills and was now Faith's last hope.

"For the last time, how many and when?" Tito said.

Each breath hurt and made Kingston's body shudder. Battling the relentless ache, he beckoned Tito closer with his right hand. When Tito leaned in, Kingston flung a fistful of sand into his face with his left hand. Tito screamed and scrubbed his eyelids with his knuckles. With eyes red with rage, he cocked his pistol and lowered it into Kingston's face.

"Don't!" Salazar shouted. "You're a fool if you don't think some of his men are up in those hills watching us right now."

Now Garza spoke. "So let's send them a message."

"No, Yago. We'll let him live and draw them in."

Kingston exhaled as Tito slammed his gun into the holster and turned towards Salazar. "What do you want to do?"

"Let's have some fun with him," Salazar said. "Give him to the ants. They have a way of making people talk."

"Ponce, Bartoli," Garza barked. Two guards rushed over. "Stake him out. Try not to let him die. Let us know if he tells you anything."

"We'll give him all the care he deserves," Bartoli said.

"When will we know how many men are coming?" Garza asked Tito.

"Tonight," he replied, tossing the matchstick away. "Diego and Paco will be back with that information no later than tonight. The brothers are also bringing the tenth girl in."

Kingston battled to remain conscious as

Ponce and Bartoli hoisted him to his feet. They dragged him along the wall of the estate and out the rear gate, each step shooting racking spasms through his stomach. Ten feet outside the wall, Kingston eyed a large mound of loose dirt sprinkled with blades of dead grass bulging from the flat earth. He slung his head to the right and saw a huddle of vaqueros dawdling by the corral. The guards let go of him, and he dropped to the ground next to the anthill. Kingston felt them stripping off his shirt and pants. The hot stones on his bare back felt like prickling thorns of flame.

Looking up, Kingston saw Bartoli unsheathe the knife in his belt, cut four strips of rope, and toss two to Ponce. They bound Kingston's hands and feet and girt the ropes to four railroad spikes jutting out of the ground.

Through his good eye, Kingston watched a wiry vaquero shuffle over from the bunkhouse sporting a crazed grin and clutching a jar of molasses. He handed the jar to Ponce, who glared at Kingston splayed on his back in the searing sun.

"If today's heat don't kill you, tonight's cold just might," he said with a derisive laugh. "Either way, we'll make sure you have plenty of company." And then he drizzled molasses over Kingston's legs, torso, and face. "Let us know if there's anything else we can do to show our hospitality."

The molasses stung Kingston's eyes, so he squeezed his eyelids shut. He smelled the sweetness of the syrup, felt it oozing down his ears, heard the vaqueros' mocking laughter above him. He was lying flat, but his head was whirling like a windmill blade. Eventually the spinning stopped, the voices quieted, and the gray light behind his eyelids faded to black.

CHAPTER 21
CHANCE ENCOUNTER

Emmet watched with rage as Salazar's goons beat his former commander and dragged him behind the back wall of the hacienda out of sight. He remembered the man in the yellow sash from the day he and the twins first arrived in town. Emmet figured Salazar was on to them, and it was critical to warn the others. He scrambled from the overlook and down to Ruby Red. Spurring the horse, he hurtled down the southern trail at a spanking speed.

After four miles of hard riding, Emmet canted Ruby Red onto the Black Angel Trail. The route was more popular and an hour shorter than the remote one he and Kingston had taken earlier that morning. After twenty minutes of level riding, Emmet noted the path descended for two hundred yards before rising again. The tree canopy thinned out, affording more views along the trail. Emmet swallowed hard when he saw four riders approaching from the second rise. He pulled up with a sharp tug on the reins, causing Ruby Red's forelegs to spray dirt and stones in a wide circle. After reining the horse towards a small draw, he dismounted and tied her up behind a copse of scrub pine.

He slid Big Betty from her sling, snatched the spyglass from the saddlebag, and positioned himself behind a large granite boulder. He focused the small telescope on each of the riders in turn. Leading the pack was a Mexican soldier riding an Appaloosa. Behind him was a young Mexican girl in ragged clothing. Two more men brought up the rear, and Emmet's blood began to simmer. He recognized them as Diego and Paco — the brothers he had saved from the Comanches that moonlit night on his way to Sabo Canyon. He whispered to himself, "Ah, *hermanos,* we meet again."

Emmet crept along the draw until the trail flattened out. No time to gain higher ground; a level plane was the best he could do. He curled his long frame behind an enormous pine. Holding Big Betty under his arm, he laid the spyglass on the ground and unsheathed the sidearm from its holster — and waited.

The clopping of hooves grew louder, as

did the riders' voices, so that now Emmet could make out what they were saying.

"We can deliver your message and save you the time," Diego said. "We have our own information to relay to him."

"My orders are to speak with Señor Salazar personally and tell him Captain Ortega will arrive a day early," the soldier said.

"How many men does Ortega have?"

"Two dozen," the soldier replied.

"How many bidders?"

"Seven."

Paco cackled and looked at the girl. "Hear that, Princess? You might end up with any one of seven different men."

Emmet waited until they all had passed and then slipped onto the trail behind them. "Stop. Don't move," he commanded. "I've got two guns on you."

The group halted.

"Hold your hands high, and don't turn around," Emmet said.

The men complied.

"What's your name, Señorita?" Emmet asked.

"Lucita."

"Where are you going, Lucita?"

"They said they are taking me to Señor Salazar's hacienda."

Emmet had both weapons balanced in his

hands, fingers on the triggers, barrels pointed at the brothers. "Turn around, Lucita."

She reined the small pinto around to face Emmet.

"Do you want to go to Señor Salazar's house?" he asked.

She looked down at the saddle horn and shook her head.

"I'm your friend," Emmet said. "I won't hurt you. Here's what I need you to do. Go back the same trail you just came down. Wait for me at the fork. I'll join you shortly. Do you understand?"

She nodded again, set her pony at an easy gait, and rode back up the trail.

"Now, you three can turn around," Emmet said. "Real slow."

The men shunted their horses to face Emmet.

"Remember me, Diego?" Emmet asked.

Recognition blazed in Diego's eyes, and he smirked. "Well if it isn't Emmet Honeycut," he said.

"I never told you my name."

"Oh, lots of people around here know who you are. I'm surprised you remembered mine."

"A face as ugly as yours is powerful hard to forget," Emmet said.

Diego's face showed nothing.

"I see you and Paco are still in the orphan-age business," Emmet said, "and tomorrow the army will visit. This certainly is — what did you call it — a new day."

The soldier sneered and said, "What do you want? I have business to tend to."

"What do I want? I want you to throw down your weapons and climb off those horses."

Paco flashed a jagged grin. "I don't think so. You've got two guns and there are three of us."

Emmet smiled back. "I just need to decide which one of you is slowest on the draw and kill him last."

"You won't have enough time to figure that out," Paco said.

"I already know who it is," Emmet said.

Paco laughed. "Who?"

"That ain't a question that needs an answer right now." Emmet figured on the soldier, given he was military-trained and not a gunslinger. "So you gonna throw down, or is dying time here?"

The riders grabbed for steel, and Emmet opened fire, dispatching Paco to oblivion with a pistol shot, while Big Betty pitched Diego backwards from the horse. Emmet dove for the underbrush, but the soldier's first shot sliced through his boot; his second hit a tree and sprayed pine bark into the air.

Emmet rolled over on the ground twice and came up firing, but the soldier had jerked his horse to the side of the trail, cutting Emmet's angle. The Mexican rapid-fired, forcing Emmet to duck behind a snarl of deadfall. After emptying his breech, the soldier turned the Appaloosa and dashed down the road, keeping his head down and his body low against the animal.

Emmet jumped up, his left leg sizzling with pain, the heel of his boot pooling with blood. He sighted on the shrinking blue and yellow target, breathed in, out, waited for the calming breath, fired. The soldier's upper body torqued forty-five degrees to the left, his face turned to the sun, and the shako fell from his head, but he remained atop the horse as it disappeared over the crest.

Emmet knew time was critical and decided against chasing the soldier down. If he was still alive he wouldn't be for long given the clean hit. He dragged the bodies of the two brothers into the underbrush and then spooked their horses into the woods. He hobbled over to Ruby Red, mounted up from the right side because of his wounded leg, and bolted down the road.

■ ■ ■ ■

Emmet caught up to Lucita ten minutes later. He could tell she was an inexperienced rider by the way she was locking her knees around the animal to keep from falling. The girl jerked her head backwards when she heard Ruby Red's hoofbeats, but her frightened look turned to a smile when she recognized Emmet.

"Are you okay?" he asked as he pulled up next to her. She nodded.

"You did good today, Lucita. Do you know how to ride?"

"No."

"Listen, we need to make tracks, so I need you to hop up here," Emmet said, patting the cantle. He scooted his body further up the seat rise closer to the horn, and the girl climbed up behind him. Emmet grabbed the reins, told her to hold on, and spurred Ruby Red to full gallop, the girl clinging to him like bark on a tree.

As they galloped along the trail, Emmet glanced down at Lucita's young hands gripping the saddle horn and felt her heated arms wrapped around his waist, and it conjured up a memory, warm and shadowed, of a sunny spring day when the trees and flowers were in full bloom, their perfume filling the air.

A different child shared his saddle, a girl who squealed to a woman sitting on a picnic blanket, "Momma, I caught a fish." The mother in the dell framed by the loblollies and dogwoods. Her beauty on full display in the blinking sunlight. Her hair black as coal, her eyes bluer than the April sky, and the mouth that whispered, "Yes, Emmet, I'll marry you." The loving smile that brightened her face after she spoke those words, and the soft lips with a trace of dandelion wine on them as they kissed. The woman leaning her head on his shoulder as they watched the girl skip through a field of blue-star and rose mallow along the shore of the lake. Enjoying the play of shade and shine on the trees. The image of the husband and father who had abandoned the mother and daughter long forgotten in the red glow of fresh love, and the wedding plans they made that day. The plans that would allow the three of them to carve out new lives. The plans that would transform Emmet from a gun-for-hire vagabond into a man of peace and place.

That was the plan. That was the way it

was supposed to be. But Fate is a marksman who never misses, and even the most rock-ribbed plans of lovers can turn into cinders and ash.

Lucita broke Emmet's reverie when she leaned forward and said, "Thank you for saving me from those men." She hugged Emmet before placing her hands back on the horn. He let go of one of the reins and patted her hand with one of the hands that had just taken the lives of three men.

"You're welcome, darling," he replied. "I promise I won't let anything happen to you."

Now his free hand moved to his pocket and he rubbed the photograph nestled there, the one that he, the mother, and the girl had posed for that same happy day. It was the last relic of a life that might have been, and he knew his promise to Lucita was a false one. His power to protect her or anybody else was limited, and he could do nothing if Fate decided to intervene again.

Emmet and Lucita encountered nobody else on the trail. It took an hour and a half of arduous riding before Reno's bungalow came into view. In the distance, Emmet could see Mariana sitting on the porch, sewing.

"Block your ears, Lucita," Emmet warned. He pulled his revolver and fired four times into the air. Soapy and Billy came out from behind the wagons, and Chiquito sprinted from beneath the cottonwoods, followed by Abe, Zack, and Frank. The door of the bungalow flew open, and Reno rushed out. As Emmet pulled up, Soapy yelled, "What in blazes is going on?"

Emmet curled his arm around Lucita and helped her off the horse. "Salazar's on to us," he said. "He took Major Kingston prisoner. We need to get out of here. Fast."

"You warned him not to go," Zack said.

"Too late for regrets. Soapy, take Billy and hitch the wagons. Everybody else, grab your belongings, and get ready to leave. Reno, we need a place to hide; somewhere that's out of view and difficult to find, but not too far away."

"I know a place," Reno said. "I'll get my things."

Mariana pointed to the girl.

"This is Lucita," Emmet said. "Please tend to her. She's coming with us."

The outside of the bungalow buzzed with activity as everybody kicked into action, hitching wagons, stashing gear, dousing the campfire. Soapy moved the horses into position in front of the cannon, while Billy yoked the mules to the Gatling gun. Emmet dismounted, ran inside the bungalow, snatched the maps and the war bag that held the major's money, and tossed them in the back of the wagon.

Reno followed him out of the house carrying a sack of his own. He sat down on the porch, took out a pencil, and scribbled on a piece of paper. He set the paper on a cushion, ran back into the house, and emerged with an armful of cans and jars. As he crammed the containers into the bag, Emmet shouted at him, "We've got enough food. Let's go."

Reno waved, scooped up his bag, and ran to join Emmet. Billy was sitting on the mule-drawn limber ready to depart when he yelled out, "Mr. Alvarez, you forgot your letter."

Reno didn't hear Billy, but Emmet did. He watched Billy hop off the chest that served as a seat, snatch the paper off the table, and stuff it in his back pants' pocket. *Just like Billy,* Emmet thought. *Always interested in other people's business.* Emmet assumed the boy intended to return the letter to Reno later — after he had read it, of course.

It took the group just ten minutes to gather their goods, hitch two limbers and a wagon, and saddle five horses. The caravan rattled north along the road away from Santa Sabino with Emmet and Reno in the lead. The horses' hooves thundered along the trail and pushed swirling clouds of dust into the air. The iron wheels on the rigs spun like tops and carved up huge clods of crusted soil and clumps of broken brush.

The group rode for half an hour until Reno directed them up a small road to the west. They switched trails three times, each one narrower than the previous, finally reached a leafy knoll. The grass and under-growth softened the thunder of the hooves but didn't slow the group's progress. Five minutes later, Reno pointed to a hollow.

"Billy, can you maneuver those mules through those trees?" Emmet asked.

"Watch me," Billy yelled back, and then he hawed the mules and snaked the limber and Gatling gun through a copse of bald cypress with Soapy right behind him. "Like threading a needle," Soapy yelled as he guided the horses and cannon through the same green spires and brought them to a halt in the shade.

Emmet studied the surroundings. The cypress trees formed a natural palisade to the south. Thick knots of alpine fir provided excellent cover to the north and west. A spring-fed pond acted like a moat to the east. The water was still, so the sound of intruders would carry, and the hollow afforded good grass for the horses to crop.

"Is this okay?" Reno asked with furrowed eyebrows.

"Perfect," Emmet replied. He turned to Frank and Zack. "Go back to the last cutoff and picket by the huge boulders on either side of the trail."

Frank bristled. "Who made you boss?" he said, his voice thick with challenge.

"I'd go, but I took a bullet in the leg," Emmet said, "and I need Mariana to fix me up. You and Zack are great long-distance shooters, and it's as good a place as any to ambush them if they've tailed us."

"Cut the butter talk," Frank said. "I'll do it for the sake of the group. For now."

"If Salazar's men show up, rain fire on them," Emmet said.

"I know what to do," Frank said.

Emmet brushed him off with a wave and limped over to Chiquito and Abe. "Would you boys mind fetching some firewood?"

"Sure," Chiquito said. Abe grunted.

Mariana grabbed Emmet's arm. "Sit down," she said, "and let's take a look at that leg."

CHAPTER 22
PRIVATE ROMERO

"Señor Salazar, come quick," Ponce yelled.

Salazar and Juanita rushed down the main corridor of the house behind Ponce. Out through the front courtyard, they saw Bartoli standing next to an unconscious Mexican soldier who was draped over the neck of an Appaloosa, harness-caught. At first Salazar thought the horse had been hit, so much blood was dripping from the saddle, but as two of the vaqueros slid the soldier off, he could see the man had suffered a sucking chest wound.

"He's bad," Ponce said. "Probably not going to make it."

"Bring him to the room off the kitchen," Juanita said, "the one next to the cabinet with the medical supplies."

Salazar brooded on the situation for several minutes. *Why was the soldier here? Was he under Ortega's command? Did he come with a message? Who shot him?* He watched as the vaqueros lifted the soldier's limp body onto the table. Juanita searched his pockets and pulled out a watch and a wallet.

"His name is Private Romero," she said, "and he is under Captain Ortega's command."

"Get Miss Wheeler and Yago at once," Salazar told her.

"He's lost a lot of blood," Faith said. She was leaning over the unconscious soldier, tilting her head back and forth as she examined him.

"Are you up to this?" Salazar asked.

She saw his eyes were fixed on the bandages on her cheek. "I'm all right," Faith said. "I feel stronger."

"Thank you for helping us," he said.

"I would never help you. I'm helping him because it's what my mother and father would expect me to do."

"Can you save him?" Salazar asked.

"No. But if you have the right medicines, I can make him comfortable."

"Juanita will get you whatever you need."

Faith set to work with diligence, using scissors to clip the soldier's blood-soaked uniform from his body. Juanita helped move the soldier up and down and left to right to remove the cut-away clothes from beneath him. As they maneuvered the soldier's half-naked body, Faith pointed to the bullet wound.

"He was shot from behind," she said. "The wound where the bullet went in is small. The front is a different story."

She pointed to the red mass of muscle and tissue mounded on the soldier's stomach. The women eased the soldier onto his back, and Faith began to stitch layers of skin together in an effort to slow the bleeding.

"You have the skill of a doctor," Salazar said.

"I'm just the daughter of a nurse," Faith replied.

She saw Juanita look away. Salazar fidgeted with the soldier's watch. Faith looked up when Garza entered the room and saw him step back when he saw her face.

Garza turned to Salazar. "Did you do that?"

Salazar shook his head. "She did it to herself."

Faith saw Garza's look turn from shock to disgust. He narrowed his eyes and snarled at her. "You stupid bitch."

Faith said nothing, smiled at him, and resumed stitching the soldier's wounds.

"Juanita, I'll station Ponce outside," Sala-

zar said. "If the soldier regains consciousness and says *anything,* let me know immediately. You understand? Immediately."

Juanita assured him.

"Yago, come to my office," Salazar said. "I
want to discuss something with you." He
closed the door harder than he intended,
leaving the two women alone with the soldier.

"Your mother must have been a fine
nurse," Juanita said.

"She had a lot of experience from the war.
When she and my father moved west, she
set up a small clinic at our cabin to help the
local farmers. She taught me many things.
How to stop bleeding, set a broken bone,
cut away bad flesh — even how to birth
babies."

"You have so much knowledge for one so
young."

Quickly, Faith sewed a continuous suture,
passing the needle in a spiral across the
length of the wound and tying it on each
end. She snipped the ends off with the scissors. "We need more bandages and linen,"
she said.

Juanita hopped up. "I'll get them."

As soon as Juanita left the room, Faith
rushed to the cabinet and scanned the
medicines. She snatched the brown bottle

marked "Chloroform," uncorked it, and poured some into a small empty vial set on another shelf. The colorless liquid gave off a sweet, pleasant scent. She capped the vial and slipped it into the pocket of her smock. Just as she returned the chloroform to the cabinet, the soldier stirred. He made a gurgling sound, his breathing shallow.

"Where?" he asked in a voice that was more wheeze than whisper.

"Señor Salazar's house," Faith answered.

"Message . . ." His voice faded.

"Tell me."

"No. I must . . ." The soldier stopped short and spit up a piece of dark tissue as smooth and slimy as a leech.

"Salazar's not here, and you're badly hurt." Faith lifted his head and gave him a sip of water. "I'm here to make you comfortable. Tell me the message, just in case . . ." This time, Faith's voice trailed off.

"Ortega . . . arrive . . . tomorrow . . . day early," the soldier said, and then he coughed with great force, causing a mixture of air and blood to froth from his mouth. His body convulsed; his head popped up from the table and then settled back. Faith knew that saliva was damming up his throat and smothering his cough reflex. She heard the last rattle exit his lungs. Juanita returned as

Faith was wiping foam from the dead man's lips.

"He's gone," Faith said.

Juanita threw the gauze on the table. "Did he say anything?"

"Yes."

"You were supposed to alert Señor Salazar," she snapped.

Faith shook her head. "No time."

Juanita crooked her head sideways and arched an eyebrow. "What did he say?"

"Captain Ortega has been delayed. He'll arrive on Tuesday, a day later than expected."

Juanita took a moment to gather her thoughts. "I suppose that's good news. We could always use the extra time. Anything else? Did he say who shot him?"

Faith didn't answer.

In a louder voice, Juanita asked, "Who shot him?"

"Indians."

"Are you sure?"

"Actually, he said red niggers. Those are Indians, right?"

Faith saw Juanita relax her shoulders after hearing her convincing canard.

"Thank you, dear," she said. "I'll bring back a clean smock after I give that message to Señor Salazar."

She opened the door and spoke to the guard: "Ponce, escort Miss Wheeler to the well so she can wash up. I'm going to Señor Salazar's office."

Ponce motioned Faith out the door with a quick hand flip. She followed him through the kitchen and into the yard's bright sunlight, the glass vial bouncing against her right leg. Big, quilted clouds cast fat shadows across the landscape. A lizard scooted across her path, and a breeze blew back her golden hair. At that moment, she didn't feel bad about the soldier dying. She didn't feel bad about lying to Juanita. The only thing she felt was a deep resolve: If the army was arriving tomorrow, she would make her escape tonight.

Salazar paced the floor of his study in front of the seated Garza.

"Ortega sent the soldier with a message," Salazar said, "and we have no idea what it is. Plus we have no idea who shot him."

"Relax, Enrique," Garza said. "We'll get to the bottom of this. It must have been Honeycut or one of his friends that shot him."

"Unless the others have already arrived." Salazar smoothed his moustache several times. "And where is Diego? Why haven't

223

he and Paco shown up yet? We should search for them."

"Patience. They're due later today," Garza said.

Salazar sat on the chair behind his mahogany desk. A black porcelain statue of a stallion reared up from the left corner. On the right corner was a cherry hardwood humidor with its edges worn smooth. "If they don't show up tonight," he said, "I want you to take some men and search for them first thing in the morning."

"First thing? Sure, Enrique, whatever you say." Garza went to the glass cabinet, removed a bottle of brandy from the shelf, and pointed it at Salazar, who waved him off. Garza poured a tumbler half full, swirled the liquid around the glass, and sipped.

"You seem calm given what's happened," Salazar said tapping his fingers on the desk.

"And what's happened?" Garza asked. "We have Kingston staked out in the yard. We know his men are hiding out at Alvarez's bungalow waiting for more men to arrive. Once Diego and Paco show up, we'll know exactly how many."

"But we don't know Ortega's message."

"Maybe he's been delayed — maybe that's the message. Maybe he's arriving early.

Either way, he'll get here eventually, too." Garza set the glass down on the edge of the desk. "You worry too much, Enrique."

"It's my job to worry. Tomorrow you search for Diego and Paco. If you don't find them, go to Reno's with all the firepower you need and bring me Honeycut and his two friends."

"Okay. I'd welcome the chance to drop in on Mariana."

"Ah, Yago, perhaps you still have feelings for her?" Salazar raised his eyebrows.

Garza circled his finger across the rim of the glass. "No," he said. "That was many years ago. I'd just like to remind her of the good life she could have had. Anyway, I have no feelings for her, unlike you, who seem to be fascinated with the Wheeler girl."

Salazar grinned like the devil, but a rap at the door startled him before he could reply. "Come," he said.

Juanita opened the door and stepped inside. "I'm sorry to disturb you, señor, but you wanted to be informed of any news. The soldier regained consciousness for several moments before he died. He said Captain Ortega has been delayed and won't arrive until Tuesday."

Garza tilted his head back and extended his arms like he was carrying a bride over a threshold. "See, Enrique," he said. "There's nothing to be worried about. Did he say who shot him?"

"Indians," she replied.

Salazar exhaled, and his body relaxed. "It looks like we have an extra day to prepare. Thank you, Juanita," he said and dismissed her with a nod.

Juanita bowed her head and left the room.

Salazar said, "Now I will have a drink."

Garza stood, removed a glass from the cabinet, and poured his cousin a brandy.

Salazar took a large gulp. "You asked me my plans for Miss Wheeler, and I will tell you. I intend to marry her."

Garza's body stiffened. "You're out of your mind."

"I'm not getting any younger," Salazar said, tapping his chest. "She's a healer. I'm going to need somebody to look after me. I believe this girl can help me live longer, just like my grandmother did for my grandfather."

Garza's face turned into a black scowl. "A longer life? You're a fool. She'll cut your throat on the wedding night."

"You're wrong. She's different. There's no evil in her."

"No evil?" Garza said with a sneer. "Everybody has the capacity for evil. They just need the proper motivation. A healer? That's nonsense, too. You could have any woman in Santa Sabino and yet you choose her?"

"I have had many beautiful women over the years, and I will have many more. This one is different."

"She's carved her face into a grotesque mask. She's a gazingstock. That scar will always remind you of how much she hates you."

"I'm attracted to her in ways you don't understand."

"You'll have to explain that to me."

"You look for one thing in a woman, Yago, and it's strictly physical."

Garza pointed his finger: "You're no different."

Salazar leaned back in his chair. "You and I have a lot of years between us. You may feel differently when you're my age."

Garza's blood was fired, and he slammed both fists down on the desk. "You're not thinking clearly; you're in a fog. You're not aware of what you're doing."

"I am aware!" Salazar shouted, his mouth spraying saliva. "I know exactly what I'm doing. She'll learn to love me." He took a deep breath and waited several moments to regain his composure. He raised his brandy and in a calmer voice said, "I'd like you to be my best man."

Garza jumped up and hurled his glass at the liquor cabinet, shattering the front pane and half a dozen glasses inside. "I want no part of this. You're jeopardizing everything we've worked for, everything we've built. I won't sit back and let you throw it all away."

"You can't stop me."

Garza stormed towards the door. "Watch me," he said with a hiss.

"Don't forget," Salazar said. "If Diego and Paco don't show up tonight, you'll start searching for them first thing tomorrow."

Garza watched his cousin swivel to look out the window and gaze at the foothills. He left the room and slammed the door behind him.

CHAPTER 23
MARIANA'S DREAM

"Lean back, Emmet," Mariana said in a soothing voice, "and let's get that boot off."

Emmet pressed his back against a rounded boulder and said, "That bullet ain't gonna improve my dancing."

Mariana laughed and then looked over to the girl. "Lucita, would you bring us some water?" The girl, eager to be useful, hurried over to the supply wagon, pulled out a metal bucket, and raced to the pond.

Mariana grabbed the top of Emmet's boot with one hand and the long heel with the other. As she wriggled it off, she dislodged Emmet's boot knife.

"I didn't even see it there," she said.

"That's the point of packing a gambler's dagger," Emmet said. "It's hard to detect a sleek weapon like that hidden in a boot." He picked up the double-edged knife and bounced it flatwise in his hand.

"I assume you know how to use it," she said.

"No point in having a weapon unless you know how to use it," Emmet said as he set it on the grass. "Abe taught me good. I'm almost as good as him."

Mariana examined Emmet's leg. The bullet had entered one side of his calf and exited the other.

Emmet pointed to the holes in his boot. "Damn, those custom-mades used to be waterproof," he said.

She turned the boot upside down to let the pooled blood drip out and then rubbed her hand against the smooth skin. "Armadillo," she said. "Expensive."

"Miss Mariana, there's two items I've always been willing to spend considerable money on. One is a good saddle and the other, good boots. That way I'll be comfortable whether I'm riding or walking."

Emmet winced when she peeled off the blood-soaked sock but didn't make a sound. Mariana lifted his foot and studied it. "You were standing on it before so it's not broken; no bones were hit."

Lucita lumbered over holding the bucket with two hands, sloshing water over the sides. "Why is water so heavy?" she asked as she set the pail on the ground.

"Thank you," Mariana said. "Could you bring me some bandages? They're in one of the small gray boxes." The girl returned to the wagon and rummaged through the crates.

Mariana rolled up Emmet's pants' leg, dunked the cloth in the bucket, and with gentle strokes wiped the blood off his calf. "It's a clean wound," she said. "Nothing complicated."

Emmet watched her as she worked. She was wearing a tiered cotton skirt with a floral print border and a simple, fitted bodice. The straight neckline was embroidered with yellow flowers. "Miss Mariana, looking at you is as easy as eating striped candy," he said.

The glow in her face grew brighter, and her left eye twinkled. "Do you believe in omens, Emmet?"

"As a matter of fact, I do."

"A couple of years ago," she said, "I had a dream where a giant eagle appeared in the sky and spoke to me. I know it sounds crazy, but the bird told me to wait for its return because it meant a deliverer was at hand who would avenge my husband's murder. So I waited. And waited. Last week, I was visiting Miguel's grave in the San Lazaro cemetery when I saw an eagle float into a treetop and look down directly at me. I knew it was the sign I'd been waiting for. I told my father, and the two of us went to town looking for strangers."

Lucita returned with a thick roll of gauze. Mariana took the knife from Emmet, sliced a long piece off the roll, and wrapped the ankle with slow delicate motions before she continued her tale.

"Major Kingston arrived in Santa Sabino that same day. When I saw his big gold ring with the eagle carved on it, I knew he was the man."

Emmet knew the ring — the King received it when he graduated from West Point — but he figured it was best not to tell her about its origin or interrupt her story.

"We approached Major Kingston and learned why he had come to our town. At last, after ten years, a man had arrived who seemed willing to take on Salazar and Garza."

She threaded a needle and stitched the gauze to hold it in place.

"It all makes sense now," Emmet said. "It explains why your father was so willing to risk his life to help Major Kingston. That's quite an omen. I had me an omen back in the war."

Mariana finished stitching, broke the

thread with her teeth, and leaned back in a way that invited Emmet to tell his tale.

"Not long after Chickamauga, the Yanks stormed Lookout Mountain and planted their flag on top of it, which was shocking to every rebel soldier who saw it. How we lost that high ground I'll never understand. But never matter, we lost it."

"Where is Lookout Mountain?" Mariana asked.

"Tennessee. Even though we were dug in good and deep, many of us couldn't shake the feeling that things weren't right — that something bad was about to happen. Soapy thought the big guns weren't positioned well and told Major Kingston, but General Bragg wouldn't listen to the major. There was a total eclipse of the moon that night. Its color turned from white to deep red. Most of us figured it was a bad sign that more blood was about to flow, and it was most likely gonna be ours."

"I think I know how this story ends," Mariana said.

"The Yanks attacked the next morning. They overran our trenches and, as we retreated, cut us down like corn stalks. Major Kingston lost both his brothers that day."

"And now he's lost his sister," Mariana said.

"Faith is all he has left. Ever since that day, I've never made fun of anybody's beliefs in signs from above. And I bet your belief in your dream was as strong as my sense of dread when I stared up at that red moon on that November night back in sixty-three."

"I'm not sure what my dream means now that Major Kingston's been captured," Mariana said. She handed the gauze back to Lucita, who returned it to the wagon.

"In fact, Miss Mariana, I find your dream reassuring. I take it to mean that there's something bigger going on here that caused me and the fellers to show up in Santa Sabino exactly when we did. It's a good feeling, like we're destined to be here, too."

"What do you plan to do?"

"I ain't sure."

"You must take Major Kingston's place."

Emmet grabbed the boot and slipped it over his toes. "There's a reason I was in the army for five years and never made sergeant. I like to go my own way. I've never been comfortable being in charge. Who am I to tell other folks what to do?"

"This is different. You know Major Kingston's attack plan."

"Yes, but . . ."

"But what?"

With a small grunt, he eased his foot the rest of the way into the boot. "I don't ever want to put myself in a position where people can question my judgment again."

Mariana helped Emmet stand. She wiped the fronts and backs of her hands on her dress and said, "You told me once that you believed my Miguel died for love."

"I believe he did."

"So let me ask you, would you die for love, Emmet?"

"I reckon I would."

"Would you kill for love?"

"Why are you asking a question like that, Miss Mariana?"

"Do you have feelings for me?"

Emmet swore that he did.

"Then kill for me. I tried to forgive Garza. Truly I did, because that's what Father Ramirez taught us. And for a long time, I thought I had, but Garza's wickedness only grows."

"What do you want me to do?"

"Lead these men against the cousins. Put Garza and Salazar out of *their* misery."

"Miss Mariana, I'd do anything for you. But you need to know there's a side to me that some folks believe ain't worth knowing."

"I know about the Baxter girl."

Emmet grimaced. "Who told you?"

"Frank."

"Why would he do that?"

"He has feelings for me, too. He said he wanted me to know what kind of man you are."

Emmet's face flushed, and the hairs on his neck bristled. "And what kind of man do you think I am?"

She reached out and clasped his hands in hers. "A strong one," she said, "and a merciful one."

"Miss Mariana, I thought that little girl's death would fade with time. It's difficult to outrace your past, but what's done is done and can never be erased. All we can do in this life is to weather the pain that comes our way."

"You have a chance to redeem yourself."

"Don't mistake yourself. I need no redemption. At the trial, I told the judge and jury that I was filled with regret because that's what people wanted to hear. And I believe saying those words cooled everybody's rage and kept me out of prison."

"What are you trying to tell me?"

"Those words I said in that courtroom

236

were lies, because if I was dropped into the same situation again, I'd do the same thing — without blinking. I know that settles hard in most folks' ears. You want to know what kind of man I am? *That's* the kind of man I am."

She released him and wrapped the rebozo tighter around her, as if she caught a sudden chill. Emmet gave her a few moments to let his words soak in.

"What do you think of me now?" he said.

Mariana grabbed the bottom of his forearms, squeezed them, and looked into his eyes. "I think you're an honorable man," she said, "and I believe that honor sometimes requires telling a few lies along the way."

Emmet took enormous comfort from her words. He knew there weren't many women who could listen to a terrible truth like the one he had just served up and not walk away.

The next thing he knew, her hands had moved up to his face, had enfolded his cheeks, and her lips were on his. He smelled lilac soap on her skin, and her kiss tasted as sweet as honey butter. In that warm embrace, Emmet knew he would need no further persuading.

They released each other, and he said,

"Killing that little girl was a terrible hard thing. But killing Garza and Salazar will be my personal delight."

"You'll lead these men?"

"Yep, and I promise you, I'm gonna do my best for your sake, and for Miguel's sake and for the major's, and for those girls' sakes and their families, and for the sake of any other person Garza and Salazar have hurt or tried to hurt."

"Thank you," she said, and she pressed her forehead into his chest.

"Miss Mariana, when this is all over, I'd like to ask you a question."

She smiled and looked up. "I hope I'll be able to answer it."

He returned her smile. "But right now, you'll have to excuse me. I got some battle plans to finalize."

"Do what you have to do," she said.

He saluted her and started limping up the hill.

CHAPTER 24
GATHERING WOOD

Emmet had asked Abe and Chiquito to get firewood for the campfire, so they grabbed hatchets from Soapy's wagon and ventured into the deeper woods. Slats of sunlight slashed through the trees, and the air was sweet with the smell of sap. After walking ten minutes on a carpet of soft pine needles, Chiquito pointed to a heap of downed timber to his left.

"Plenty of fuel here," he said. "Let's grab some."

Abe joggled his head. "I shouldn't be helping you," he said. "My brother hates Apaches."

"You said that earlier, but you never said why."

"He got caught in an Apache ambush. Hid out to save himself and saw a group of them torture a defenseless cowboy. Witnessed the whole thing. They fashioned a small metal cage from barrel hoops and cooked him over a fire."

"I've never done that to anybody. As for you and your brother, prejudices are what stupid men use for reason."

Abe lifted a six-foot length of pine, its bark rotted off, the trunk as smooth as a saddle, and set it against a rock. With a fierce stomp of his boot, he snapped the log in two. "An Apache's upbringing ain't Christian," he said. "You people are savages, so that's why I think you're so clever when it comes to torture. In fact, you redskins must spend a lot of time dreaming up new ways to make people scream."

Chiquito raised his hatchet and hacked at a rack of dead branches spiking out of another log. "We redskins can be quite resourceful," he said, with a sneer. "But red, black, or white, never underestimate man's ability to be cruel."

"My brother said the man screamed for hours before he gave up the ghost," Abe said. "Is that how long it usually takes? Hours?"

"Already told you," Chiquito said. "Never done it, so I don't know. I guess it depends on how big the fire is." He stooped to pick up another branch but then stopped and straightened up. "Wait a minute. You're not upset about the guy who died; you're actually curious about what it's like to roast somebody alive."

Abe shrugged. "It ain't wrong to be curious." He set his boot on the log a second time and let the weight of his body break off another piece. "You folks do it for fun, but imagine if you had somebody you really hated perched over that fire."

Chiquito held up his right hand. "Shhh," he whispered. "We've been followed."

Abe spun around but saw nothing. He fixed his eyes on the tree line and listened. The wind swept through the upper pine boughs, and a bluejay squawked before taking flight. Otherwise, nothing. Abe turned back to Chiquito. "I don't hear nothing," he said, but Chiquito had disappeared into the forest shadows.

Now Abe heard a familiar voice snarling at him from behind.

"Who you talking to?"

Abe turned on his heel again, but this time found himself face to face with Danny Brown, who was pointing a Springfield Indian carbine at his stomach. Abe was stunned and put his hands up.

"So, we meet again," Brown said. "Now, which red-headed sack of shit are you?"

Abe swallowed hard. "Does it matter?"

"Not to me. Where's your injun friend?"

"What do you want with him?"

Brown laughed. "What do you think we want? The price on his head."

"He's a wanted man?"

"Hey, Lonnie," Brown yelled. "Looks like we got ourselves a real scholar. He don't even know he's hanging out with an outlaw."

Brown's blond-haired companion limped from behind a swath of thick underbrush clutching a Winchester, his straw hat scrunched on his head. Lonnie sluiced a stream of spit between his two front teeth. "That's funny, given you said his pappy was an outlaw. Got himself hung for robbing a stage, ain't that right, Danny?"

"True enough," Brown said. "Spent the stolen money buying drinks for everybody in a saloon only four towns away. A vagrant spending money like he was a banker caught the attention of a couple of U.S. marshals."

Abe's body trembled with rage, but he had to wait for Chiquito to make his move. In the meantime, he figured he'd best distract the bounty hunters.

"Hunting down men is the lowest job I know," he said.

"It pays real good," Brown replied.

"How's the leg?" Abe asked Lonnie. "I intentionally missed the artery when I stabbed you. I wish I had it to do over again."

Lonnie squinted and said, "Hand over the hatchet and your pig-sticker."

Abe tossed them both on the ground.

"The boot knife, too."

Abe did as he was told.

"Know how an Apache gets into an honest business?" Lonnie asked.

Abe shook his head. "Don't know, Goldilocks, but I have a feeling you're going to tell me."

"Through an open window," Lonnie said with a laugh. "We were tracking another wanted scoundrel when we got news your friend Rago was headed this way. A red nigger perched atop that much killing power was sure to draw a lot of attention. A buddy of ours rode all the way up here from Sweetwater to tell us. Pocketed twenty dollars for his trouble."

Danny Brown scratched his stubbled chin. "Never would have put you and the redskin together in a million years. You going red? Or is Rago going white?"

"You sure have a problem with names, don't you, Brown," Abe said. "His name is Chiquito, not Rago."

"Enough of your sass!" Brown yelled and brought the stock of the rifle down on Abe's head, dropping him to the ground. "Tie him up."

Lonnie set the Winchester down, removed a small coil of rope hanging from his belt, and bound Abe to a nearby tree in a sitting position.

"Now we'll see how loyal an Apache is," Brown said. "He was just here, so I know he's within the sound of my voice. Rago," he yelled at the treetops. "You've got two minutes to get out here. Otherwise, we're going to do some serious damage to your friend."

Brown leaned in and said, "Your brother is down at the cutoff looking to ambush somebody, but it ain't going to be us, so I wouldn't plan on him coming to your rescue again. That is, assuming you're really Abe."

Abe could smell thick tobacco smoke on Brown's clothes. "Assume whatever you want," he said. "But maybe you've got your names wrong again, and I'm Zack, and it was me that swived your daughter."

"Keep at it, lowlife," Brown said. "You and the redskin ain't leaving these woods alive." He drove the toe of his stovepipe boot into Abe's stomach so hard the boy threw up.

Abe was panting for air but knew he couldn't quit. "Your fair-haired daughter was one fine toss in the hay, I'll say that," he said, forcing a fake snigger, his breath rolling in painful heaves, strands of bile dripping from his lower lip.

"Her hair was black, you fool."

"Who cares?" Abe asked, and then he braced himself for the next assault.

"Why, you miserable . . ." Brown exploded in a violent fit, beating and kicking the boy in a wild frenzy. Just as Abe was about to pass out, he heard a faint buzzing as Chiquito's hatchet zipped through the air, followed by a rich *whomp* as it embedded in Danny Brown's spine. Brown collapsed on top of Abe's legs, his body twitching like a speared fish, until he shuddered one last spasm.

Abe heard Chiquito let loose with a war whoop and saw him barreling down at Lonnie like a stampeding steer. Before Lonnie could raise his rifle, Chiquito collided with him at full tilt, knocking him on his back. Chiquito charged again, but Lonnie had recovered and, being a taller man with longer arms, flipped the Apache over his hip. Both men jumped to their feet with knives drawn. Lonnie lashed out first, but Chiquito back-heeled and then lunged, slicing Lonnie's shirt. As Chiquito concentrated on his opponent's knife hand, Lonnie swung a mighty blow with his left and knocked the Apache off-kilter. Chiquito shook off the daze just as Lonnie thrust at his midriff. The Indian parried with his own knife and slid the weapon off and away.

Now Chiquito crouched, his knife held low to attack the soft spot of Lonnie's belly. The blond man made a stabbing motion, but the Apache didn't react. Instead, he spun two steps to the right and lashed out at Lonnie's face. Lonnie ducked and then lurched toward Chiquito, but the Apache was ready. As he pushed his opponent to the ground with his free hand, Chiquito plunged the knife into Lonnie's back and twisted it to good purpose. Lonnie fell on his stomach, both arms flailing at the wedged-in knife, unable to reach it. After a minute, his body buckled and calmed. Chiquito placed his foot on the blond man's back and yanked the knife out.

"Didn't know when I'd see you again," Abe said. He was unable to keep his head up and it listed to one side. "Thought you might have headed back to the reservation."

The Apache cut the ropes and lifted Abe to his feet. After the redhead had steadied himself, his temper tripped, his energy surged, and he scooped his knives off the ground. With a blade in each hand, Abe stabbed at both sides of Lonnie's corpse as he screamed at him, "You want some more of this, Goldilocks?"

Abe felt Chiquito's hand on his back.

"Maybe you should use the hatchet," the Indian said. "It does a better job, although I'm pretty sure he's dead."

Abe relaxed his arms and flopped back on his rump, panting like a boxer who has just gone ten rounds, beads of sweat the size of match heads dripping off his nose. Chiquito helped Abe to his feet again and brushed him off. The boy had difficulty straightening his body and said, "It hurts powerful. I think I got a couple of busted ribs."

"Let's get back," Chiquito said, his words spoken as if trying to calm an agitated animal. "There could be others hunting me. I can come back for the fuel later."

"Sorry," Abe said. "Got carried away. Too bad Brown wasn't still alive so we could try that Apache roasting thing. Would have been fun."

Chiquito cleared his throat. "No need to apologize," he said. "It's actually comforting knowing I'm not the only savage walking around these woods."

Abe threw Chiquito a quick glance and asked, "How come I didn't know you got a bounty on your head?"

"It wasn't important. It has nothing to do with why we're here."

"Hellfire, it's important to know if someone's out there coming for one of us."

"Well, from what Danny Brown said, it seems they were after you first — or at least, after your brother."

"Don't know anything about that," Abe said with a quick wave.

"That's what I mean," Chiquito said. "It doesn't matter." He pointed at the bodies. "Should we bury them?"

Abe shook his head. "Not worth the bother."

"So much for your Christian upbringing," Chiquito said.

Abe offered no response. Instead, he draped his arm around the Indian's shoulder for support, and the two of them shuffled back to the camp.

CHAPTER 25
REVELATION

Emmet gathered up the King's maps, picked up the new Spencer, and hiked to the top of the hill so he could get his bearings. His foot bothered him only a bit — Mariana had done an excellent job dressing the wound. The ascent was gradual, except for the last fifty feet, where the trees thinned out and the rock outcropped at drunken angles. Using the rifle as a hiking stick, Emmet scrambled up the steeper incline until he reached a bench that opened for a dozen yards.

The view was breathtaking. The foothills wrapped around Santa Sabino like loving brown arms, with the higher mountains, hard and timeless, looming behind them like sentinels. Clouds ribbed the sky, and the San Rafael River curled through the valley like a shiny, blue-green ribbon.

Emmet moved back from the edge of the cliff and the two-hundred-foot drop to the talus below. He spread a map across a flat rock and oriented himself with the surroundings. As he studied the map and the terrain, he heard sand and gravel scattering under footfalls. He grabbed the rifle just as Reno clambered over the rise.

"You spooked me," Emmet said. "Men have died coming up on me quick like that."

"Sorry."

Emmet swept his arm from left to right. "Quite the view, huh?"

Reno gave a quick glance and nodded. "I've seen it before."

"There's rain coming tomorrow," Emmet said. "I can smell it in the air."

"You'll make a good farmer someday," Reno replied. "Mariana told me of your intentions to settle down."

"That's my plan."

"She also told me you intend to take Major Kingston's place and lead the attack on the hacienda."

Emmet set his rifle against a rock and picked up another map. "Yep."

"And you're going to attack first thing tomorrow morning."

"Yep."

"I'd advise against it. You said they're on to us."

"They know about the twins and me from

when we first showed up, but I don't think they know much else."

Reno leaned against a slab of sandstone. "They likely suspect Major Kingston has other men."

"Let them suspect. They could never imagine what Soapy brung."

"You can't be sure of that."

Emmet glued his eyes to Reno. "Are you playing with me, or do you know something I don't?"

Reno fidgeted with the leather bracelet on his wrist. "All I'm saying is that they could be sitting there just waiting for us. Why attack early tomorrow morning?"

"Because the army is due to arrive later tomorrow, and we want to be long gone."

"A day early? How do you know that?"

Emmet squinted and tilted his head. "I just know. And here's the best part: Salazar and Garza don't. We'll go in early and take them by surprise."

"Rethink this. You're making a mistake," Reno said in a louder voice.

"No. This is a great vantage point. From here, we've got easy routes to position the cannon and Gatling gun. We get into position tonight and attack first thing tomorrow."

Reno straightened up, pointed his Spencer at Emmet, and cocked it. "I'm sorry, but I can't let you do that."

Emmet's bones went cold, and a sick feeling penetrated to his bowels. It wasn't fear but something else, a reaction to not wanting to think the worst.

"What are you saying?"

Reno kicked Emmet's rifle out of reach and said, "Your crusade is over."

Emmet fixed his eyes on Reno's seamed, brown face. "You're with Salazar?"

"Trust me. You're no match for him. He'll kill us all, Mariana and myself included. I refuse to let that happen."

"You betray your own daughter?"

"I'm saving my daughter. She was foolish to even consider going against the cousins."

Emmet took a step towards Reno.

"Don't," Reno warned.

Emmet froze. "Mariana loves me," he said.

"No, she doesn't. She wants you to think that because she needs your rifle to kill Garza and avenge Miguel."

"Not true." Emmet could not slow the furious pounding of his heart. He thought about reaching for his boot knife and then realized he didn't have it. The blade was lying on the grass where Mariana had bandaged his leg. "What about Faith?" he asked.

"She's not my concern."

"What about the other girls?"

"Even less a concern."

"You know that unless somebody stands up to the cousins, the people of Santa Sabino will never be free."

"They'll survive. Mariana's safety is all I care about."

"What do the cousins know?"

"Everything. They know about Soapy and the others, the cannon, the Gatling gun, the wagons of ammunition. Everything. Your situation is hopeless."

"When did you turn?"

"I went along with Mariana's madness until you showed up, and Major Kingston said others were on their way. I decided to stop this before things went too far. I believed that once the major was out of the picture, the rest of you would go home."

Emmet shook his head in disgust. "What kind of man are you?"

"A good father."

Emmet doffed his slouch hat and ran his fingers through his hair, his mind racing to buy some time. "Who have you been feeding information to?"

"Diego."

"What do you intend to do with me?"

"Kill you. One shot. Close range. Then

I'll shove your body off the cliff. I'll tell them one of Salazar's men ambushed us."

Emmet put his hat back on. "Mariana will find out, and she'll hate you for it."

"She won't find out."

"Everybody will be able to tell your gun's been fired."

"My Spencer will go over the cliff two seconds after you." Reno lifted Emmet's rifle off the rock. "Then I'll tote your unfired one back with me."

Emmet realized he was running out of time and seized on one last idea.

"When did you last speak to Diego?"

"This morning."

"Then Salazar and Garza don't know about the big guns. Listen to me, Reno. I killed Diego and Paco earlier today before they reached the hacienda."

"Lies."

"Where do you think I found Lucita? Ask her who she was with."

"Lies. She wasn't with Diego when I met him today."

"She must have been with Paco. Before you kill me, check and ask her."

"Don't you see, Emmet, it doesn't matter. I can't let you attack Salazar. If you fail, he'll think I double-crossed him, and both Mariana and I will end up dead."

"But, if we prevail?"

"Mariana is all I have left; I can't take that chance. I'm sorry. Move closer to the edge."

Emmet had faced death many times during the war and acted with courage and equanimity. This time would be no different, even though his heart throbbed at the base of his throat. He sidled closer to the edge of the cliff, raised his arms as if to embrace the clouds floating above him, closed his eyes, and waited.

A shot rang out, but Emmet felt no impact, no pain. Instead, he opened his eyes and saw Reno fall forward, a hole the size of a silver dollar in his back oozing blood. Twenty yards away, cloaked in the shadows of the trees, Soapy lowered his rifle. Emmet went limp and leaned on a rock for support as Soapy emerged from the shade into the sunlight.

"It's been quite a spell," Emmet gasped, "since I was so close to death. Thanks for showing up when you did, Soapy. I owe you a life."

Soapy scrambled up the rocks. "You owe me a bundle of nothing," he said. "Thank Billy instead." He reached into his pocket, removed a sheet of paper, and handed it to Emmet. "Billy saw Reno leave this behind and thought he'd do a good deed and return it to him. Showed it to me first."

"I saw Billy take the letter off Reno's porch," Emmet said. He looked at the paper. It wasn't a letter, but a map showing the exact route to their present location.

"When I saw the map, I knew something was rotten," Soapy said. "Why draw a map of where you're going and leave it behind? That is, unless you're trying to tell somebody else where you're going. When I saw Reno making his way towards you, I figured I'd follow him."

"He had me fooled," Emmet said.

"He had all of us fooled. What are we going to tell Mariana?"

"Almost always better to tell the truth."

Emmet remained still for a few minutes to let his heartbeat return to its normal pace and then stooped to pick up the maps and both Spencers.

"You sure you're up to telling her?" Soapy asked.

"What do you mean?"

"I've noticed the way your eyes picnic on her."

Emmet nodded. "I'll manage it," he said, "if you manage hefting him back to camp."

"I got him," Soapy said, as he grabbed Reno's body by the arms, stood him up, and then let gravity flop the dead man over his shoulder. "Let's go deliver the bad news."

CHAPTER 26
DINNER

Once again, Faith found herself sitting in the hacienda's spacious dining room, except this time a fire crackled in the marble fireplace. Once again, it was she and Enrique Salazar sharing a meal alone, except this time it was dinner. Because they sat at opposite ends of the long table in the huge room, the effect was comical, although neither was laughing.

"Thank you for joining me, Miss Wheeler."

"Did I have a choice?"

Faith watched Salazar break off a piece of bread from a small round loaf and spread a generous lump of butter on it.

"You always have a choice," he said. "You showed great skill tending to the soldier."

"He died."

While Salazar chewed on the bread, he shook his head and said, "I'm scouring my brain trying to figure out a way to convince you that I want only good things for you."

Faith didn't respond. She spooned some stew into her mouth. The stew was a delicious blend of beef and onions and potatoes, but she refused to give Salazar or his household the satisfaction of a compliment. She gazed at the flames flickering from the candelabra nearest to her.

"You've scarred your face," Salazar continued, "but your inner beauty — your inner power — is intact. It can never be damaged."

Faith shifted her eyes to look at him. He was staring at her.

"What can I do," he said, "to show you my good intent."

"There's nothing good inside you."

"What if I free one of the girls?" Salazar offered.

She dipped the spoon into the bowl again, raised it to her mouth, but stopped when it was parallel to her lips. "That would be a start," she said and then swallowed the mouthful.

Salazar set his knife on the tabletop and knitted his hands together. "Even better," he continued, "I'd like you to select the girl."

Faith was dabbing her mouth with a

napkin but stopped. "I get to pick who you let go?"

"Yes, Miss Wheeler. Who will it be?"

Her limbs tingled at the thought of saving the pregnant captive.

"I suppose Calida," she answered with as little expression as possible.

Salazar laughed and turned his head towards the fire, which danced soft orange shapes on the wall. "She's the girl who's been sick the past few mornings."

"The rich food doesn't agree with her."

Salazar threw her a doubtful look and resumed eating without looking up.

"That's one possible explanation," he said.

"You don't want to be selling off a sick girl."

The ends of the older man's mouth curled into a smirk. "No, we don't want to be doing that," he said. "A woman in her condition would be best cared for at home." He winked, picked up a small cast-iron dinner bell, and rang it. Armando appeared at the door, but when he saw Faith's bandaged face, he held a hand to his mouth.

"I'm over here, Armando," Salazar said with a growl.

The boy's eyes slid sideways and shrank into a hard glower. "Yes, señor?" he said.

"Bring Calida here."

As Armando exited the room, he looked back at Faith, shook his head, and shut the door.

"You will see I'm a man of my word," Salazar said, "especially when it comes to making promises to you."

"If you'd like to please me," Faith said, "free them all."

"All of them?"

Faith stood and pounded both hands on the table. "All of them. And then promise to end this awful business once and for all."

Salazar stroked his beard with his right hand. "That's quite a request, Miss Wheeler. What would you offer in return?"

The question took Faith aback. She squinted at him, softened her voice, and asked, "What do you want?"

Salazar leaned back in the chair and sipped from his wine goblet. "I want you to become my wife."

The words stunned Faith and made her stomach clench up. She flopped back into the chair and canted her head to one side. The fire was snapping, and the grandfather clock in the corner was tolling, but, at that moment, she was in a daze and heard nothing.

"Imagine. You would be a hero to all these women, because they would know they are free because of you," he said. "Then you could live here like a queen. And you could put your healing powers to work for everybody's sake."

Faith tried to control her eddying thoughts. She steeled herself and focused her concentration. "What will your cousin say?" she asked.

"He has no say."

"What about the money he'll lose?"

"I'll make it up to him."

Faith could not stop her hands from quivering. She was scared, confused. Could she really save all the girls by sacrificing herself? Her parents taught her that there was no greater love than to do that for others, but could she spend the rest of her life with this vile man?

"Let me sleep on it," she said.

Salazar's face brightened. "You'll give me your answer in the morning?"

She swished her head from side to side, trying to shake her discomfort away. "Yes."

"Promise?"

Now she gave a slow nod. "Yes."

A door knock and then Armando appeared with Calida beside him.

"Come, Calida," Salazar said and motioned her into the room. "I have good news. Tomorrow morning we're sending you home to your parents."

The girl's eyes bugged out, and she squeezed her hands together. "Thank you," she gushed.

Salazar tilted his head towards Faith. "Thank Miss Wheeler. She picked you."

Calida rushed to Faith and hugged her. "Thank you, thank you, thank you," she whispered.

"Armando, escort Miss Wheeler and Calida back to their room. And tell Ponce he'll be taking Calida home tomorrow."

Faith trailed Armando and Calida as they moved towards the door, but as she passed Salazar, he grabbed her hand. She tried to yank it away, but his grip was firm. He bowed and kissed the back of it. "Until tomorrow," he said and then released her with a graceful motion, as if setting a small bird free.

The short, stocky guard posted outside the girls' quarters opened the door for Calida and Faith to enter. He was as ill tempered as all the other guards. When he saw Faith's face, he asked, "What happened to you?"

"I'm not used to eating with such sharp knives," she said.

"You did that to yourself?"

She smiled at him.

"You're a fool," he said and then pointed to a tin-gilded mirror hanging on the wall. "Look at yourself."

He grabbed her arm with one hand and whirled her in front of the mirror. Faith refused to look, so he grabbed her chin with his other hand and forced it up so she could see her reflection. In a pang of self-consciousness, Faith raised her hand to her cheek but stopped short of touching it.

"Stop it!" Armando yelled. "Let her go."

The guard turned and said, "I don't take orders from whelps like you. Who do you think you are?"

"I'm the person that brings Señor Salazar his coffee every morning," Armando answered with a scowl. "You heard what he did to Moco — and that was just about his dog. Imagine what he'll do when I tell him you tried to pluck his favorite flower?"

The guard glared for several seconds and then released Faith. He pointed at Armando and said, "You keep your mouth shut."

Armando pointed back. "You keep your hands off."

Faith turned away from the mirror and moved towards the door behind Calida.

"Wait," Armando said. "This bully's paws have caused your wounds to open up. You'll need fresh bandages." He reached into his pocket, pulled out a roll of gauze, and handed it to Faith. "I've already cut the strips for you," he said with a small smile, "because I know they won't let you have scissors."

Faith took the bandages, thanked him, and went inside. As the door closed behind her, several girls rushed over to ask if she was okay. She assured them that she wasn't badly hurt, that the wound stung, but that Salazar hadn't laid a finger on her.

"Thanks to her, I'm going home tomorrow," Calida said. The pregnant girl's face was radiant.

Faith spoke in a voice laden with sadness. "Salazar said he would free all of you if I married him."

Valencia grabbed Faith's arm. "Don't do it," she said. "We'll be all right."

"You can't be sure of that," Faith answered.

"I think you should marry him," Fabiana said. She was a wide, squat girl with long, dark braids. "Better they let eight of us go than none of us."

"No!" Toya yelled. "I don't trust him. Why would he let any of us go?"

"Why do you think, you idiot?" Fabiana said. "Because he wants Faith, and it's the only way he can get what he wants."

"He could take what he wants by force," Toya said, and then she looked down at the floor.

"He doesn't want me that way," Faith whispered.

Belinda spoke next. "He still wants to marry you after you cut yourself like that?" She stroked Faith's bare arm as a sign she didn't mean to offend her by the comment.

Faith patted Belinda's hand and said, "I promised him an answer tomorrow."

"You said your uncle would come for you," Toya said. "Let's wait for him. Maybe he'll come tonight."

Fabiana stood and pressed her point. "If he was coming at all, he would have been here by now. Our only way out of here is for Faith to marry him. If it were me, I'd do it."

Faith looked up at Fabiana. "You would?"

"If it meant all the rest of the girls could go home," Fabiana replied. "Unless you think you're better than us."

"No," Faith said, "I'm not better than any of you, just better than Salazar."

Valencia leaned in and pressed her forehead against Faith's. "Don't do it," she said, her voice soft and low. "Please don't do it."

The two girls held that position for several seconds. Finally, Faith clasped her hands on the sides of Valencia's head. "I mean to save you all, but not by marrying him." She pulled the bottle of chloroform from her pocket and held it up. "See this? It's powerful medicine. Later tonight, I'm going to put the guard to sleep, escape over the wall, and bring back help."

"But if you run away," Calida said in a frightened voice, "they won't let me go home."

"None of us will go home," Fabiana said with a snarl. "What if I tell the guard what you're planning to do?"

"Trust me," Faith said. "The best thing all of you can do right now is trust me."

CHAPTER 27
A SECRET REVEALED

It was late afternoon when Frank and Zack returned from the cutoff and assured the group that nobody was in pursuit. Zack's gait slowed when he saw Abe's bruised and swollen face. "What the hell happened to you?" he asked.

"Ran into your old friend Danny Brown and his pal," Abe said. "They done me bad, Zack. They busted a few ribs and broke some teeth." Because of the damage to his mouth, the word came out as "teef."

Zack stared at his brother. "You ran into them out here?"

"Turns out they were bounty hunters looking for Chiquito," Abe said.

Frank looked at Chiquito. "You're a wanted man?" he asked, half question, half groan. "Well, if that don't beat the dutch."

"Chiquito saved my life," Abe said. "I guess all Apaches ain't bad, Zack."

"He's the one that put your life in danger,"

Zack replied. He turned to the Indian. "Looks like my brother took a vicious beating. Exactly when did you step in? And how come we didn't know about the bounty on your head?"

Chiquito stood and pawed the knife in his belt. "You'd like to discuss this now?"

Zack looked back at Abe, who shook his head.

"Maybe later," Zack said. He looked at Mariana. "What's wrong with her?"

Mariana sat in silence, wrapped in a green and orange rebozo, her face puffy and red, wiping tears from her eyes.

Emmet pointed to the body shrouded in a yellow, cotton blanket in the back of the wagon. "Turns out Reno was working with the cousins."

"Well, ain't today full of surprises," Frank said. "Never would have made him out for a turncoat, the good-for-nothing."

Emmet watched Mariana absorb the comment with a shiver.

"You don't know who you can trust around here," Zack said, flipping a wary eyebrow at the Apache.

Lucita ran up to Mariana and sat next to her. "I picked some flowers for you," she said, "because you look so sad." The girl held out a fistful of firewheels.

"They're beautiful," Mariana said, admiring the fiery red centers ringed by yellow outer bands. She set the wildflowers in her lap, removed two of them, and pinned them in her hair, one over each ear. "You're kind, Lucita."

"They made you smile," the girl said, "so I'm going to pick some more," and she flitted back into the field.

Behind the child, the sun was moving towards the horizon. A cool wind was sweeping down the slopes and chilling the air, so Soapy lit a campfire. As the group reclined around the snapping flames, Emmet explained to everybody how Reno's body came to be in the back of the wagon and the implications of taking the next steps.

"This is what we know," Emmet said. "The army and the bidders will arrive sometime tomorrow, Sunday, but Salazar doesn't know it. I killed the soldier who was on his way to deliver that message. The cousins still believe the army will arrive on Monday. If we attack tomorrow, we'll have the element of surprise, and we can avoid an encounter with the army."

"How much surprise?" Soapy asked. "You said the cousins already know about us."

"They know about me and the twins," Emmet said. "But I don't believe they know about the rest of you. Reno was funneling information to Diego and Paco, and I killed those two brothers on their way back to Salazar's before they could deliver Reno's message."

"Busy morning," Chiquito said.

"I'm an early riser."

"We're down two and a half men," Zack said. "Abe's pretty busted up and won't be much help."

"We still have enough men to pull this raid off," Emmet said. Catching himself, he added, "and women."

Mariana's mouth formed a small scribble of a smile. Emmet touched the tip of his hat to compensate for his unintended slight. He would have done anything to dispel her freight of pain right then and ease her sorrow about her father. But he figured the best thing to do was keep talking, even though it wasn't his way.

"The King explained the battle plan to me before he was captured, and now I'm gonna tell it to you. Chiquito, tomorrow, before sunrise, Salazar's kitchen help is expecting a wagon of Pedro's baked goods. The major fashioned the baker's wagon with a fake compartment on the underside that'll hide you. It's a snug fit, but you're wiry enough."

271

"I've been in tighter spots," Chiquito said.

"Once you're inside the gate, take out the two guards roaming the yard, and the two guards in the tower. Go back and unlock the gate. With Reno gone, we need someone to drive the bakery wagon into the compound. Any volunteers?"

Now Emmet looked at Mariana.

She met his gaze, and her eyes brightened. She shifted the rebozo onto her shoulders, and said, "I'll drive the wagon."

Emmet touched his hat again. He hated to put Mariana in danger, but it was the only way the plan would work. "Take Lucita and your father's body to Father Ramirez. Then go to the baker's and swap wagons. Hide Chiquito in the fake compartment, and then bring the wagon of food into the hacienda. Do you understand?"

Mariana nodded.

"But listen to me," Emmet said with a dose of urgency in his voice. "After you set Chiquito free from the wagon and deliver the food, get the hell out of there as quick as possible. You don't want to be anywhere near that place once the music starts."

Emmet then looked at Zack. "You'll position yourself on the ledge I showed you yesterday that overlooks Salazar's den. He rises early and goes there every morning.

Don't attempt anything by the light of Salazar's lantern, because it can cast misleading shadows. Wait for sunrise, and then make your head shot."

"Will Garza be with him?" Abe asked.

"No way of knowing," Emmet replied. "But Salazar's the brains, so if we kill him first, we cut the head off the snake. I bagged a lot of Yankee officers during the war. It's really an act of sabotage — it disrupts the enemy's usual lines of communication and spooks the troops."

Frank spat the long blade of grass he was chewing into the fire and stared at the flames. Emmet ignored him and continued. "Abe, can you at least load shells into the cannon?"

"I can try."

"Soapy and Abe, you'll position the cannon about nine hundred yards from the compound on the west side." His finger tapped the location on the map.

"Perfect spot," Soapy said.

"Frank and Billy, go in the back way and position the Gatling gun at the humpback bridge. After those vaqueros hear the report from Zack's rifle, they'll come pouring out of the bunkhouse like bugs inside a burning log. Keep them pinned down. After we free the girls, we'll put them in the second wagon that Pedro will be driving and make our escape. Any questions?"

"Yeah, I got one," Frank said. He rose and took a deep breath, inflating his chest for effect. "Who the hell put you in charge?"

Emmet didn't move, didn't speak.

"Major Kingston was the brains behind our operation," Frank said. "You ain't no Major Kingston."

"Emmet can lead us," Soapy offered.

"Like hell," Frank bellowed. "Honeycut ain't qualified to shine the major's boots." He pounded his chest. "If anybody should take charge, it's me."

"You're crazy," Emmet said.

"Don't ever call me crazy!" Frank shouted.

When the big man started for Emmet, Soapy jumped up and extended two arms to intercept him and said, "Emmet has been in a lot of battles."

"So have I," Frank replied. "The difference is we won ours."

"You Yankee dog," Emmet said with a sneer.

"Honeycut, let's settle this once and for all. It's about time I carved you off an honest slice of truth." Frank began to roll up his sleeves.

"Quit it!" Soapy yelled. "Enough. You

both saw war. But, Frank, you're the only man in this outfit strong enough and experienced enough to manage that Gatling gun. Without you, we lose a major part of our advantage. If you don't operate that gun, then, truly, all of us might as well go home."

Frank would have none of it. "Forget it, Soapy. I'll take my five hundred dollars for showing up, just like Major Kingston promised."

Emmet realized that without Frank, the group's odds of success had greatly declined. He let his temper cool and then said, "It's hard for me to ask a Yank for help, but that's what I'm doing. Why don't you join us and take home two thousand dollars?"

"Why don't I join you?" Frank asked in a mocking tone. "Maybe I think this whole operation is jinxed, what with Major Kingston being captured, Reno turning traitor, and bounty hunters breathing down our necks — but that's not the reason."

A vein in Frank's temple throbbed as he glared at Emmet.

Emmet looked at the ground. "Spit it out."

Frank pointed his finger at Emmet's nose. "I don't follow kid-killers into battle."

Emmet's hands fell limp at his side, and he bowed his head. "Is that really the way it is?"

"Yeah, that's the way it is," Frank replied and returned to his seat by the fire.

"Then I'll fetch your money — and everybody else's."

Emmet strode over to the wagon, just as Lucita returned with more flowers. He shoved a few boxes of shells aside to get at Kingston's war bag, leaned in, and pulled it out. He returned to the campfire, dropped the bag, knelt down, and removed a burlap sack that held packets of money wrapped in string.

"I've got all of your boodles right here," Emmet said, "in crisp, neat one-hundred-dollar bills sealed with the stamp of the U.S. government." He held up half a dozen thick sheaves of cash. The sight of the money stunned everybody into silence.

"I know you got issues with me," Emmet said. "Let me meet them head-on."

Emmet approached Billy. "First up, I know I ain't the soldier that the major is. Never will be. But I'm damn accurate shooting from a galloping horse, which is gonna come in mighty handy tomorrow. Ruby Red is a good chopper, and she can turn on a biscuit and never cut the crust. I'll be as fast and frisky as anybody sitting around this campfire."

Billy's eyes popped when Emmet handed

him two thousand dollars, and he gave a loud *yee-haw.*

"Second, it's not my battle plan, but the major's." Emmet dropped a packet in Abe's lap, who picked it up and dandled it in the palm of his hand. "The King told the plan to me, and I think it's a corker. Major Kingston crammed a lot of sober thinking into it, and it'll work if each of us does his job."

Emmet tossed a packet to Zack. "The battle starts after you take out Salazar through the window. Think you can make that shot?" Emmet knew the answer but wanted the rest of the group to hear Zack's reply.

"Mr. Honeycut, you spent a lot of years teaching me how to shoot. Don't worry. I'm gonna part Salazar's hair with this here Spencer."

Everybody laughed except Frank.

"Third, I want to tell you why we have to fight this battle." Emmet presented a packet to the Apache, who received it with both hands.

"Chiquito here will tell you that revenge is a sacred duty. I cotton to his thinking, except I prefer the word *reckoning* instead of revenge. Salazar and Garza are demons of the first stripe. They steal and kill and profit off the misery of others."

Emmet handed Mariana a packet and looked into her eyes as he spoke his next words.

"They murder innocent people. They kidnap innocent children and sell them off as slaves. They're animals. Lower than animals, because animals don't kill for pleasure."

Mariana lifted her chin and nodded.

Emmet approached Soapy and flipped him his money. "My friend, you and me saw a lot of action together during the war. I believe with the weapons you brung, the element of surprise, and enough gumption, we can beat them. What do you think?"

Soapy waved the money back and forth in front of his face like a fan. "I stood beside you at Chickamauga, brother, and I'll stand beside you now. I believe we can best them, but our chances would be considerably better if Frank would help us." Soapy looked at Frank, who once again shook his head.

Emmet approached Frank, tugged five hundred-dollar bills out of a packet and handed it to him. Frank jammed the cash into his pants. Then Emmet dipped into his shirt pocket and, with a trembling hand, removed the photograph that he kept so close to his heart.

"Your hand is shaking, Honeycut," Frank said. "You nervous about something?"

"I'm gonna tell you something I've never told anyone before," Emmet replied.

"That don't make *me* feel privileged," Frank said.

Emmet handed him the photograph.

Frank examined it and said, "It's a picture of you with a woman and a girl. Means nothing to me."

Emmet took the picture back and said, "Those two meant the world to me. For all your bluster about what I did in Dixville, you sure don't know the story too good." He handed the photograph to Mariana, who studied it for several seconds.

"The woman is beautiful, and the girl looks just like her." She passed the picture back. "Mother and daughter?"

Emmet nodded and then pressed the picture into Soapy's hand.

Soapy jumped to his feet and cried out, "Damn me to hell if that ain't Amy Baxter and her mother! I almost didn't recognize her because they're both gussied up. The only pictures I ever saw of them were the ones they put in the paper. Emmet, what's this mean?"

"That was my engagement picture, Soapy. Me and Polly Baxter was supposed to get hitched. That's why she and Amy were at the Dixville Hotel that Saturday night. We were gonna get our license the next morning and get married later that afternoon."

Soapy smoothed the palm of his hand over his bald head. "How come nobody knew about this?" His voice was a shaky mix of bewilderment and distress. "It never came out at your trial. Nobody knew anything about it."

"Three can keep a secret when two are dead," Emmet said. "Polly's husband abandoned her and Amy two years before. She was still married according to the law, so we kept our relationship secret. Nobody knew about our engagement, especially not in Dixville. We agreed not to tell anybody we were married until it was done."

A puzzled look came over Chiquito. "What happened to the woman and the child?"

"They died in a hotel fire along with several others," Emmet said, "including her brother, who was gonna be my best man. Amy was gonna be her mother's maid of honor."

Chiquito lowered his head as if to let the enormity of the tragedy soak in. Tears rimmed Mariana's eyes. Everybody remained silent as Emmet turned back to Frank.

"I came to Dixville to start a new life, Frank, but that night, fate turned my new life into cinders and ash. Amy was gonna be my stepdaughter, and I shot her. I killed my own kid. I killed the little girl that I loved so much. Now, what do you think of that?"

Frank stared at Emmet with eyes as cold as cairns. The big man rose and, in an uncharacteristically soft voice, said, "If I ask you an honest question, will you give me an honest answer?"

"I almost always tell the truth."

"When you shot that girl, did you know her mother was already dead?"

Emmet ran a sweaty hand through his hair and looked up at the sky, steeling himself, trying to keep the bitter memory from besting him. He bit back tears, tasted blood in his mouth, and looked back at Frank.

"No, I didn't know her mother was already dead. I was hoping she had made it out alive." He took a deep breath. "And if I was willing to answer to her for what I did, I sure as hell don't need to answer to you."

Frank's shoulders drooped, and he stared at the tops of his boots. He exhaled a slow sigh that shrank his big body.

"I don't know if you've done things in your life that you wish you hadn't, Frank, but I have," Emmet said. "And rare is the day when a person gets a chance to make up for it. But I'm in that position now, and tomorrow is that day. Not that I believe what I did was wrong, but to answer to those people who've believed I was wrong. People like you. Now, will you help us free those girls?"

Frank lifted his head, stood tall again, and said, "Honeycut, I guess my motivation is a lot simpler than yours — I joined this posse for money, so, if it's okay with you, I'd like to take the rest of my two thousand dollars right now." He extended his doughy hand, palm up.

Emmet supported the bottom of Frank's outstretched hand with his left palm, slapped the packet of money into it with his right, and said, "Frank, thanks for letting me think dangerously noble thoughts again."

Soapy ambled over and wrapped an arm around Emmet's shoulder in a gesture that appeared to be one part admiration for his confession, and one part condolence for his loss. "Looks like you're heading up a shooting party," Soapy said. "Looks like it's time for a reckoning."

Emmet offered a weak smile. "Then let's get going."

The group bolted into action, removing

the contents of the supply wagon to make room for the girls they hoped to free, hitching the animals, and stashing the packets of money. As Mariana turned to go, Emmet reached for her arm.

"If nothing else," he said, "I'm gonna prove to you that I'd kill for love and, if necessary, die for it, too. There ain't a greater testament I can make to you, Miss Mariana. And just in case something happens to me, I want you to keep my money."

"I can't," Mariana said. "I'm superstitious. It could jinx you. Better that you keep your money and take this."

She removed the cross from her neck. "Miguel gave it to me as a wedding present." She pressed it into Emmet's palm. "Promise me I'll see you again."

"I promise I'll do everything possible to try and make that happen."

Their lips and tongues met in a salty, bittersweet kiss, and Emmet felt all his past sorrows evaporate in that one tender moment. He clung to her a bit longer, her mouth soft and warm, unsure of whether he'd ever see her again.

"I'll pray for you," she whispered, and then she took Lucita by the hand and led her to the wagon. They climbed into the seat just as Chiquito lobbed himself into the back next to Reno's body. Through the trees Emmet followed Mariana with his eyes as she guided the wagon along the trail until it disappeared over the ridge. Now it was time to saddle up, get into position near the hacienda, and wait for morning.

Chapter 28
Pedro's Bakery

Mariana, Chiquito, and Lucita rumbled down the road to Santa Sabino. Dusk had blackened into night, and high thin clouds surrounded the risen moon.

"I'll hide under the blanket when we get to Santa Sabino," Chiquito said.

"Why do you have to hide?" Lucita asked.

"People are looking for me," the Apache replied. "People who want to hurt me."

Mariana added, "Just like those bad men who took you away from your father and mother."

"But you didn't do anything bad, did you?" the girl asked.

"Some people think I did," Chiquito replied, "but I don't think I did."

Mariana glanced up at the darkening clouds and lifted the rebozo over her head.

"It must be strange, Chiquito," she said, "spending your days knowing that men are hunting for you, that death could be right around the corner."

"Death is around the corner for all of us."

"True," Mariana said. "Better to focus on life."

"What is life?" the Indian said. "It's the flash of a firefly dancing in the twilight, the sound of a bird singing at dawn." He pointed to the sky. "It's a perfect pale ring around the moon telling us that tomorrow will bring rain."

"You strike me as a man of fierce dignity," Mariana said.

"I seek to become a good ancestor."

Mariana sat contemplative for a few minutes and then said, "My father was not a good ancestor."

"I'm sorry about your father," Chiquito answered, "but, from what I understand, he was only trying to protect you."

"By killing Emmet? By betraying all the people who trusted him?" Mariana's words blazed with anger. "Garza murdered my husband."

"I did not know that."

"It was years ago, but I've never forgotten Miguel, and I'll never rest until he is avenged."

"I am grateful that I can help you with your sacred duty," Chiquito said.

"My father was not an honorable man,

but I believe you are, even with a bounty on your head. And I believe Emmet is an honorable man, chivalrous even."

Lucita turned to Mariana and asked, "What does 'chivalrous' mean?"

"Emmet told me that back in olden days, knights in shining armor swore oaths to be chivalrous," Mariana explained. "That meant they would try to be brave and honest and do nice things for people."

"Then Emmet is chivalrous," the girl said with a smile and a bounce of her head.

"I think so, too," Mariana said, and then she stroked the girl's black hair.

"What about Dixville?" Chiquito asked. "Was that chivalrous?"

Mariana's smile faded as she considered the question. "I think he did what his conscience told him to do. I think he has always remained true to himself."

"Sounds like a lot of people hate him for being true to himself."

"Emmet told me that he'd rather be hated for who he was than loved for who he wasn't," Mariana said, "which I find strange, because I believe most people want to be loved."

"Do you love him?"

"I do."

"Your feelings for him have nothing to do

with his willingness to take on Salazar and Garza and avenge Miguel?" Chiquito asked.

"It's not like that. I would feel the same if he had decided not to fight." Mariana looked back and saw Chiquito arch an eyebrow. "You don't believe me?" she asked.

"Whatever you say," the Apache replied. "You realize he comes across as cold and quiet to people who don't know him."

"Every person has his secret sorrows that none of us knows about. Emmet has a scar on his heart. A lot of times people call a man cold or quiet or aloof when he is only sad."

"Do you have secret sorrows?" Chiquito asked.

"I do," Mariana answered, "just like you."

They fell silent, and Mariana returned to her own thoughts until they reached the outskirts of town, where Chiquito concealed himself under the blanket. The wagon rolled along dark, empty streets. Mariana detoured around the Ox-Bow Saloon to avoid any encounters with early morning carousers and squeezed the wagon along an alley next to the church. She escorted Lucita to the back door and knocked several times.

"Father Ramirez will keep you safe until I return, Lucita. And I will keep these beautiful flowers in my hair to remind me of you."

The little girl grinned, and they hugged, just as the sleepy priest opened the door. Father Ramirez had a long face shaped like a shoe with a wide, round forehead and a smaller, curved jaw line. Even through drowsy eyes he radiated kindness. As soon as Mariana explained Lucita's situation to him, he yanked the girl inside out of sight. Then he helped Chiquito remove Reno's body and place it in his office and drape a blanket over it.

"Nobody will see him in here, Mariana," the priest said. "I'll get the undertaker later."

"I'll explain what happened to my father later, too," Mariana said. "In the meantime, if all goes well, Pedro will be bringing you the rest of the girls in this same wagon in a few hours."

"I'll be ready," he said.

She climbed back into the wagon and wove her way through the side streets. She could tell she was nearing Pedro's bakery because the aroma of fresh bread filled the air. When he saw Mariana pull up, the baker sprang through the front doorway to meet her. Pedro was a short, clean-shaven man in his mid-thirties, with a wide nose and thick eyebrows.

"Right on time," he said wiping his floury hands on his apron. "Time to swap wagons.

But where's your father?"

"Dead," Mariana said. "It's a long story that I don't have time to tell right now."

"But who will drive the wagon with the food into the hacienda?"

"I will."

"No," Pedro protested. "It's too dangerous. Does Major Kingston know about this?"

"No. Salazar took him prisoner."

Pedro's forehead dripped with sweat from the heat of the ovens, and he wiped his brow with the back of his hand. "And yet we're still going through with this?"

"Yes. The army is arriving later this morning, but Salazar doesn't know it."

"A day early," the baker said, rubbing his hairless chin. "So we need to get in and out before they arrive."

"Listen to me, Pedro. I can do this. I will get Chiquito inside the compound and deliver the food before the shooting starts. I'll be safe."

"I don't like it."

"Believe in me. I plan to be out of there as soon as these supplies are unloaded."

The baker gazed at her for several seconds and then nodded.

"You're a good man, Pedro. Don't worry. You're the one who is taking a big risk. You are willing to drive the getaway wagon with the girls inside in the middle of a gunfight."

"I was blessed with two sons," he said. "If they had been daughters, who knows? Maybe the cousins would have abducted them, and then where would I be? Come, let me show you the trick wagon; it's a clever design. Major Kingston told me he used it several times during the war to sneak spies behind enemy lines."

Mariana alerted Chiquito with a light tap on his moccasin, and he slid from beneath the blanket. Pedro flipped the tarp back on the bakery wagon. It was loaded with baskets of tortillas and sweet breads.

"You'll miss Salazar's business when this is over," Mariana observed.

"No, I won't," Pedro said with a snort of disgust. He reached beneath the wagon and pulled out a wooden pin that held the trap door up. The door dropped and thudded against the hub band of the wheel.

"Mariana, the door opens from the outside only. When you let Chiquito out, let the door down gently to avoid making any noise. Don't do what I just did."

She practiced several times to get it right. Once she was comfortable maneuvering the trap door, Chiquito climbed in and scrunched himself into the cramped quarters. Mariana handed the Apache his rifle and knives, which he tucked against his side, and then she slipped the pin in, locking him inside. She noted that the freeboard above his head extended less than three inches.

"Do not forget about me," Chiquito whispered.

"How could I forget somebody so willing to help me with my sacred duty?" Mariana whispered back.

She turned and embraced Pedro. The baker handed her a bag of pastries. "Use these to distract the guards. And give my regards to Mrs. Medina in the kitchen. She's as ornery as they come."

Mariana stepped on the toe board, climbed into the seat, snapped the reins, and steered the horses towards the hacienda.

CHAPTER 29
WAITING FOR SUNRISE

Even with the gathering clouds, the moon provided enough light to guide Emmet's night travel. He maneuvered into position an hour early to make sure the baker's wagon got through. Ruby Red was tied up fifty yards behind him, pawing at the ground, itching to go.

Emmet wiped the dew off Big Betty with his hand and then unwrapped the spyglass. It felt as cold as an icicle lying across his fingertips. Squinting through the eyepiece, he saw the front gate through the trees. The breath of two guards positioned behind the campfire puffed out in little white clouds in the early morning chill. The frosty air forced Emmet to wrap the blanket tighter around his torso.

He hoped everybody would soon be where they needed to be: Mariana driving the wagon to the compound, Chiquito hidden inside it, warming the cold metal of his knife and rifle with his body heat; Zack perched on the ledge looking down on Salazar's window; Soapy swabbing out the cannon while Abe stacked shells; Frank and Billy maneuvering the Gatling gun near the humpback bridge; Pedro positioning the getaway wagon near the hacienda.

For now, all he could do was sit. Trees around him swished in the occasional breeze, and a great horned owl hooted several sad notes in the distance. Emmet had never felt more alert. Blood was coursing through him like spring snowmelt, and the hairs on his arms extended like brush bristles. But his excitement was tempered by the knowledge that lives could be lost — innocent lives.

As he waited in that dark surround, it struck Emmet as strange to know that this night of peace was about to explode into a morning of cannon blasts and gunfire. But then he realized this was just like so many of his war experiences: crouching in the woods at night, eager to attack at first light, hoping that all his friends would make it out alive.

Now Emmet heard the *wee-wah* of wagon wheels. Mariana rolled up to the main gate, and a shiver of anxiety came over him as his first minutes of worry commenced. Emmet believed nothing should divert a man's attention when he goes into battle. Nothing. And here was Mariana, more than a beautiful distraction; she would be a source of constant worry to him as long as she remained in harm's way.

The guards walked around the campfire and stood on each side of the wagon. Even in the dim glow of the firelight, Emmet admired her beauty. She offered each guard a sweet roll. *If Mariana's good looks don't divert your attention,* Emmet thought, *your empty stomachs might.*

The guards each plucked out a roll and munched it as they circled the wagon. They hefted the tarp to make sure it was only food being delivered and half-glanced at the underside of the wagon. If they were on high alert, they didn't show it.

The guard on the left rapped on the big wooden gate. As it creaked open, the guard on the right waved Mariana through. Emmet let out a sigh of relief when the gate closed behind them, and he knew they were safely inside the compound, and Chiquito was free to go about his silent knife work. Now Emmet waited for sunrise, and the first report from Zack's rifle.

CHAPTER 30
THE WATER BARREL

Faith dozed in and out most of the night and woke in the predawn hours. She lay on her cot for several minutes, summoning her courage. The room was dark and quiet except for the soft buzz of several girls snoring. Faith sat up and looked out the window. Clouds scudded past the moon, but enough light filtered into the room through the iron bars to allow her to make out the white sheets on the cots. She grabbed the sleeve of her smock and, after several tries, ripped off a piece the size of a face cloth. Next she removed the vial of chloroform from her pocket.

Leaning over the cot next to her, Faith nudged Valencia and whispered, "It's time."

Valencia shifted several times, rubbed the drowse from her eyes, and sat up. Faith rose and padded to the door, avoiding bumping into any of the cots. Valencia followed her across the room. Uncorking the bottle, Faith sprinkled a generous amount of the anesthetic on the torn piece of smock, which tinged the air with a sweet, pungent odor. She pointed to the doorknob.

Valencia tapped on the door with two fingers.

"What?" the guard mumbled from the other side, his voice muzzy with sleep.

"Calida is sick again."

Faith plugged the vial and passed it to Valencia. A minute passed, and then the door opened, and the guard entered. Valencia said nothing but pointed to a cot in the middle of the room. As soon as the guard cleared the door, Faith sprang from behind it and jumped on him, locking her legs around his waist, clamping the cloth across his nose and mouth. The guard spun and tried to throw her off like a wild horse tossing a rider, but Faith clung to him like moss to a river rock.

The guard lunged at his back and made a frantic grab for her hair, but his arms couldn't reach. Faith felt a brief relaxation in his body, and then a sudden burst of strength as he squirmed and twisted his frame back and forth in a wild attempt to flip her off. He slammed his back against the wall, almost crushing her, but Faith held her grip. Again, she felt his body relaxing,

his motions slowing, until he pitched forward and fell across several cots, waking
half a dozen girls.

"Help me flip him on his back," Faith told
Valencia.

The girls awakened by the fall said nothing, listening as Faith told Valencia what to
do: "If he starts to stir, sprinkle more of this
on the cloth and hold it to his nose and
mouth for a minute or so. Too much will
kill him, so use it lightly."

Valencia took the cloth and nodded. Faith
turned to the girls who were staring at her
from their beds, including Fabiana.

"I'm going to get help," Faith told them.

"No you're not," Fabiana said. "You're
running away."

"I intend to save us all," Faith said. "I'll
send people to rescue you."

"Please don't be long," Valencia pleaded.

Faith opened the door, scanned left and
right to see if anybody was there, then
stepped into the hall. Soon Mrs. Medina
would be starting her day and preparing
coffee for the early-rising Salazar. As Faith
inched towards the kitchen, she heard the
raspy growl of another guard snoring in the
dining room. With her back pressed against
the wall, she felt her way along the hall, past
the sleeping man, and into the kitchen,

where she accidentally kicked one of Viper's large water bowls. Ducking under the kitchen table, she waited to see if she had stirred the guard and listened for footsteps — or the scratch of paws. Nothing . . . only the slosh of water back and forth inside the bowl.

She peered out the kitchen window and jumped back when she noticed a third guard smoking a cigarette by the well. He tossed the butt on the ground, ladled water from a bucket, and drank. Faith remained hidden, surrounded by hanging pots and pans. When the guard sauntered around the corner towards the small courtyard, she cracked the door open several inches. The chilly air bubbled gooseflesh on her bare arms. To generate some warmth, she chafed her arms with her hands.

When she figured it was safe, she dashed to the east side towards the well and hid behind a water barrel under the ramada. It took several tries to remove the plug from the barrel and get the water flowing. Once the barrel was empty, she planned to roll it across the yard and use it to scale the wall.

The guard returned to make another pass, whistling as he walked. Faith watched him as he stopped to flex his knees and then looked at the water draining from the barrel. He came towards her with his gun drawn, so she slid deeper into the shadows and balled her body up to make it as small as possible.

She watched him peer around several barrels and under a wooden bench. Her hopes sank once he found the plug on the ground, picked it up, and jammed it back inside the barrel to stop the flow. Faith didn't breathe, didn't budge. The man dawdled by the barrel for several more minutes before walking back to the well pump. When Faith saw him lean against it and roll another cigarette, she realized she was trapped, and her stomach knotted up in defeat.

The smell of the damp oak wood reminded her of the rain barrel beside her house, the one she would hide behind to fool her parents when playing hide and seek. Her parents? What would they do in this situation? Pray. She rested her head on her arms and lifted a heart-felt plea to heaven to send a deliverer to show her a way out.

CHAPTER 31
MRS. MEDINA

Mariana steered the wagon along the west side of the main house but stopped halfway between the kitchen and front gate when she realized neither of the guards in the yard could see her. She jumped to the ground, reached under the wagon bed, undid the pin, and, with a gentle hand, let down the trap door. Chiquito slipped out, rolled between the wheels, and vanished into the shadowscape, just as the guard in the rear came around the corner.

"You there," he yelled. "What are you doing?"

Mariana pushed the door back up and repositioned the pin as he closed in. "I thought something was snagged on the wheel," she said, "but I was wrong. I'm here with the food." She grabbed the bag of sweet rolls and offered him one. He peered inside the bag and pulled one out.

"Where's Pedro?" he asked as he bit into

the pastry. The tip of his thick moustache turned white with frosting.

"Baking," Mariana said. "He's still got a lot to do before your guests arrive on Monday."

"They've been delayed a day," he said.

"Nobody told us."

The guard shrugged. "Kitchen's around the corner."

Mariana hopped into the seat and guided the wagon outside the kitchen door. Before she could climb down, Mrs. Medina walked out holding a lantern. She was an older, stunted woman, with a round face, pug nose, and short, curly hair that thinned at the sides. A cook for thirty years, she had spent the last five trying to please the palates of Salazar and Garza.

"Where's Pedro?" she snapped.

"He has a lot more food to prepare but sends his regards," Mariana said. "I just learned from the man in the yard that your guests have been delayed."

Mrs. Medina ignored Mariana, yanked the tarp off, and swung the lantern around the inside of the wagon. "Well, *I'm* not unloading these baskets," she said. "Armando."

The teenaged servant popped his head out the doorway.

"Bring the food into the kitchen," she

said, and then she handed the lantern to Mariana. "Make sure he gets everything."

Armando sprang into action, grabbing a basket and lugging it inside. Mariana remained in the seat, shining the light for each of Armando's trips. Dawn was just outlining the curves of the mountains. *My time is running out,* she thought. She jumped from the wagon, set the lantern down, and brought a basket into the kitchen, passing Armando on the way. There was no room left on the table, so she set the basket on the floor.

"Not there, here," Mrs. Medina said, pointing to a wooden bench next to the fireplace. As Mariana moved the basket, the cook handed her a bucket. "Tell Armando to fetch some water."

Half a dozen baskets remained in the wagon. "I'll get the water, Armando," Mariana said. "You keep unloading."

She turned the corner expecting to encounter the guard with the frosting moustache again. Instead, she saw his body stuffed behind a horse trough and knew Chiquito had made his acquaintance. She lifted the bucket to the pipe and jacked the pump handle. The brisk air had made the metal as cold as marble in her hand. As water purled from the spout, Mariana sensed movement out of the corner of her eye. When the bucket was full, she set it down and moved deeper under the ramada.

"Chiquito?" she whispered. No answer. She peered around the barrel and saw a girl huddled in the shadows. In the darkness, Mariana could just make out the blonde hair on the top of her head.

"Faith?"

The girl's pupils went wide as buttons at being recognized. "Who . . . who are you?" the girl stammered.

"I'm Mariana — a friend of your uncle's."

Faith hopped up and buried her head in Mariana's bosom. "I knew my uncle would come for me."

Mariana thumbed the girl's chin and gasped when she saw the bandages. "Those animals," she said.

"It's not their fault," Faith said, pressing her fingers against the bandages. "Is my uncle okay?"

"Yes."

"Do you know the army is coming today?"

"Yes. Listen: We have little time. I'm going to get you out of here. Now."

Mariana turned and studied the compound. All clear. She grasped Faith's hand, and they ran across the yard, pulling up next to the house. Mariana's heart raced at the prospect of whisking Faith away before the shooting started.

"Around the corner there's a wagon with a hidden compartment underneath," Mariana said. "If you climb into it, I can sneak you out of here."

They waited until Armando carried the last basket inside, and then they scurried to the wagon. Mariana set the bucket down, reached under, and released the pin, but, because of her shaking hand, the door slammed down before she could catch it. Armando heard the noise and stuck his head outside. Mariana froze when their eyes met, and her heart dropped like lead. She had been so close to rescuing Faith and had failed. Her sorrow changed to puzzlement when she saw Armando smile at Faith and raise his index fingers to his lips. Faith smiled back before scrambling inside the compartment. Mariana reset the pin and brought Armando the bucket.

"Thank you for your help," she said, dazed yet relieved.

Armando leaned in and whispered, "Garza took my sister two years ago."

Mariana gave a sympathetic nod.

Then the boy reached into his pants pocket and removed a roll of gauze, placing it in her hands.

"In case her bandages need freshening."

"I'll see to it," she said. "I'm leaving now."

"Not so fast," Mrs. Medina said, pushing Armando aside. "I think we're missing a few items."

"Write them down," Mariana said, "and I'll get the list tomorrow."

"No, no, no," Mrs. Medina clucked. "We'll go over it together right now, and tomorrow you'll bring me what's missing."

Mariana rolled her eyes and peered up at the eastern hills backlit by the rising sun. She knew Zack was up there preparing to fire the bullet that would start the attack. There was nothing she could do to escape the wave of destruction that was about to roar down. She followed Mrs. Medina into the kitchen.

CHAPTER 32
SUNRISE

Garza rose from his bed in the dark, lit the flat-wick kerosene lamp, and fished a light-green *guayabera* and brown pants out of the closet. After tugging on his boots, he lifted his holster and gun from the bedpost and buckled them on.

He knew his cousin would already be up, expecting him to search for the missing men and girl. He walked down the hall to the den and could tell Salazar was inside from the lamplight reflecting off the polished wooden floor behind the door. He knuckle-rapped twice before opening it.

"Good morning, Yago," Salazar said. He held a goose quill pen and was scratching figures in one of his tally books. Viper sat next to him, sphinxlike.

Garza didn't respond and slid into one of the two chairs in front of the desk.

"Good to see you up early," Salazar continued. When he looked up, he noticed the gun. "Hardware before breakfast?"

Garza stared at his cousin in steely silence.

"What's going on?" Salazar asked.

Another knock on the door, and this time Armando entered carrying a metal coffee pot and two clay mugs. The servant splashed coffee into the mugs and handed one to Garza, who took a long sip and swirled the warm liquid around his mouth before swallowing.

"Tell Mrs. Medina to delay breakfast today," he told the boy.

"Since when do you interfere with meals?" Salazar said. "Armando, tell her we'll have breakfast as usual."

"Do as I say," Garza barked at the boy. "My cousin and I have important business to resolve."

Salazar set the pen down and dismissed Armando. The servant nodded and left the room. Salazar flipped his hands up, arched his eyebrows. "So?"

"Tell me it's not true."

"What?"

"You're letting one of the girls go."

Outside, the darkness continued to dissolve, and gray clouds filtered the emerging light, bathing the hills in a soft, dull glow. Further beyond, black rain clouds massed at the edge of the sky.

"It's true," Salazar said. "You must have spoken with Ponce."

Garza slammed the mug on the desk.

Salazar took a quick sip of coffee. "And now I'm going to tell you something else that will vex you, Yago. I've asked Faith to marry me, and, if she consents, I promised her I would set all the girls free."

Garza exhaled a long, slow breath, drew his Peacemaker, and said, "You've finally lost your mind."

The dog rose from the floor and began to growl.

Salazar let out a short laugh. "What do you intend to do with that?"

"Stop you."

Garza watched as Salazar's right hand eased toward the inside pocket of his jacket. "Leave the derringer where it is, Enrique."

Salazar's hand froze and dropped into his lap.

Garza stood and said, "You carry such a small gun, a girl's weapon, really. Real men wear more metal."

Salazar swallowed and stared at his cousin.

"You never thought I'd agree to free the girls, did you?" Garza asked.

Light continued to seep through the window and bleach out the remaining shadows. Salazar picked up the lantern, blew out the flame, and set it back on the desk. He steepled his fingertips and squinted at Garza through dark berry eyes.

"It doesn't matter what you think," he said. *"Vibora."*

The dog deepened its growl and bared its teeth.

"Oh, but it does matter," Garza said. He cocked the pistol, pointed it at the dog, and fired into its head, killing it instantly.

Salazar recoiled in the chair and shouted, "What have you done!"

Tito and Ponce burst through the door, looked at the dead animal, and then over at Garza.

"You never did like that dog," Tito said.

"Seize him!" Salazar shouted. "He plans to shoot me next."

The two men turned and smiled at Salazar. Tito sidled over to the desk, drummed his fingers on it, and then pushed the black porcelain stallion off the edge. He was still smiling after the statue hit the floor and shattered into pieces.

Garza's teeth were clenched, his eyes focused. He cocked the pistol again. "Tito and Ponce are with me on this."

"Are you really going to kill me?" Salazar asked, a puzzled look creeping across his face.

"You've left us no choice."

Salazar sat still as a gravestone, except for the corner of his upper lip, which was twitching. Garza had seen the tic once before — when a *pistolero* was holding a knife to his cousin's throat. Garza knew Salazar was scared.

"Last chance to change your mind," Garza said. He pointed the Peacemaker at Salazar's nose. "What's it going to be?"

With his lip quivering even faster, Salazar placed both hands on the desk and took a deep breath. He opened his mouth to answer, but no words came out. Instead Garza watched his cousin's head explode in a spray of blood and bone. Instinct made Garza, Tito, and Ponce dive on the floor as the last echo of the rifle shot drifted into the hills. Garza skittered away from the window and rammed his back against the wall. Tito and Ponce stared up at Salazar's body slumped on the desk, his brain exposed, a red stew soaking the papers and journals and dripping onto the dead dog.

"Sniper in the east woods!" Garza screamed. "Find him."

Tito and Ponce rolled across the floor, stood, and bolted down the stairs. Garza felt something warm and sticky dripping down his cheeks. When he realized it was spatter from his cousin, he wiped his face with an arched hand. Just then a huge explosion jostled the house and rattled the coffee pot and mugs. Above him, between the wooden rafters, dust and adobe flakes drifted down like snow.

Garza crouched in the corner, bewildered. *Cannon fire? Is the army here? Are they attacking us?* He slithered across the floor and stood when he reached the door. The next sound he heard was the unmistakable thumping of a Gatling gun being added to the mix of war noises punishing the estate. His next impulse was rapid and urgent. Get out of the house. Now.

CHAPTER 33
THE ATTACK

Emmet was already in the saddle when the two outside guards heard the first boom from Soapy's cannon. He and Ruby Red bore down as the men rushed to get inside the gate. Emmet could feel the mare's power stronger than ever.

"Girl, you've got your dancing slippers on this morning," he yelled at the horse.

As a rule, Emmet didn't shoot men in the back, but he was always willing to make exceptions. He snapped off two shots with his Spencer, pitching one guard into the fire pit and the other against the gate. Emmet breathed another sigh of relief when the dead man's weight pushed the unlocked gate open. *Good work, Chiquito,* he thought.

Right then, Mariana was foremost on his mind. He'd seen her enter the compound but never leave. Gunfire screaming from the main courtyard temporarily sidetracked his concern. Through the open gate Emmet saw

Chiquito pinned down by a vaquero hunched behind the fountain who was firing a steady stream of bullets. The Apache couldn't get a clear shot at the man from his angle, but Emmet could.

He aimed through the water splashing in the fountain, breathed in, out, waited for the calm, squeezed off. The vaquero never expected a shot from outside the perimeter. The bullet hit him in the chest, dropping him on the flagstones, and leaving him gasping for breath like a netted fish. Chiquito finished him off using the stock of his rifle to crush his skull.

Emmet charged Ruby Red up to the gate and kicked it wide open so Pedro and the wagon for the girls would be able to get through. The body of the guard behind the wall was splayed out in the yard, his throat sporting a red gash as thick as a buffalo tongue. A wet pool showed how ably Chiquito had bled him out.

The Gatling gun was *rat-a-tatting* like hail on a tin roof when another cannon crump shook the earth. Emmet yelled to Chiquito to go for the girls. The Indian ran through the main courtyard peppering the front door with buckshot until he was able to kick it in.

Fretting again about Mariana, Emmet

headed towards the kitchen to see if he could find her. As he rounded the corner, a bullet buzzed by his ear. He twisted the reins to get Ruby Red back to the front of the house and out of the line of fire. Peeking through a narrow slit between the roof spout and the edge of the house, Emmet spotted a vaquero nested behind a water trough. Further back, another man crouched behind the short wall that squared the side courtyard.

Emmet removed the Walker Colt on his leg. With both the rifle and pistol balanced in his hands, and a galloping start, he and Ruby Red peeled around the corner again. Emmet's rifle spat lead at the vaquero behind the trough while he fired his pistol at the other man in the side courtyard. It took Emmet just two shots to kill the trough vaquero. The man in the courtyard was trickier and required five. He lay there coughing blood, taking a bit longer to meet his Maker. Emmet shot him again to hasten the divine reunion and then resumed his search for Mariana.

Mrs. Medina and Mariana were halfway down the list of food supplies when they heard guns blazing, felt the house shake, and heard Armando tell them to hide inside the pantry.

Mariana wasn't sure what to do. Faith was tucked inside the wagon. What if a stray bullet hit? Or, worse, a stray shell? She realized she had to act.

"I'm sorry," Mariana said. "I can't stay here."

Mrs. Medina grabbed her arm. "It's too dangerous," she said, shaking her head.

"I have to get out," Mariana said, ripping her arm away. She opened the pantry door and ran through the kitchen and out to the wagon.

Garza eased into the hallway as gunfire raged below him on the first floor. A vaquero was pinned down in the great room behind a tall oak armoire. As he peered around the banister, Garza saw an Indian rapid-firing from behind a hutch. Not wanting to betray his position, Garza inched along the railing without shooting.

The Indian sprinted into the adjacent dining room and dove under a birch-wood table. The only way the vaquero could get a good angle was to drop to his knees. When he dropped, the Indian's gun was already barking shots that were on target. The firing ceased, and the house turned as silent as a church, a gray haze of gunsmoke floating to the ceiling like incense.

Garza figured the Indian's eyes were scouring the upstairs hallways and doorways for any hint of movement, so he remained statue-still, holding his breath. When he heard the Indian enter the kitchen, he slipped into the guest room directly above it. Through the floorboards, Garza heard the muffled voice of the intruder assuring Mrs. Medina and Armando that everything was going to be okay.

Garza sidled over to the window, and what he saw stunned him. In the distance, a cannon ball exploded in front of the bunkhouse. A Gatling gun by the bridge was peppering his men with fierce fire. All around him he heard head-splitting thunder and saw red pistol blasts. Closer to the house, he saw the bodies of three vaqueros — one behind a trough, another by the fountain, the third against the wall. He knew he had to escape, but how? Looking down, he flooded with rage when he recognized Mariana climbing into a wagon. *Reno's double-crossed us,* he thought.

He pushed the bottom pane up, flipped his sombrero back, and climbed through the window, making sure to hook the heels of his boots into the edge of the gutter for balance. He extended his arms and jumped feet first into the back of the empty wagon, rolling to break his fall. Mariana screamed and spun around to see Garza's Peacemaker pointed at her face.

"Drive," he said.

She snapped the reins but not hard enough to please Garza.

"Drive!" he screamed.

She lashed the horses with force, and they lurched forward, gathering speed.

As Emmet rounded the corner heading towards the kitchen, he nearly collided with the wagon rushing by in the opposite direction. The back wheel grazed Ruby Red, frightening the animal. She reared up, tossing Emmet to the ground. Chiquito dashed from the kitchen door to help him.

"One of Salazar's men just took off with Mariana," he said.

Emmet jumped up and raced around the corner as the wagon sped down the side yard.

"Take him!" Chiquito yelled.

Emmet dropped to a kneeling position and sighted on the bouncing wagon. Mariana's black hair rippled in the air, and Garza's head bobbed up and down. Emmet aimed but couldn't get a clean bead. Each time he sighted on Garza's head, it would jostle to the side and expose Mariana's head. Emmet lowered his rifle as the wagon rattled out the front gate and towards the bend in the road.

"He's getting away!" Chiquito screamed.

Emmet tried sighting again, but Mariana and Garza's heads kept overlapping. The thought of hitting Mariana sent a shiver up his spine. *Too much at stake,* he thought, *too much to lose.* He lowered the rifle a second time. As the wagon rounded the corner and disappeared from view, Emmet could feel Chiquito's stare on his back, cold as Canadian ice.

"Explain," the Apache said.

"No clean shot," Emmet said. "No room for error."

Heated gunfire by the bunkhouse grabbed Emmet's attention next, leaving him no time to fret over Garza and Mariana.

"How many more vaqueros inside?" he asked.

"At least one more guarding the girls," Chiquito answered.

"Find him, kill him, and bring the girls out. I'll signal Pedro."

Emmet remounted Ruby Red, raced to the front gate, and let loose an ear-piercing whistle. A minute later, Pedro looped around the corner with Soapy's empty wagon.

"Mariana just roared down the road in my wagon," Pedro yelled, "and Garza's with her."

Emmet nodded and pointed to the doorway off the side courtyard.

"Put the wagon there. The girls will be coming through that door any minute."

As Pedro maneuvered into position, Emmet rallied the length of the inner yard on the west side to make sure it was safe. When he reached the rear gate, he peered over the wall just in time to see a cannon shot make a direct hit on the bunkhouse. A huge pillar of black smoke and red fire shot up through the building, strewing flaming timbers and dead men on the ground in front.

The Gatling gun flashed red in the blue smoke. Frank had the rest of the gunmen pinned down like bugs in a blizzard. They crouched behind anything they could find for protection — barrels, wagons, saddles on fence posts. One of Soapy's first lobs had blown up part of the stable. The carcasses of three horses lay on the ground twisted into awkward positions. The rest of the animals had run off, leaving Salazar's remaining men no quick way to escape.

Emmet spotted one man ducking behind

a buckboard who intended to make a dash across the road to the main house. After the next cannon shot exploded, the man burst through the smoke, scrambled to the rear gate, and banged on it like a crazy man.

"Let me in!" he shouted.

Emmet opened the gate.

"It's a massacre!" he screamed.

Emmet raised his Spencer and said, "I prefer the word reckoning." He dropped the man with a hole in his chest the size of a hen's egg.

As the Gatling gun resumed its spray, Emmet made a sickening discovery outside the wall: a man staked to the ground like a buffalo hide. The cannon shots had covered him with a blanket of dust, and he wasn't moving. Emmet knew who it was as soon as he saw the big gold ring on the man's finger. Rescuing the King meant dodging the Gatling gun, because Frank would assume he was the enemy. Was it worth the risk? Was the King even alive? He couldn't decide what to do until he saw the King's hand twitch.

Emmet opened the gate and crept along the hacienda wall towards Kingston until a barrage of bullets from the Gatler started popping little balls of dirt around him. Emmet hit the ground, dug his belly into the earth, and covered his head with his arms.

After several minutes, Frank jerked the gun back towards the bunkhouse, and Emmet raced over to his former commander. The King had a pulse. But beneath the blanket of dust, Emmet could see his body was covered with hundreds of welts and boils, oozing white pus. Emmet brushed the last few fire ants off Kingston's eyelids and nostrils, cut him loose, and dragged him by one arm back against the wall.

At that moment, the big gun was inside a drift of powder smoke, so it was hard to determine which way the machine was pointed. Emmet grabbed Kingston under the armpit, steadied himself, and made for the rear gate. As the smoke around the Gatling gun cleared, he saw the six long barrels were trained on him. Emmet waved his hat hoping that Frank would recognize him. He ducked just as Frank cranked the handle and bullets burst forth in zipping streams. Emmet lost his balance and toppled, losing his grip on Kingston as he fell. Kingston groaned as the next stream of bullets ripped through his body. Emmet remained motionless until Frank turned the big gun back towards the bunkhouse and then dragged the wounded man to the other side of the wall.

Blood leaked from four holes in Kingston's side and feathered out his nose. Emmet knew the King was done for.

Kingston lifted a limp hand, beckoned Emmet closer, and in a raspy voice asked, "Faith?"

"We're rescuing her," Emmet said, and then he watched as his former commander widened his eyes, exhaled, and did not breathe again. Emmet knelt there for a moment in the silence of the breath not taken. He thought about the man he had followed into battle so many times, who had proven himself a master military strategist, who had shown every soldier under his command what it meant to be strong, courageous, and unflinching in the face of almost-certain death. Emmet closed the King's eyelids.

"Goodbye, soldier," he whispered, "another Johnny Reb killed by friendly fire."

Now, a screech of metal grinding against metal filled the air as cartridges mis-fed into the Gatler's hopper, and the rotary barrel jammed, silencing the big gun.

In the distance, Frank was screaming at Billy.

Forget Billy, Emmet thought, *blow the bridge up and get out.* No longer pinned down, the remaining vaqueros reopened fire and surged forward. Emmet picked up his rifle and pot-shotted several of them from the rear gate to buy Frank and Billy time. In between shots, he saw Frank light the fuse on a stick of dynamite.

An enormous explosion shook the earth, and a black cloud of rubbled rock and wood shot into the air. When the haze cleared, Emmet saw the bridge was gone. The force of the explosion had knocked the Gatling gun into the river. Frank and Billy had already mounted up and were riding down the back road, their job finished.

After he climbed atop Ruby Red, Emmet rode along the eastern wall, noting that Zack's marksmanship had created four more corpses on that side of the compound. Emmet raised his eyes to Zack's vantage point and waved his gun. When Zack waved back, Emmet pointed to the rear gate, where a half-dozen men remained. As Zack opened fire to keep them at bay, Emmet returned to the side courtyard, where Pedro waited with the wagon.

Chiquito reentered the kitchen, crept past the pantry, and stopped just outside the hallway. Silence. He eased his head around the corner. No sound. He moved five feet further along and stopped. The house remained in a dead hush. Chiquito held his breath and finally detected a faint creak in a floorboard at the end of the hall.

"It's over!" the Apache shouted. "Give yourself up."

No answer. But Chiquito sensed what was coming next and dove into the dining room just as a vaquero leaped from a side room with both guns blazing. In the hall mirror, the Apache watched the gunman unlock the door to the captives' room and duck inside.

Chiquito positioned himself to the left of the door. He tapped on a door panel with the gun muzzle. A blaze of bullets from inside the room sent splinters of wood flying through the air and made the girls shriek.

Chiquito tapped again. "Still here," he said.

"If you come in, I'll kill these girls," the vaquero shouted.

"No, you won't," Chiquito said. "You know Salazar wants them alive. This fight is between you and me. You need to ignore the girls and pay attention to what I'm going to do next."

The Apache stole back to the dining room and dragged one of the corpses back down the hall. He bore the dead man upright, propped himself behind the body, and kicked the door in.

More gunfire exploded, and the girls screamed again. Using the corpse as a shield, Chiquito fired three close-range shots. The next sound was the flump of the vaquero hitting the floorboards. The Indian let the corpse drop to the floor. Several girls rushed to Chiquito and hugged him. He noticed they were stepping around another man sprawled to the side.

"This makes him sleep," one of the girls said, holding up a cloth and bottle of chloroform.

"I bet it does," Chiquito said. "Girls, it's time to leave. Follow me."

The girls trailed the Apache down the hall, past the great room, and through the side courtyard to the waiting wagon. Several of them cowered when they first stepped outside and heard the gunfire, their faces tense, their eyes flitting side to side, but Pedro spoke reassuring words as he helped lift each of them up.

One of the girls pointed at Emmet. *"Yo lo conozco,"* she yelled.

"What's she saying?" Emmet asked.

"She says she knows you," Pedro replied.

Emmet gazed at the girl for a moment, and then a flash of recognition hit him —

she had been in the back of the wagon he had stopped on his way to Sabo Canyon. Sitting next to her was the other girl that Paco and Diego had abducted that moonlit night. He nodded and smiled at both of them, and they smiled back. Knowing the two girls were safe brought Emmet great satisfaction, but his warm feeling didn't last long.

"Where's Faith?" he asked.

Chiquito shrugged. "Nobody left inside."

Emmet turned to the girls. "Where's Faith? Where's the blonde girl?"

"She escaped," several girls said at the same time.

Emmet scratched his ear, unsure of what to do. *Is she hiding nearby? Could she have made it back to town?*

"Where's Major Kingston?" Pedro asked.

"Dead," Emmet said.

Two shots pinged the ground in front of Emmet's boots. The man with the yellow sash had figured another way into the yard. It wouldn't be long before the others followed. Emmet returned fire to knock them back. "Go with Pedro," he told Chiquito, "and bring the girls to Father Ramirez. Soapy and the twins will meet up with you in town. And tell everybody to keep their eyes open for any sign of Faith."

Chiquito hopped up next to Pedro, who hard-reined the horses. As they pulled away, the Apache shouted at Emmet, "Where are you going?"

"After Garza."

CHAPTER 34
TRACKING GARZA

Emmet and Ruby Red raced down the road to catch up to Garza and Mariana. He hoped she was alive, that Garza had not harmed her. To the north, he saw thunderheads bulked high, rolling south over Santa Sabino. He knew it was only a matter of time before the heavy rain reached him.

Emmet was a good judge of time. Garza had a thirty-minute head start, but a man on horseback could cover twice as much ground as one in a wagon — as long as the rider didn't take any wrong turns. Emmet came to the first fork in the road, slowed the horse, and studied each trail for clues. There, in the road heading south, almost undetectable, were the fresh, faint grooves of wagon wheels. He switched off and urged the horse back to top speed.

The road twisted through the rolling foothills and down to the floodplain of the San Rafael River. As Emmet descended, the pines and alders thinned out, and the vegetation changed to scrub and catclaw. Thirty minutes later, he reached another fork. The dirt in the road was packed harder and yielded no signs as to which way the wagon had gone. Emmet dismounted and walked fifty yards up the road searching for a sign. Nothing. He returned to the fork and walked up the smaller road angling to the southwest. About twenty yards up, he spotted it — a bright red firewheel by the side of the road. Emmet recognized it as one of the flowers Lucita had given Mariana, which she had pinned in her hair. He picked it up and stuck it into the pocket of his denim shirt next to the photograph.

Emmet climbed back on Ruby Red and galloped down the southeast trail for five more miles before reaching another fork. This time, he didn't have to stop and dismount. A second firewheel shimmered like a tiny setting sun against the brown dirt on the westerly road. Emmet swung down and picked up and pocketed the blossom before switching off and continuing his descent. In the distance he could see the blue-green river flowing between banks of red rock. A mile later, the road crested, affording a wide view of the terrain. Emmet sat his horse, grabbed the spyglass from the saddlebag, and peered through the instrument. Panning from east to west with a slow, deliberate motion, he found what he was seeking. The wagon was so far away that it appeared no bigger than a matchbox, but Emmet could make out a man in a red sombrero driving, with a dark-haired woman sitting in the back. As he watched them drop down and disappear behind a treeless hillock, his spirits brightened, knowing that Mariana was alive and unharmed — at least for now.

CHAPTER 35
FATHER RAMIREZ

A cold rain poured from thick clouds as Pedro and Chiquito rumbled the wagon towards Santa Sabino. Pedro directed the girls to cover themselves with the tarp to stay dry and hidden as they neared the village. Chiquito pointed to a solitary rider approaching from the east and readied his rifle. When the horseman got closer, the Apache announced, "It's Zack. He's one of us."

Zack pulled up, and Chiquito told him to follow them into town.

Now Soapy and Abe flashed into view, cutting down a wide draw that intersected the road from the west, the cannon jangling in tow behind them.

"How'd we do?" Soapy asked.

"There's only half a dozen or so of Salazar's men still breathing," Zack said. "Between the cannon and the Gatling gun, you thinned the herd to a handful."

Soapy looked please with the results. "Where's Major Kingston?" he asked.

"Emmet said he's dead," Chiquito answered.

Soapy shook his head at the sad news. "Long live the King."

"Where's Emmet?" Abe asked.

"Garza escaped with Mariana," Chiquito replied. "Emmet's gone after them."

"Frank and Billy?"

"Making tracks back to Sweetwater," Zack said, "and dreaming up ways to spend all that money."

"Well, thank God we got all those girls out of there in time," Soapy said.

"Almost all," Chiquito said. "Faith escaped, but we don't know where she is."

Soapy rubbed his chin. "Well if that don't take the rag off the bush. So this thing ain't over."

"One step at a time," Pedro said. "Let's deliver these children to Father Ramirez."

Soapy and Abe fell in behind the wagon. A mile up the road, they saw the shadow of another rider coming from the opposite direction. "He's racing like the devil beating tan bark," Zack said. "Something's up."

The shadow grew large and distinct enough for Pedro to recognize him. "It's Pepe."

"The army's at the bridge!" Pepe shouted. "They'll be in Santa Sabino in fifteen minutes."

"There's just enough time to get these girls to Father Ramirez," Pedro said. "You know what to do, Pepe. Ready the streets."

"The streets are ready," the tailor assured him.

"What's going on?" Soapy asked. "You fixing to take on the army?"

"Major Kingston was a smart and thorough man," Pedro said. "Thanks to him, we have a few surprises of our own for Captain Ortega."

"Wait a minute," Soapy bellowed. "Captain Ortega? Captain *Javier* Ortega?"

"Know him?"

Soapy let out a booming laugh. "Why, him and me have done wagonloads of business over the years. He loves munitions even more than me. He's one of my best customers."

"Well, he's not your customer now," Pedro said. "He's your enemy."

"We'll see about that," Soapy answered. He swung the limber and cannon around the wagon and raced down the muddy road, with Zack hurtling on horseback behind them.

"Hang on, girls," Pedro said as he whipped

the reins, "we're heading for the home stretch."

Ten minutes later, Pedro and Chiquito whirled the wagon to the side of the church where an anxious Father Ramirez was waiting in the pouring rain. He pulled the tarp off, and when he saw the girls, he clasped his hands together in delight and looked up at the black sky, water running down his chin. "God be praised," he said. He looked at Chiquito and Pedro. "Bless you both for getting them here."

The girls looked around their new surroundings, bewildered. "Is it safe?" Toya asked the priest.

"Yes," Father Ramirez replied. As he helped each girl off, he pointed to three women waiting by a tiny grotto where a statue of the Virgin Mary gazed out.

"Those women will hide you in their houses."

The girls raced to the welcoming arms of the smiling women, who hugged the children, stroked their faces, smoothed their hair with their hands, and uttered reassuring words.

Valencia was the last to leave the wagon. She eyed Pedro. "Will you find Faith?" she asked.

"I'm not sure," Pedro admitted. "I think

there's a better chance of Faith finding us."

Valencia gave a nervous nod and ran to the grotto. Pedro watched the older women split the girls into three groups and lead them away in different directions.

"Who's your friend?" Father Ramirez asked. Pedro turned to introduce Chiquito, but the Apache had vanished like vapor on a prairie wind.

"That was Chiquito," he said. "But somehow I don't think you'll ever get the chance to meet him. Keep the wagon here, Father, in case we need it later."

"Where are you going?" the priest asked.

"To take on the army," the baker replied, and then he leaped from the step board and dashed down the main street, his sandals splashing through the puddles and slapping against the wet cobblestones.

CHAPTER 36
THE ARROYO

Garza steered the wagon off the road and down a gentle slope until he reached the dry bed of an arroyo. The wheels made a slushing sound as they came to rest in the soft sand. He jumped down, looked up at Mariana, and swept his arm across his chest. "Beautiful spot, no?"

Steep walls of sandstone rose from the bed of the arroyo. Even with the black sky, the landscape appeared illuminated. Flash floods had carved the walls into soft, undulating curves, marbled with multicolored layers of rock laid down over thousands of years. The arcs were gentle, giving no clue of the turbulent forces that had created them. Over time, rain water had deepened the passageway and smoothed the hard edges so it appeared the walls themselves were flowing.

"This is sacred ground to me," Garza said. "My father died here. It's also where I killed my first man." He studied the ground like he was reliving the memories. Then he barked, "Sit over there."

Mariana climbed down and sat on the ground where Garza was pointing, in the middle of the arroyo, about ten yards downslope from the wagon.

"I was fourteen years old. Me and my father helped his best friend steal a strongbox from a pay wagon headed to the copper mine. They decided this was a safe and secluded spot to divvy up the money. When my father's friend saw how much money there was, he changed his mind and tried to keep it all. They shot each other over it. My father died instantly, but his friend didn't. I finished him off with a good-sized rock, and I kept all the money."

"I never knew that," Mariana said. "It proves you've been a bad man for a long time."

Garza shrugged. "Here's something else you don't know. This is also the spot where Tito and I drowned Miguel."

She saw his flinty eyes waiting for her reaction, felt her face turn pale as tallow, and swallowed a tight knot in her throat. She remembered her Miguel — kind, patient, so eager to help, so easy to please, his warm smile and gentle touch.

"We staked him right where you are," Garza said, "just before the rains came. The water runs off the slot canyons and picks up speed as it rushes into the narrow passages. You'd be amazed at how quickly this bed fills up."

"You bastard!" Mariana screamed, and then she unleashed a bone-wracking sob.

Garza ignored her. "Once the rains came, it was too dangerous to stay here," he said, "so Tito and I waited down by the banks where the arroyo empties into the San Rafael. We bet how many cigarettes we could smoke before Miguel's body washed down. I bet four. Tito bet six. He won."

Garza retrieved a long thick branch of juniper that had been carried down the arroyo during a past storm and snagged on some sagebrush. A long rumble of thunder forced his gaze to the sky. "Heavy rain soon," he said and smiled.

"Why are you so filled with hate?" Mariana asked.

"I'm not."

"You hate me."

"No," Garza said. He snapped several branches off the main one and tossed them aside. "But you should have married me when you had the chance."

"I didn't love you. I could never love you."

"What is love?" Garza gripped the main branch and kept breaking it over his knee until he had made eight sticks. "You could have been wealthy."

Mariana shook her head and sneered. "What is wealth without love?"

"Wealth without love," Garza replied, "is wealth." He unsheathed his Bowie knife and, with long, powerful strokes, whittled sharp points on the ends of each stick. He then retrieved a length of rope from the wagon, cutting it into eight pieces. He knotted a rope around each stick and tossed two of them to Mariana. "Slip your wrists through the loops and pull the rope tight," he said. "Then lie back on the ground."

Mariana was terrified, but she obeyed, easing her head back into the soft, pink sand. Garza walked to the edge of the arroyo, picked up a rock the size of a beer mug, and knelt next to Mariana. More thunder, and now the rain began to fall. He hammered the handmade stakes into the ground, pinning her arms.

As he maneuvered to stake her legs, she asked, "Why didn't you unhitch one of the horses and escape by yourself once we were free of the hacienda? Why did you let the wagon slow you down? Why are you keeping me with you?"

Garza pointed to the remaining pile of four sticks. "Because I want to meet the man responsible for my cousin's death."

"Who's that?" she asked.

Garza looped the ropes around her ankles and pounded the stakes in.

"You know who it is," he said. "Emmet Honeycut."

"No!" she shrieked. "No." Her neck muscles turned spongy, and her bones were no longer able to support her frame. She felt dizzy and laid her head down to stop the feeling.

"I know he cares for you, Mariana."

"How do you know that?"

"Your father told us."

With renewed energy, she pitched back and forth in a frenzied attempt to rip the stakes out, but they held.

"Why did your father betray us?" he asked.

She scowled. "He didn't. He gave himself away, and now he's dead."

"Who killed him?"

"Why do you care?"

"It would be a sweet justice if it was Honeycut."

"It wasn't."

"Too bad. Anyway, if he's as good a tracker as I think, he'll find us," Garza said. "If not, I'm sure he'll be grateful for the

341

flowers you left behind."

She lowered her head to the ground again, and a cold shudder went through her body as she sobbed hot tears through unblinking eyes.

"You didn't think I'd notice the missing flowers in your hair?" Garza said with faked surprise. He stood over her spread-eagled body. "You know, it would be easy to take advantage of you right now." With the toe of his boot, he lifted the hem of her dress several inches off the ground. "But it seems these days I've acquired a hunger for virgins."

His laugh echoed off the sandstone walls as he let the hem drop. "Now I think you hate me just enough. Time for me to move into the rocks and wait for your hero to show."

"What makes you so sure he's coming?"

"Men of his stamp always do. It's pathetic — letting a woman get the better of a man — but it happens all the time. Now, don't you go anywhere."

Garza scrambled up the slope, the Peace-maker slapping against his right leg, and disappeared from Mariana's view.

Mariana waited five minutes, hoping that Garza was out of earshot. In a voice a bit louder than a whisper, she called out, "Faith, are you okay?"

From inside the wagon came the girl's frantic reply: "Get me out of here. Please." Her voice was shrill, fretful.

"Shhh," Mariana warned. "Garza is still nearby."

"Please. I can't move!" Faith cried out. "It feels like I'm inside a coffin."

"You must lower your voice. Help is coming," Mariana assured her.

"When?"

"Any time now. Keep your eyes shut. It will make that closed-in feeling go away."

"My heart is racing, and I feel like I can't breathe." Mariana heard her clawing at the wooden boards.

"Take slow, deep breaths," Mariana said. "Tell me about your home. What was it like?"

It took several minutes, but Faith finally answered.

"Our cabin was tiny, but the canyon was beautiful," the girl began, "especially the sunsets. The colors would blaze like fire if a strong wind kicked dust into the air, or if clouds showed up on the horizon at just the right time. Mariana, I need to get out."

"Did you like living out there?" Mariana picked her head up as she spoke, even

343

though she knew Faith couldn't see her.

"I like people," the girl answered, her voice only a little less panicked. "My father was a preacher, so folks would come to listen to him. And my mother was a nurse, so neighbors would bring sick members of their family out. But I wished we lived closer to a town. The big sky made me feel small."

They conversed in hushed tones for another few minutes, about how kind and gentle Faith's parents were, how she wished she had a sister or brother, and the toy flute that was her favorite Christmas present. Mariana sensed that Faith had calmed a bit, until a deafening crack of thunder startled them, rekindling the girl's distress.

"What's going to happen to us?" Faith moaned.

"Help is coming," Mariana said as she closed her eyes, leaned her head back, and felt fat, cold raindrops splatter against her face.

Chapter 37
The Army Arrives

The parade of men, horses, and carriages clomped up the main road into Santa Sabino, rain pouring off their hats and uniforms. Luis Muñoz's warning had already dampened Captain Ortega's mood, and the weather was making it worse. *Time to cut ties with Salazar,* he thought. *Too many trips to the same well. If this is my last opportunity, I might as well take home as much money as I can.*

Ortega had traveled to Santa Sabino three times before. Normally, some of the villagers would come to watch the procession, but not this time. Nobody was expecting him today, and, even if they were, it was raining.

Fifty yards ahead, two men emerged from a side yard, waved to Ortega as they crossed the street, and disappeared behind the wall of a cantina. The captain detected the aroma of fry bread in the air and saw smoke puffing from the chimneys of several houses. He sighted two more villagers walking across the plaza.

Here the road changed from packed dirt to cobblestone, which amplified the creak of each wheel and the clop of each hoof. The group had drawn within fifty yards of the plaza when a peasant on horseback darted in front of them from a side street towing a barricade of log poles and sagebrush lashed together with barbed wire and straw line. Ortega's horse bucked in fright, and the soldiers drew their weapons. The people in the plaza scattered.

The barricade was as tall as a man and extended the width of the street. There was no way to advance. The horses in front lurched side to side, startled at being corralled without warning. Ortega raced to the back of the column just in time to see another rider tow a second barricade behind them. The metal wire flashed sparks as it scraped across the wet stones. Realizing they were trapped, the captain yelled, "Form a phalanx around the carriages and wait for my order."

A voice above him shouted, "Captain Ortega." The officer glanced up and saw men walking to the edge of the roof with their guns trained on his soldiers.

"Steady, men," Ortega said. "Don't fire until I give the order."

"Don't fire at all," one of the men on the roof yelled back.

"Who are you?" Ortega asked.

"Pedro." He motioned Ortega back to the middle of the column in front of the building where he was standing. "Time to talk."

"So talk," Ortega hollered. In a quieter voice, he warned his soldiers, "Be ready for anything, men."

"Somebody will be coming out of the front door below me," Pedro said. "He has no weapon. Tell your men to hold their fire."

Just then, an unarmed Soapy Waters strutted out of the tailor's shop with his hands clutching his suspenders.

"Remember me?" Soapy asked.

The wary expression on Ortega's face turned to surprise. "Señor Waters," he exclaimed. "Don't tell me you're part of this ambush?"

"Ambush?" Soapy said with mock surprise. "No. You mean new lease on life."

The door of the lead carriage opened, and a well-dressed man stepped out on the footboard in fancy leather boots. "What's going on?" he asked, obviously irritated by the holdup. "What do these people want?"

Ortega held his hand up to silence him.

"What do you mean a new lease on life, Señor Waters?"

"Salazar is dead," Soapy replied. "Garza has run away. Just about all of the gunmen are dead, and — most important to your feisty friend over there with the expensive footwear — the girls are gone. There's nothing left for you here."

"You dare to confront the army?" Ortega said. "I can order my men to open fire at any time."

"And so can I," Soapy said. He pulled on his suspenders. "We took care of Salazar and Garza and their men, and, if we have to, we'll take care of you and yours."

Again, Ortega scanned the rooftops and the wooden faces of the men brandishing Spencer repeating rifles. "These people are peasants," he said. "My guess is that most of them don't know how to shoot those guns."

"Enough of them do," Soapy assured him. He looked up at a red-headed man standing on top of the blacksmith's shop. "How do you like our chances, Zack?"

"Like shooting catfish in a birdbath," the man replied. "And the boss man in the fancy uniform will be the first to go."

In a slow, deliberate motion, Soapy took his fingers off the suspenders and let them drop to his side. "Captain, the choice is yours. Death, if you push forward, or life, if you go back the way you came. Life for your soldiers. Life for your rich friends sitting in those carriages. Life for you — and your political future. In fact, I think you would be rewarded with a lot of votes in Santa Sabino if you make the correct decision today, as well as a sizable contribution from me. Helping rid this town of the cousins has made me a richer man."

Ortega wrinkled his face. "You're telling me to surrender?"

"I never said surrender, and I'm not telling you what to do. These people have been under the heels of the cousins for too long. They want their freedom, and they almost have it. Only you and your men stand in their way. We're asking you to grant them their freedom by simply going home."

As Ortega mulled the situation, Soapy added, "I've got a gift for you as a sign of good faith. I know your passion for military hardware — for heaven's sake, you and me have done enough business together." He raised his hand and waggled his fingers. Outside the barricade, a man drove up in the limber with the cannon behind it.

Ortega's eyes widened. "A light twelve-pound Napoleon."

Soapy beamed. "It's a pleasure to be in the company of a man who knows his weaponry. It's been fired a lot today, so it needs a good cleaning, but it's my gift to you. So what's it going to be?"

Seconds passed, and then Ortega glanced back at the gentleman standing on the carriage step, who shook his head and then tipped it back in the direction they had come. Ortega turned back to Soapy. "That cannon explains how you bested Salazar."

"Partly explains," Soapy said. "I'd have given you the Gatling gun, too, but it ended up in the river. Do we have a deal?"

Ortega gave a half smile. "I accept your offer, Señor Waters."

"Then tell your men to lower their weapons."

"You tell your men to do the same."

Soapy pushed his arms down several times, signaling the men on the roof to put down. They did so.

Ortega barked the order, and his soldiers did the same.

"Now we'll remove the barricade behind you," Soapy said. He signaled to Pepe on the roof by spinning his right hand in the air like he was twirling a lasso. Pepe faced the rear of the caravan and made the same sign. The back barricade slid across the road, the metal wire screeching against the cobbles.

"Have your men lead the way home," Soapy said, "and your rich friends can follow."

On Ortega's command, the soldiers single-filed along each side of the carriages and retreated down the street. As the vehicles turned around, Soapy gave the signal to remove the other barricade. When the man in the limber wheeled in the cannon, Soapy told Ortega, "You'll need a driver."

"Gonzalez," Ortega yelled. "Take the cannon." A soldier dismounted, passed his reins to the soldier next to him, and climbed into the limber.

Ortega turned back. "Tell me, Señor Waters. How did you come to be in Santa Sabino with your weapons?"

"Long story. I'll tell it to you when we next meet. Maybe next month? I've got another Napoleon at my shop. I could bring it out to you — but you'll have to pay for that one."

Ortega nodded, turned the horse around, and trotted down the street behind the carriages. He heard Soapy shout, "A cheer for Captain Javier Ortega."

Ortega heard the men roar and welcomed their expressions of gratitude. He turned back and doffed his shako only to see they weren't cheering for him — they were cheering for themselves. His cheeks flushed with embarrassment, he quickly donned his hat and moved more rapidly along the street, listening to the hooting and hollering growing fainter as the caravan rumbled down the hill, around the corner, and back towards the Santa Sabino bridge.

CHAPTER 38
THUNDERSTORM

Emmet discovered a good location to conceal Ruby Red — a trough that was out of sight and stippled with blackberry bushes, one of the horse's favorites. He didn't tether the reins in case he needed a quick escape. As Ruby Red nibbled on the berry bush, Emmet scuttled along the open landscape keeping low. He could see the cut Garza had taken led to the bottom of an arroyo, the lowest land feature for a quarter of a mile.

He slipped through a cleft in the rocks and slid down the rain-slickened embankment until his boots hit the sandy bed. He crept along the canyon wall, his hand moving across the smooth sandstone for balance. Every ten feet, he poked his head out to see what was ahead. With each step, he neared the spot where he had seen the wagon disappear.

It was barely audible, but Emmet picked

up the sound of a woman's voice. Was it Mariana? He stopped, listened, and eased his head around the arc of the wall. It was Mariana, but she was staked out in the middle of the creek bed. Who was she talking to? There was nobody else in sight. He leaned back against the wall. Even though she was bound, the sight of her alive gladdened him. That feeling didn't last, because the next sound was the voice of Yago Garza from behind, ordering him to drop the gun and put up his hands. Emmet dropped the rifle.

"Turn around."

Emmet obeyed. He watched Garza slowly pick up the rifle, never taking his eyes off his enemy.

"A new Spencer, Mr. Honeycut," Garza observed. "Aren't we lucky?" He checked to make sure the rifle was loaded before holstering the Peacemaker. "Walk towards Mariana."

Emmet advanced to the center of the creek bed where Mariana could now see him. Her initial look of joy turned to one of crushing resignation when she saw his hands up and Garza following behind.

"Look who's here," Garza said with exaggerated excitement. Mariana blinked back tears of despair. After Emmet had walked five paces beyond her, Garza ordered him to sit down and slip the ropes over his wrists. He tossed two stakes into Emmet's lap and told him to lie back in the sand, facing Mariana. "One wrong move," he said, "and I'll shoot her."

Emmet lay on his back, looking up. The pelting rain made him squint his eyes. With one hand, Garza stabbed a stake into the ground and then hammered it deeper with the rock. When he had set the last stake, he stood. "Isn't this romantic? Now you can watch each other die."

The rain intensified, and larger drops cratered the sand. Emmet heard the runoff first, a gentle seethe from upstream. Then he saw it: long fat fingers of flowing foam slithering along the creek bed.

"This canyon is about to flood just like that," Garza said, snapping his fingers. "The water rushes fast through this narrow reach."

The bubbling rills raced each other downhill, seeking out the lowest points in the bed and filling them, swirling in circles in a relentless search for a faster route to the river below.

Emmet watched a thin sheet of water wrap itself around Mariana's head, envelop her ears, and move towards him. The sky-fresh runoff felt cold as it lapped against his skin. He and Mariana lifted their heads to keep water off their faces.

Garza stepped through the shallow stream to the wagon and unhitched the two horses. He slapped one horse on the croup, and it clambered up the slope. Holding the reins of the second horse, he peered down at the captives. "What a beautiful place to die," he said.

A bigger surge of water bore down the slope, this one six inches deep. It smacked stones and clumps of debris against Emmet's head and poured up and over his face, forcing him to hold his breath for several seconds, until the swell passed.

"Time for me to go," Garza announced. "I'll be waiting for you two to join me down by the river."

He led the horse up the slope, to the top of the bank, and then he disappeared over the rise.

"Faith, are you okay?" Mariana called out.

"Get me out," the girl screamed. "I hear the water, and I can't swim."

Emmet was stunned by the revelation that Faith was inside the wagon, but his shock disappeared when he saw another wall of water surging at them.

"Brace yourself!" he shouted. He closed

his eyes and mouth just before the wave of brown soup engulfed him.

Submerged and holding his breath, Emmet centered his energy on his right side and yanked on the rope in an attempt to rip the stake out. The surge passed, the stake held, and the rope fibers sliced his wrist open, mixing blood into the water.

After Emmet caught his breath, he heard a fresh threat above him: water tumbling from an overhanging slab of caprock ten feet up, the flow sizzling like raw meat tossed on a hot grill. The sizzle was soon drowned out by another upstream roar as a two-foot wall of cocoa-colored slurry spiraled down the riverbed in uneven waves.

Mariana screamed, but the water — more violent now, and pushing larger pieces of wood — swamped and silenced her. The surge shunted the wagon several yards down the creek, frightening Faith. "Save me!" she screeched. "I don't want to die."

The wave passed, and Emmet looked at Mariana, who was choking for breath, her hair plastered with mud, her face flushed. He kicked his right leg to dislodge the stake, but the deluge had done nothing to loosen the tether. Rain continued to pour in thick sheets and gargle down the walls. Emmet knew time was running out.

The next wall of water was even higher. It sloshed back and forth against the sides of the canyon and slammed into the wagon, crushing it against the hard wall, breaking off one of the wheels, and shattering the compartment that trapped Faith.

Emmet's last sight before the water overwhelmed him was Faith kicking out broken boards, scrambling out of the wrecked wagon, and clinging to it from the outside. After the water swamped him, the furious roar of raging water changed to the muted sound of bubbles fizzing in his ears. He held his breath for ten, twenty, thirty seconds. When he felt his lungs were about to explode, he thrust his head up for air, but the water was too deep, and he couldn't break the surface. Foam and water shot into his mouth and throat, making him gag. The contents of his stomach pushed up his windpipe, and he vomited into the water column.

Again, the water subsided. Emmet, dizzy and losing consciousness, channeled all his remaining strength into his right arm and gave a mighty tug. The stake lifted and popped out of the wet earth.

Emmet flipped on his side and slammed his bloody fist back and forth against the other stake until it dislodged. With both hands freed, he jumped up and kicked the leg stakes out just as the next surge of water came sweeping down the canyon.

He saw Faith in her sodden smock, kneeling next to Mariana, straining to pull out one of the stakes with a piece of deadwood.

"You can't swim," Emmet shouted. "Get to high ground." As she ran to the embankment and began climbing, he hurried over to the unconscious Mariana.

Emmet tensed himself for the impact. He shielded her from the brunt of the wave with his body but couldn't stop the water, now spiraling in flumes around his legs, from submerging her. As he thrashed and clawed at the stakes, her body floated with the rising water, pulling the ropes taut. The stake that pinned her left arm popped out, and Emmet tried to lift her head higher up so she could breathe, but the water was too deep. He watched as air bubbles floated up from her mouth. When he saw her body sink, he knew her lungs had filled with water, and his desperate thoughts turned to despair.

The swell subsided, and Emmet pried out the three remaining stakes. He swept Mariana up in his arms, carried her to the bank, and, with Faith's help, shoved her up on a higher ledge. Another powerful surge exploded down the canyon as Emmet climbed up, and a six-foot-long section of embankment crumbled and collapsed into the churning waters, almost taking Emmet with it.

As he pulled himself onto the ledge, Faith placed her ear next to Mariana's mouth. "She's not breathing." She swished two fingers around Mariana's mouth to unblock any obstructions and to scrape the thin clay layer coating her tongue. Emmet flipped Mariana sideways and slammed her back with his open palm. "Live!" he thundered. "Live."

For five minutes he shook her wildly and slapped her back to no avail. Again, Faith put her ear to Mariana's mouth, looked up at Emmet, and shook her head. Emmet flopped back on his rear, pulled Mariana's body against his, and rested his head on top of hers. Grief wracked his brain, and he sat there, stunned and broken-hearted. Minutes passed before he spoke.

Without looking up, he said, "I only knew her for six days, but she changed my life."

"I only met her this morning," Faith replied, "and she saved my life."

"I was gonna ask her to marry me." The fact that Fate had thwarted Emmet once again marbled his sadness with rage. "I lost the first woman I loved to fire, and the second one to water," he said through gritted teeth.

"I lost both my parents to gunpowder," Faith said softly.

Her words snapped Emmet's mourning in half; he lifted his head and looked directly at the girl. "Faith, I'm Emmet. I am so sorry you lost your parents. Forgive me for not considering what you've been through."

"I'm sorry about Mariana," Faith said. "So very sorry. You must be one of my uncle's friends, too."

Emmet nodded.

"Is my uncle okay?"

"I'm sorry to tell you that your uncle's dead, darling."

Faith lowered her head but did not cry. "Are the girls safe?"

"Every last one of them."

The force of the water had ripped the bandages from her face. Emmet stared at the cross carved into her cheek, which was oozing a mixture of blood and pus. His eyes turned into slits, and he pointed two trembling fingers at her face. "Who cut you?"

She shied from his hand, looked away. "I did."

"Why?"

"My own reasons."

Emmet nodded, studied her face. "Your uncle told me about you. Know what he said?"

Faith shook her head.

"That you have a smile that can melt butter."

It was as slow as a slack tide turning, but the corners of Faith's mouth curled towards heaven. Emmet was pleased when he saw the gentle arc of her smile counter the sharp, straight lines of the knife cuts and said, "I can see your uncle was right."

Then he reached out and wrapped his arm around the girl. When she rested her head on his chest, he kissed her on the temple and said, "You knew your uncle would come for you, didn't you? And because he did, you're safe now."

"And because of Mariana and you."

They held their soggy embrace for several silent minutes. Then Emmet released the girl, rested his head against Mariana's blue cheek, and rocked her like a sleeping child, ignoring the chittering of two long-billed thrashers in the tree above him, and the roiling water below.

CHAPTER 39
BY THE RIVER

Garza sat on the bank of the San Rafael smoking his fourth cigarette. Water plunged from the arroyo into the river, creating coffee-colored swirls in the deeper, slower-moving water. The torrent would sometimes include pieces of deadwood or chunks of drabbled underbrush scoured from the creek bottom. He thought about his next move. Should he return to the hacienda? Wait for Tito? Intercept Ortega? Flee to Rio Rojano?

The rain had stopped, and a small break in the clouds had appeared. Garza flicked at some midges that had swarmed around him. "Damned bugs," he said. He turned back to the arroyo in time to notice Emmet's slouch hat skimming along the surface of the water like a brown otter. He knew the powerful rush of the current would eventually dislodge the stakes. He took one final pull on the smoke, flicked the butt into the river, rolled another, and waited for Emmet and Mariana's bloated bodies to wash down next.

Five minutes passed before Emmet released his grip on Mariana. He stood, lifted her body, and carried her further up the embankment before setting her down behind a patch of *palo verde.*

"Wrap her tight in this blanket to keep the flies off and stay with her. I have one final piece of business to take care of."

"Garza?"

Emmet's sorrowful eyes turned cold and unblinking. "Yep."

"But what about the commandment 'Thou shalt not kill'?"

"My grandma used to read the Good Book to me when I was little. I remember the story that God sent avenging angels to kill the evil people in Sodom and Gomorrah."

"That's true," Faith confirmed.

"Today, I am the avenging angel sent to kill Garza. Do you understand?"

Faith nodded.

Emmet whistled twice, and Ruby Red emerged from the bushes, her coat shiny from the rain. As he slid his boot into the stirrup and swung up, Faith yelled, "Wait."

Emmet looked at her.

"Maybe you should leave me one of your guns to protect myself. You know, in case . . ."

"You mean in case I don't come back?" Emmet asked.

"Garza's a dangerous man."

"Have you ever fired a gun, darling?"

"No."

"Now's not the time to be teaching you."

"What should I do?"

"Three things." Emmet unrolled his wet-weather poncho and handed it to her. "First, put this on." He watched her find the neck hole and slip the poncho over her head.

"Second, stay well hidden." He pointed to the *palo verde.*

The girl scooted behind the bushes next to Mariana's body.

"And the third?" she yelled back.

"Trust your avenging angel."

Emmet spurred Ruby Red up the slope to higher ground to find where the arroyo emptied into the river. It didn't take long. After tracing the path of the watercourse for ten minutes, he came to a crest and saw the confluence six hundred yards to the east.

Garza was standing by the river's edge next to where the arroyo was disgorging.

Emmet dismounted and pulled the horse out of sight. Slipping Big Betty from her sling, he took up a position on a horizontal slab of pink granite overlooking the vista. He wet his left pointer finger and held it in the air. A strong breeze was still blowing from the north. Several breaks of sunlight shone between the dark clouds, sparkling the western reaches of the San Rafael with diamond flecks.

He gazed down at Garza, the red sombrero on his enemy's back forming a perfect target. Emmet steadied the rifle atop the rock, and with a fiery eye, he aimed . . . *You were so right, amigo . . .* breathed in, out . . . *what a beautiful place . . .* waited for the calm . . . *to die . . .* squeezed off.

From that distance, it took the bullet less than a second to reach its destination. Emmet had considered the topography, factored in the arc of the earth, and compensated for the wind. What he didn't account for was the biting gadfly that Garza bent down to swat off his leg just as Emmet pulled the trigger.

The shot stung a stone in front of Garza, who dove on the ground and rolled behind a downed cypress trunk for protection. Emmet cursed under his breath. Big Betty was a breech-loaded weapon. Garza had the

Spencer and could fire many more shots without reloading. From here on, every bullet counted.

Emmet eyed Garza's horse grazing in a field fifty yards away. He sighted on the tip of the horse's ear and fired. The bullet's impact made the animal rear several feet in the air before it bolted across the field and out of sight. Garza's means of escape was gone.

Quickly, Emmet reloaded. He figured Garza knew the shots had come from his right side, so he maneuvered towards Garza's left. The terrain where Emmet was hiding was studded with boulders. He duck-walked behind the larger stones and crept on his belly behind the smaller ones.

Garza had not returned fire yet. Instead of fifty yards to his right, Emmet had now re-positioned himself thirty yards to Garza's left, still six hundred yards away. He decided to bide his time behind a ten-foot-wide chunk of silkstone. As he waited, he watched a striped whip snake slither by his boot and into the long grass. After ten minutes, he eased his head over the rock; Garza was still crouched behind the cypress. Emmet contemplated the situation. Was enough of Garza's body exposed to form a target? No.

Several more minutes passed. Emmet

looked again and saw Garza had shifted his body close enough in Emmet's direction for another try, a small slice of his pants and vest now in view.

He scraped Big Betty's muzzle against the siltstone to form a small sighting groove in the rock. He aimed, breathed in, out — but before the calming breath came, three shots popped the boulder, spraying sand and pulverized rock into Emmet's eyes. He rubbed them with his fingers until the specks watered out. When three more shots pinged the rock, Emmet decided to change plans.

He scrambled down the backside of the hill, sliding on his boots and balancing himself with his free hand. He was able to straighten himself when he reached the ledge that ran above the arroyo, scurrying along the narrow bench.

Now that he was hidden from view, Emmet intended to follow the arroyo and surprise Garza from behind. The ledge sloped down to meet the riverbed. Emmet stepped into the brown water, now only two feet deep. A piece of hickory driftwood came sloshing down, and he grabbed it with one hand as it passed, holding his rifle out of the water with the other.

He floated along with the log, feet first,

and wended his way down several sharp curves. The height of the canyon walls shrank as he neared the confluence, and eventually the walls merged with the bank. At times, his boots snagged on a submerged rock or tree root, but he would thrust his legs up to maintain his balance and continue his downstream passage.

As he neared the location where the arroyo emptied into the San Rafael, he dug his heels into the streambed and let go of the log to stand up, but the surge of the water was stronger than he realized. It tossed him off balance and dropped him in the water, submersing Big Betty and the sidearm in his holster. He sprang from the water and boosted the rifle into the air, but the damage was done — his weapons were wet, and he knew they would not fire. *If Garza had any idea the advantage he now has,* Emmet thought, *he would hunt me down and shoot me like a dog.*

Emmet grabbed onto a jut of sandstone and climbed out of the stream. The only edge he had now was the element of surprise. He was amazed at how much distance he had covered in so short a time and figured he had positioned himself behind Garza. Here, the bank dipped down, allowing him to climb out of the ravine and attack. Removing the socket bayonet from its scabbard, Emmet fixed it to Big Betty's muzzle and took a deep breath.

It was Chickamauga all over again, waiting in a trench, bayonet fixed, ready to go over the top. He hoped he had reached this location undetected, but, for all he knew, Garza could be standing on the other side of the crest waiting to blast him to kingdom come. There was only one way to find out.

Emmet stormed up the slope, jumped over the edge, and ran at Garza, whose back was to him, the sombrero staring at him like a big bloodshot eye. Garza did not hear Emmet's footfalls until he was just twenty feet away. When Emmet saw Garza turn around, he unleashed a piercing rebel yell and lunged. Garza raised his rifle to fire, but Emmet parried it away and, with a great upward swing, knocked the gun out of his hands and out of reach.

The twisting motion put Emmet off-kilter and forced him to one knee. Garza grabbed Big Betty's barrel, and the two men struggled in a tug of war for control of the long gun. Emmet back-stepped several paces and twisted the gun so the bayonet pointed at Garza's midriff. When Emmet thrust, Garza let go and flipped sideways, causing Emmet to propel forward and embed the bayonet four inches into the dead cypress.

Before Emmet could unstick the bayonet, Garza's fist hammered him on the side of the head and knocked him to the ground. Emmet was dazed, and a second powerful blow almost reeled the sky into darkness, but he knew this was like every battle he had ever been in — a fight to the death. He jumped up, and both men assumed wrestler stances.

The hated enemies made several feints at each other, but then Garza side-kicked Emmet's left leg, dropping him to one knee. Garza charged, forcing Emmet to shield his head with his arms from the assault. "This is for my cousin!" Garza screamed as he delivered punch after brutal punch.

Blindly, Emmet groped for Garza's shoulders and, with great force, shoved him back. Garza lurched forward again, the momentum tumbling both men into the river. Garza's hands were as strong as iron, and he grabbed Emmet by the throat and forced him underwater. Emmet twisted and turned to break the vise-like grip, but his left leg was pinned beneath his body. He held his breath and tried to pry Garza's hands from his neck. He rocked his body back and forth until his leg slid out from beneath him, allowing him to shift his weight to his right side.

Emmet tomahawked Garza's face with both fists, knocking him backwards. With his right foot wedged between two rocks for purchase, Emmet sprang from the water with a sudden surge of power and clamped his hands around Garza's throat.

Garza struggled as Emmet extended his fingers and locked them in place. Garza thrashed in the water, but Emmet's arms were two solid rails of steel, and he channeled all his fury into them — fury at the man who murdered Faith's parents, abducted innocent girls, tortured the King, killed the woman he loved; fury at the men who stole from the poor, bullied the humble, and left a wake of sadness and grief behind them. All this raw emotion strengthened his resolve and the grip of his fingers, and he squeezed with such force that he felt Garza's windpipe crack under his thumbs, and even then, even after the last air bubbles broke the surface and the body went still, he held him under for another minute.

He released the body, and the wind nudged it back to the bank. Emmet stumbled onto the shore and flipped himself on his back. "That," he panted, "was for Mariana."

He lay there for ten minutes, spent. Eventually, he tilted his head up and gazed at the purling water. Dragonflies with colorful wings flitted across the sawgrass. In the shallow waters of the opposite bank, a blue heron stood motionless on its reedy legs. As he viewed the tranquil scene, he realized any new life he made for himself from here on would be without Mariana, and then his hollowing grief returned, forcing his head back to the ground.

CHAPTER 40
THE ROAD BACK

"Faith, you can come out now," Emmet shouted as he dismounted.

The girl eased herself from behind the bushes. "Is he dead?"

"Yep."

She raced to him and hugged him around the waist.

"It's over, darling," he said. "This whole nightmare is over."

"Are we going to bury Mariana?"

"No. I'm bringing her back to town. She was a churchgoer and deserves a proper burial. Hop up on Ruby Red."

She mounted the horse and said, "I'll make room so you can fit her body on."

"No. I'm gonna carry her. You ride."

"It's a long way back," Faith warned. "It would be much easier to let the horse do the work."

"Listen, I never got to hold the first woman I loved after she died because I lost her in a fire. This time will be different. I'm gonna hold on to Mariana as long as I can. Let's go."

They set out for Santa Sabino in silence, Emmet holding Mariana in his arms, lumbering side to side, Faith atop Ruby Red, moving at a slow pace. Emmet thought about everything that had occurred since he had received the telegram seven days ago. Conflicting emotions battled inside him: his sense of redemption at having saved Faith and the rest of girls, swamped by his grief at losing Mariana; the warmth of his heartfelt reunion with the King after so many years, chilled by his torture and accidental death; his relief at coming into so much money so quickly, darkened by the realization that he still had no home or place to go.

They walked for two hours without stopping before Emmet needed a break, the front of his denim shirt black with sweat from the heat of the blanket he had wrapped Mariana in. He sat on a rock, still holding her, while Faith uncorked the canteen. She took a swig and handed it to him. He took a long pull, handed the canteen back, and wiped his mouth. When he passed it back, he noticed her eyes were fixed on the road ahead.

"Somebody's coming," she warned.

Emmet turned and saw a wagon rolling towards them from the opposite direction.

"Could be trouble," he said. "Bring me the spyglass."

She dismounted and handed it to him.

"Hold Mariana while I take a look." Faith sat on the rock, and Emmet gently rolled the dead woman into the girl's lap. He peered through the eyepiece and sighed with relief when he recognized the driver approaching them in Soapy's wagon.

"It's Pedro," he said.

When he got nearer, Pedro shouted from the wagon, "Is Garza dead?"

"Yep," Emmet yelled back.

"Then we did it!" Pedro yelled. "All of us. The cousins are dead, and the army has gone home." He pumped his fist into the air, and screamed, "Santa Sabino is free!" He immediately lowered his hand and rolled to a stop when he saw Mariana's lifeless body. "What happened?" he asked, the excitement draining from his voice.

"Garza," Emmet answered.

"We couldn't save her," Faith added. "I couldn't pull the stakes out in time."

He looked at Emmet. "I'm so sorry for her, and for you. Come, let's bring Mariana's body to Father Ramirez."

Emmet and Pedro took the body from Faith and placed it in the wagon as if it were a fragile piece of art. Emmet climbed in the back. Faith tied Ruby Red to the back of the wagon, jumped onto the toe board, and sat next to Pedro.

"You must be Major Kingston's niece," he said. "I'm glad you're safe. Now, let's get you back, too."

And then with a flip of the reins, Pedro roused the horses and turned the wagon back toward Santa Sabino.

The muddy roads slowed them down, and they entered the village from the south in the early afternoon. The clouds had cleared away, and the strong sunshine made the adobe buildings shimmer. Emmet heard noises of celebration as they approached the center of town. Hundreds of villagers swarmed the main plaza, chattering excitedly, exploding firecrackers, and dancing in groups.

Emmet eyed Soapy standing on the edge of the crowd. He waved to him, catching his eye, and pointed to the church. Soapy waved back and pointed to the same place. Pedro maneuvered the wagon next to the San Lazaro church. Soapy scooted around the edge of the crowd toward them, only to slow his pace to a crawl when he saw Mariana's body.

Soapy looked at Emmet and asked, "Are you okay?"

He nodded.

"Poor Mariana," Soapy condoled. "She was a brave woman to go into battle with us."

"I met her six days ago," Emmet replied, "but I felt like I knew her for twenty years."

"I know you had feelings for her," Soapy said, wrapping his arm around Emmet's shoulder.

Emmet nodded again.

Next Soapy looked at the girl. "You must be Faith. I'm sorry about your parents and your uncle."

"Thank you."

"Garza?" Soapy asked.

"In hell," Emmet replied.

"Good," Soapy said with a hard toss of his head. He took his arm from Emmet's shoulder and slapped him on the back. "This thing is finally over."

Father Ramirez appeared in the doorway and directed Emmet to place Mariana's body in the sacristy next to her dead father. Emmet had not been inside many churches in his life. He studied it as he carried Mariana down the aisle. The building was dimly lit, with rows of wooden benches and a simple wooden cross hanging behind the altar. The smell of burning candles was strong. It was as quiet as a crypt, save for the muffled din of the villagers celebrating outside in the plaza.

A tapestry depicting the Virgin of Guadalupe hung on the wall. Emmet recognized it, because Mariana had once described it to him: a lady dressed in a blue-green mantle with stars on it, supported by an angel at her feet. Emmet felt a pang of peace as he carried Mariana past the tapestry.

After Emmet set the body down, the priest said, "I will make arrangements for her Mass and burial." He exhaled a loud sigh, shook his head, knelt down next to her, and began praying. Emmet walked to the back of the church and rejoined Soapy, Faith, and Pedro.

"What are your plans, Faith?" Soapy asked.

"I want to be a nurse. My mother taught me well. I birthed a calf when I was six and a real baby when I was nine."

"What about returning to your parents' home in Diablo Canyon?" Pedro suggested. "Your mother healed the sick there."

"That place is just my parents' cemetery now," she answered. "It was hard for folks to get there. I need to be where the people I want to help are."

"Well, then stay here with us in Santa Sabino," Pedro said. "We have great need of someone with your skills."

"I don't know anybody in Santa Sabino," Faith said in a dull tone. She pulled down a lock of her hair, stroked it, and shrugged. "But, then again, I don't know anybody in any other towns."

As Emmet listened, he knew she wasn't pitying herself, just speaking the truth.

"Stay with me and my family," Pedro pleaded. "We have two sons, and my wife has always wanted a daughter."

Faith hesitated and said, "I need to think on it."

"Stay with us until you decide."

"You have one huge factor working in your favor," Emmet offered. "Your uncle told me that if anything happened to him, he wanted you to inherit the family money. He wrote a letter to that effect. I have it in my saddlebag."

"Lawdy!" Soapy yelled and then caught himself. He looked back to see whether Father Ramirez had heard him. In a quieter voice, he said, "I mean, that's a lot of money."

The expression on Faith's face didn't

change. "I don't care about money."

"You do realize you're set for life," Emmet said, "and can do anything you want. That money can buy a lot of medical supplies and a lot of education so that you can do a lot of healing."

As Faith pondered Emmet's words, the church door flew open, and an excited Armando rushed in and ran up to Emmet. "Everybody knows you're in here!" he shouted. "They want you to come out. You are heroes. They want to thank you."

Armando recognized Faith and approached her. "I am so glad you are safe. Do you remember me?" he asked.

"Of course I do," Faith answered. "You were kind to me."

"Armando, you reek of kerosene," Pedro complained, swishing his hand back and forth in front of him.

"I know," the boy replied. "I warned everybody to get out of Salazar's hacienda, and, after they did, I set it on fire. I hope my sister is able to see the black smoke from wherever she is."

"Such a huge place," Faith said. "It will burn for a while."

"Such an evil place," Armando said with a scowl. Then he caught himself, and his grin returned. "What will you do now, Faith? Go back to your family?"

"My family is gone."

"I'm sorry. Will you stay in Santa Sabino? Please stay."

Faith turned to Emmet. "I just met you today, and I don't know anything about you. But my uncle put a lot of trust in you, so let me ask: What do you think I should do?"

"When in doubt, darling," Emmet answered, "it's best to heed your heart. And it sounds to me like your heart wants to heal people. Santa Sabino is as good a place as any, plus you speak the language."

Soapy grabbed Faith's arm and said, "I can send you all the medical journals and books I can get my hands on. Plus, Doc Blackmore is a close friend of mine back in Sweetwater, and he'd surely take some time to teach you some of what he knows. What do you say?"

Faith let out a playful laugh. "Okay, okay. I'll try it. I'll stay."

Emmet believed that might have been Faith's first genuine laugh since the day she lost her parents, and it heartened him. Pedro gave her a rib-cracking hug, followed by Soapy and Armando with softer hugs.

"What about you, Emmet?" Soapy asked. "Where are you headed?"

"I ain't sure."

"You heard Armando," Soapy continued. "You're a hero. The people here love you. You've been yapping for years about how you want to change your life and settle down. Here's your chance. Now's the time. Time to seize the life you've been aching for."

"I ain't sure where to begin," Emmet offered.

"Start by buying Mariana's house," Soapy said. "You got money now."

"And many of the townspeople will help you grow the vegetables," Pedro added.

Soapy leaned in and whispered, "It also may be a chance to regain a daughter."

Emmet studied Soapy's face for several seconds. "You are a devious salesman, Mr. Waters." He turned to Faith. "What do you think about me staying in Santa Sabino?"

"Look, I'm sixteen years old," Faith answered. "I don't know anybody here, and nobody knows me. I will help anyone who wants me to help them. I hope they will all be good people. But what if they're not? I'd feel a lot safer if there was an avenging angel around. You know, just in case."

At that moment, warm fatherly feelings for Faith flooded over Emmet. He hugged her and said, "Maybe I better stick around. You know, just in case."

A fist pounded on the outside of the door. "Is Faith in there?" a girl shouted. "Somebody said they saw her arrive in a wagon. Is she in there?"

Faith's face brightened. "It's Valencia."

Armando opened the door, and Valencia stepped into the church. She blinked her eyes several times to adjust to the darkness. When she recognized Faith, she screamed with joy and raced over to embrace her. "I'm so happy you're safe!" she cried.

Now, the other girls who had been held captive rushed through the door. More shrieks of glee shattered the quiet of the church as the girls reunited. They rushed to Faith and buzzed around her, telling her how they were freed, how happy they were to be going home, and their relief that their ordeal was over. Valencia, in particular, kept bubbling with joy, clinging to Faith like a burr, hugging her between bouts of crying and laughing.

The noise of the outside crowd intensified. Armando opened the door again and peered out. "Everybody has crossed the plaza and is outside," he said.

And then Emmet heard it, and he couldn't believe his ears. It was soft and scattered at first, but then it grew louder, more unified, more distinct, a giant swell of energy filling the air: "*Queremos* Emmet! *Queremos* Emmet!"

"They're chanting for you to come out,' " Armando said.

Emmet shook his head in disbelief.

"Brother," Soapy said as he extended his right arm towards the door. "Give the people what they want."

Emmet stepped through the door and outside into the bright piercing sunlight and the happy shouts of a mob of men and women waving straw hats and rebozos. Grateful villagers engulfed him, and the church bells began pealing in joyful celebration. "You're the savior of Santa Sabino," a man yelled. Emmet felt pats on his back, saw beaming brown faces at every turn, heard them thanking him for setting them free. He had never been on the receiving end of such adulation from so many people at once, and the warm and welcoming reception moved him. And, for the first time in his life, here in this small village, on this crowded plaza, among these friendly faces, and the chants and the cheers, he knew he was finally home.

ABOUT THE AUTHOR

David C. Noonan worked as an environmental engineer for thirty-five years, taught graduate engineering classes at the Massachusetts Institute of Technology and Northeastern University, and published more than three dozen technical journal articles before turning to creative writing. Thomas Nelson (now part of Harper Collins) published his first book, *Aesop & the CEO: Powerful Business Lessons from Aesop's Ancient Fables,* which is now available in eleven languages. His work has also been published in *Parents* magazine and *Civil Engineer* magazine. He lives with Clare, his wife of more than forty years, in a suburb south of Boston. They have three grown children and one grandchild.